Betrayals

of Spring

L.P. Dover

The Prophecy

Summer, Fall, Winter, Spring
Two Courts to Four is what it will bring.
Without the Four the evil will spread,
The Land of the Fae will fall into dread.
The next generation will provide the Four,
The maiden souls and nothing more.
The Power of Four will start with the first,
If he gets the power, only then will you be cursed.
The Power of Four will be drawn to the others,
Their power is strong, the power of lovers.
The moment they become one,
Only then will the change have begun.
Two Courts to Four is what needs to be,
To save the Land, so shall we see.

Prologue

Meliantha

"A letter has arrived for you all the way from the Winter Court, Your Highness," Naida says as she bows. My heart about jumps out of my chest at the mention of the Winter Court. I look at her smiling face and then down to her outstretched hand holding out the letter.

Naida is my servant, and although I have no need of one she chose to serve willingly. She is also a wood nymph that loves nature just like me. Her brown hair is pulled back in a bun, and her eyes remind me of the deep green color of grass. Naida helps me in the gardens along with my sprites now that Calista has become Queen of the Fall Court and can no longer join me. I enjoy her company just as much as I do my best friend, Elissa.

I hastily reach for the letter. The envelope is smooth and thick. My fingers twitch with the need to tear it open to see if the letter is from *him*. Could it be from Kalen?

I look up at Naida and she has a huge smile on her face.

"Thank you, Naida, for bringing this to me. Do you mind if I open it in private?" I ask sweetly and pout my lips. Naida and I share numerous secrets, but this one I would like to keep to myself for now.

Her delicate laugh makes me smile.

"Of course, Your Highness," she replies. Naida bows her head and leaves the room, shutting the door quietly behind her.

I am excited, but nervous to know what the contents of the letter. I turn the envelope over and there sealed in wax is the Winter Court crest symbol. I gently slide my finger under the paper to break the seal, and it breaks with an audible snap. Closing my eyes, I lift the flap. I take in a calm breath as I reach in to grab the letter inside. It's folded over once so the anticipation of seeing the words will be short lived. I peek in from the bottom of the paper and my breath ceases as I see his name. What if he is professing his love to me in this letter? We had a great time at Calista and Ryder's wedding. We enjoyed numerous hours of talking about his wolves and my animals. His joking manner caught my attention from the very beginning and I have been waiting impatiently for the chance to see him again.

I groan in annoyance at myself. I need to stop stalling and read the letter. I feel like a lovesick adolescent pining over a boy. I am twenty years old and have had many crushes on the warriors over the years, but what I feel for Kalen surpasses all of those ridiculous crushes. I open the envelope slowly and I'm disappointed to see that there are only a few words on the paper. I guess I was thinking there would be more.

Dearest Meliantha,

Please meet me out by the gardens. I'll be waiting. Yours Truly, Kalen.

I can't believe he's actually here! I jump up and down with joy and dance across my room in excitement. I had asked Calista what the connection to Ryder felt like, and she had described it to me. I couldn't believe it, but it is exactly how I feel about Kalen. Could he be the one I am supposed to be with?

Calista and Ryder had their vision when they touched hands, so maybe that is what I have to do with Kalen. I rush to my closet, almost tripping along the way, and I pull out the purple tank top that matches my amethyst-colored eyes. I grab a pair of khaki shorts and a pair of sandals.

Satisfied with the way I look, I head straight for the gardens. The gardens are a short distance away and it only takes me a few minutes to get there. When I arrive I can see a tall frame and black, shoulder-length hair, and I know it is him. He must hear me coming because he begins to turn around slowly. My heart stops along with my feet, because I'm mesmerized by the sight of him. He's breathtaking with his muscular body encased in his warrior uniform. It hugs the planes of his body, and I can see the extent of his muscles. His breastplate is silver, and it covers his entire chest and back. The Winter Court symbol is engraved on the chest. He's also wearing black leather vambraces to protect his forearms and the usual black leather pants and tunic underneath the armor.

I begin to walk toward him since my feet seem to be cooperating now, but I notice that something seems different about him. He walks toward me to close the distance, but he stops a couple feet away. My fingers ache to touch him to see if the vision will appear.

His lips turn up in a smile.

"Good morning, Meliantha. Thank you for meeting me."

I fidget from nervousness, and my voice squeaks when I say, "Good morning to you, Kalen. I was going to head out this way anyway to tend to my gardening, so it was no problem at all. What brings you to the Summer Court?" I ask.

He pulls out a small silver box from his pocket and extends his arm out slowly to hand it to me.

"I brought you this," he replies coolly.

His eyes lock with mine when I reach for the box. I'm scared to touch his skin, but I'm also excited to see if he's the one. He has to be the one, I just know it. I close the distance to grab the box, and then our fingers touch. I feel the coldness of his Winter skin, but then…nothing. I release the breath I didn't realize I had been holding to look down at the silver box resting in my hands. I don't want him to see the tears that are beginning to form in my eyes. I open the box to see a beautiful amethyst-colored jewel encased in a silver setting with a silver chain. It's very lovely, but it begins to blur as the tears build in my eyes. I can't believe I was wrong about him being the one. My heart shatters and it's taking every ounce of my being to keep it together.

My voice quivers when I ask, "Why did you bring me this?"

I instinctively look up to meet his eyes when I notice him stepping forward. Kalen is a tall man who is about 6'2" which makes him tower over me about five inches.

He laughs and shrugs his shoulders.

"I brought it as a gift for you. I thought things were going to change, but it doesn't look like that's going to happen. I guess I was wrong."

My mouth hangs open and I stare dumbstruck at his audacity. I can't believe he would be so flippant. He acts as if it's not a big deal and that he doesn't care. I should have known from the beginning that he wouldn't take this seriously. I've heard stories of the flirtatious Prince Kalen, but with me I thought it was different. I thought *he* was going to be different.

I can't believe how stupid I was thinking that Kalen, the prince of heartbreak, would actually settle down with me and be the one the prophecy had foretold would be mine. I thrust the necklace out to him.

"Take it back! I don't want it! I thought you were different… that you actually cared," I scream.

Kalen rushes over and pulls me into his arms. I stand motionless as he leans down to place his cold, Winter lips onto my forehead. The searing pain of his frozen kiss has branded me a fool. I want him gone and out of my life.

He lets me go but holds me by the shoulders.

"I did care, my sweet princess, but I can see now that it was a wasted effort. Besides, you're a little too timid for my tastes. I'm sorry it has to be this way, but it's a good thing we found out now before things were taken further." He reaches down and touches the necklace in my hand. "Keep the necklace. It's the least I can do for the heartache I have caused. You need to forget about me, Meliantha."

I look into his piercing blue eyes, but I see nothing. He smiles again, but instead of seeing his playful smile, I see one of mischief and deceit. Even though I'm dying inside, it takes everything I have to muster up the strength to say what needs to be said.

"I want you to leave… now! I will forget you and think nothing more of you from this day forward. I can guarantee you that. Leave!" I yell.

He bows.

"It's been a pleasure, Princess, but I will do as you

wish. Again, I'm sorry."

He gives me one final glance and walks away, never looking back. The sounds of his footsteps are silent as he leaves. I can no longer breathe from the anger taking over my body. Why did I fall for him? Why can't I be strong like Calista? The heartache feels like a poison slowly travelling through my body and killing everything in its wake. Why does it have to hurt so much? I take one last deep breath and the world seems to stop as I let out the loudest, guttural scream imaginable.

I know the whole Summer Court can hear me, but I don't care. The scream lasts for what feels like an eternity. When my lungs are spent I collapse to the ground out of breath and heartbroken. A broken heart is something I never want to feel again, and from this moment on, I vow to keep my heart safe.

Chapter One

Meliantha

- Five years later -

I jerk awake covered in sweat while the memory of the dream comes flooding back to me. I have tried to forget that day, but it always comes back.

"Mel, are you OK?"

I look over to see Finn's amber-colored eyes staring at me with worry. I try to force a smile to reassure him that I'm fine.

"I'm alright, Finn, it was just another nightmare. Go back to sleep," I reply softly.

He quirks his eyebrow to let me know he doesn't believe me. He leans up to give me a kiss and I gently kiss him back. His tongue traces my bottom lip and he moans against my mouth. Satisfied with the kiss, he rolls over on his side and slowly drifts back to sleep. The deep rumble of his breathing lets me know he is sound asleep. I wish I could fall into the realm of dreams that fast. These days I am lucky to get even a couple hours of sleep.

Finn is one of our warriors in the Summer Court and has been for one-hundred and fifty years. We've been lovers for almost five years. It began not long after the ordeal with Kalen. I guess you could say he was there to mend my broken heart. According to the prophecy, I am one of the Four. That means I will be drawn to another to complete the magic I am destined to fulfill, just like Calista and Ryder. They are now King and Queen of the Fall Court and have expanded their powers in the Land of the Fae.

Finn knows that one day I will no longer be his, and that he has to accept that. Our time together is amazing, and I enjoy his company as well as the intimacy. His attitude changes in bed sometimes from being soft and sensual to being rough and possessive. It has concerned me on numerous occasions. On the rough nights, our encounters tend to be a little wild and heated. I can honestly say I have enjoyed some of those nights, but sometimes it gets a little too rough. My sense of danger spikes to a whole new level when he gets like that. Every time I mention it to him he seems to not understand a word I'm saying. It's like he can't remember some of the things he's done. It doesn't happen often, but I have learned to be more alert around him when his mood changes.

I stare at Finn. He's lying peacefully in my bed. I wish that I could love him, but the feelings never come. I care for him and have a deep respect for him, but I know in my heart that I will never fully love him. I reach over to play with his silky, long, blond hair that flows past his shoulders and is splayed across the pillow. He always keeps it pulled back when he trains, but when we're in bed together he lets it hang loose because he knows that is how I like it. He looks ethereal when he has his hair down. His face is always smooth and his smile is angelically beautiful. He may have the face of an angel, but his fierce temper and battling skills would claim otherwise. Sometimes I wonder why he stays with me knowing it will never last. There are so many Summer faeries here that would kill for a chance to be with him. Maybe one day he will find one. His hair glides through my fingers as I gently twist it around. His blond hair is so white it illuminates in the glow of the candlelight in my room. It's so white it looks like snow.

I silently groan at the thought of snow and it sends a sharp pain straight to my stomach. I wish to all the heavens and the stars that I could just forget about a certain Winter Prince and that dreadful day in the past. I close my eyes and I lean back on my pillow. I can't stop my mind from recalling all of the events from the last five years.

Calista and Ryder's court has flourished with love and life. They now have a two-year old son named after her fallen Guardian, Merrick. He is the cutest little boy and what's strange is he looks exactly like a little version of Merrick, except for the eyes. His golden blond hair is long and it curls at the ends, giving him a cherub look. His big, round eyes are the ice blue color of Ryder's and it's the first thing everyone notices in his tiny face. I can almost see Merrick looking out through those eyes, and it makes me wonder if some of his essence inside Calista was passed on to him. I haven't been able to see him much until recently, now that I have been allowed to travel. I was on house arrest for years because of the threat of the dark sorcerer. It's been five years now and nothing has gone amiss. Being cooped up in this palace for that long has left me in a foul mood. I'm twenty-five years old and I refuse to be treated like a prisoner.

I am no longer the shy and timid princess of before. I now train for battle with the warriors, thanks to Calista and her demands to my father, King Oberon. She disclosed how she trained with Merrick for all those years and how she's a skilled dagger thrower. I knew she was strong, but I had no clue she was that skilled. It hurt that she didn't trust me enough to tell me, but I know she had her reasons. I train every morning with my brother, Drake, and my Guardian, Ashur. Training has made me strong, both mentally and physically. I have found that I'm excellent with the bow and arrow, and just like Calista, I never miss my target. There is one secret I have kept to myself and told no other. I have always had my ability to do anything I desired with nature, whether it's with plants, trees, grass, or land.

I still have an affinity for animals as well, but a new magic has occurred in me. I didn't figure it out until a couple of years ago when one of my sprites had a flying accident by running into a tree. Her wing was severely damaged, and it didn't look like she would ever be able to fly again. I heard her wailing in the garden, so I ran over to see what had happened. I saw her lying on the ground screaming in agony. Since sprites are very small, I scooped her up in my hands and began looking at her wing. I remember feeling a strong emotion surging through my body. I wanted to help her so badly. Then, almost instantly, the magic happened. I could feel a buzzing throughout my body like it was travelling through my bloodstream, and then out of nowhere it blasts from my fingertips. The power exploded into the sprite's wing, and then, a few moments later, the wing was miraculously healed. I haven't used my healing capabilities since. I don't know if it was a fluke, but I haven't actually tried to heal anything since then. This type of information would be valuable to the dark sorcerer and it's not something I want spread around the Land of the Fae.

When I turned twenty-one four years ago I had my Guardian Ceremony. I expected to see Kalen there, but he didn't show up. He had come to the palace one day long before the ceremony asking if he could see me, but I strongly declined. Why he came to see me again, I don't know. Ever since that day at the gardens, I wanted to avoid him at all cost. King Madoc and Queen Mab came, so I guess there was no need for Kalen to attend. It's definitely a good thing he didn't come, because now if he says anything cruel to me, I will gladly show him how I'm not weak anymore. Training and eating more has filled my body out with curves and muscle. I had to get a whole new set of clothes to fit my newly formed body. My old frame was frail and breakable and thinking back to how I used to be disgusts me. How could I have been so weak? Nothing and no one is going to hurt me now. I have never felt more confident than I do in this moment. It'll definitely shock Kalen when he sees me tomorrow.

The Winter Solstice Ball is tomorrow night and we are headed to the Winter Court in the morning which happens to only be a few short hours away. Once the sun peeks over the horizon I will be packing and loading up to head out with my family, my Guardian, Elissa, and Finn. I have asked Naida, my servant, to stay behind so she could spend some time with her family while I was gone. We are scheduled to stay for two days and I can already feel deep within my gut that it's going to be a visit from hell. I will be staying in one of the guest houses with Ariella and Elissa during the visit.

My eyes feel heavy and they burn like someone has

thrown a handful of salt in them. I rub them to help clear the feeling, but I know it is from the lack of sleep. My body feels tired and it's beginning to wear down on my sanity. I need to be in top shape when we leave to go to the Winter Court. I turn over on my side toward Finn's back and I drape my arm across his stomach as I move closer to his warm body. The golden band wrapped around his upper arm feels cold against my chest. It was given to him as a gift a couple years ago from the Dwarf Kingdom when my special arrows were delivered. I found it odd they would give him such a fine gift, but I was told from the messenger that Durin, the Dwarf leader, had made it for him in honor of me. I haven't seen Durin in years, but he'll be at the Solstice Ball. I will have plenty of chances to catch up with him. Finn moves his body back against mine and lets out a contented moan in his sleep. I breathe him in deeply, and the smell of a summer breeze fills my lungs along with his heady scent of being pure male. I close my eyes and slowly drift off into a much needed dreamless sleep.

Chapter Two

Kalen

"Are you excited about the ball tonight?" Breena asks.

Not really, I think to myself, but unfortunately I have to be. I'm already out of bed and picking out clothes to wear to meet my parents. I look over at Breena lying in my bed, and she gives me a seductive smile. She sits up slowly and lets the sheet fall from her perfectly sculpted breasts to below her waist. The way she's biting her lip lets me know she is ready for round two, but right now I can't think of anything else other than the auburn-haired beauty with the amethyst-colored eyes. Her face has haunted my dreams for years, and last night happened to be one of those nights. I turn my head away from Breena and walk over to my closet. The woman sure knows what she's doing. Breena is a beautiful Winter fae woman with long, straight brown hair that is the color of cinnamon. Her round, hazel-colored eyes stand out from her creamy white complexion, but the more I look at her the more I know I do not love her.

Tonight is the Winter Solstice Ball, and it's also the night we celebrate our engagement. With my back turned, she can't see the lie in my eyes when I reply, "Yes,

Breena, I am ready for the ball tonight."

I don't know how I ever let things get this far. I was distraught over finding out about how close Meliantha and Finn were getting, so I ran to the first girl I could find. Breena has always been interested in me, so it wasn't hard to get her into my bed. What makes things harder is that she's a councilman's daughter which practically makes her royalty. Our union will be looked upon as greatness, but if anyone finds out about my distaste for her, it will cause turmoil within the court.

My parents are happy with my arrangement to marry Breena, but they have also had reservations about it. They can obviously see the torment in my eyes, but it's my decision and I am going to uphold it. The meeting with my parents will begin in thirty minutes, so I grab a pair of jeans from my closet and I pull them on. I got the jeans from the mortal realm, because everyone was wearing them when I visited not too long ago. So many things have changed in the mortal realm from the last time I visited. I grab a red t-shirt from the closet, and I slip it over my head. It hugs my muscles which seem to be what the ladies go for now these days. I run my hands through my long black hair, and I grab the thistleburch chord that I always use to tie my hair back in. The tie comes from the thistleburch trees here in the Winter Court and is known for its strengthening powers. Most of the warriors here have some part of the thistleburch tree on their body to give them strength and luck when in battle. It looks like a thin piece of brown leather, and it always feels cold resting up against my skin.

I silently groan in annoyance when I hear Breena getting out of bed and walking toward me. The woman surely doesn't have any issues with being naked. She wraps her arms around me and squeezes. I can feel her breasts pushing up against my back, but it does nothing for me in this moment. The thought of Meliantha takes all my focus, and to know I'll be seeing her for the first time in five years has me a little on edge.

Breena moves around to face me and says, "I think I'm going to get dressed and head to my quarters to get ready for the ball, unless…" She rubs her naked body against mine as she continues. "You want to have a little fun first." She raises her eyebrows in question and licks her lips. If only the eyes looking back at me were purple would I be all up for it, but I just can't seem to get my mind focused.

I shake my head no and regretfully reply, "Not right now, Bree. I have much to do before tonight, and I have to be at the meeting with my parents in half an hour."

She narrows her eyes at me and I can see her jaw tighten as I speak, but she quickly brushes it off and goes to fetch her clothes. I think she knows deep down that I don't love her, but she hasn't mentioned anything to me about it. I watch her pull on her clothes, and it's hard to believe that I've been with her for almost three years. I love the ladies, and I never actually thought of settling down with one until I met a certain Summer faerie that I was deeply attracted to, but look how that turned out. She is now in the arms of another man every night, and the thought sends a burning anger through my chest. I grip the closet door and I don't realize what I was doing until Breena raises her voice to get my attention.

"Kalen! Are you OK? What are you doing? You almost broke the closet door in half," she exclaims.

I shake my head to clear my thoughts and I relax the tension in my face to force a smile.

"I'm sorry. I didn't realize I was holding it so hard." I loosen my grip on the handle and slowly drop my hand.

She doesn't look like she believes me, but she shrugs her shoulders and comes over fully dressed to give me a kiss on the cheek. With a concerned look she says, "You looked like you were about to kill someone. What were you thinking about?"

I shake my head, laughing it off while I kiss her on the lips. I hold her face in my hands to assure her.

"It was nothing. Enjoy the rest of your day, and I'll see you soon." I kiss her again quickly before she leaves the room.

Now that Breena is gone I can have a few minutes of peace before I meet my parents. These past five years have been long and brutal. I am twenty-six years old, but I feel like an eighty-year-old man in mortal years. The only enjoyment I have out of life is training my warriors—since I'm now leader of the Winter Court Army—and spending time with my white wolves. I've kept quiet about my thoughts of Meliantha and haven't spoken about her to anyone other than my wolves.

I walk over to my bedroom window to look out at the snowy landscape beyond. I've seen the same land all the years of my life, but something feels like it is missing. I look at the fountain that's frozen like always, and I use my magic to turn the ice to water. I watch it flow rhythmically throughout the fountain. My magical abilities are with water and animals. Using my magic used to make me feel free and alive, but now all I feel is hollow inside. I would give anything to be able to feel whole like I did five years ago.

I am no longer carefree and easygoing. I am dead to the world with no sign of life. The Winter cold seems to be flowing inside my blood turning everything to ice. Meliantha was beginning to thaw me out with her warm glow, but now that she has forsaken me the ice has taken over and left me freezing inside of a cold shell. One way or another I will talk to her tonight. I have to find out what went wrong.

Chapter Three

ALASDAIR

- Dark Sorcerer -

I appear in her room just as she's changing out of her clothes to head to the shower. I can hear the water running and the steam from it is billowing into the room. It looks like I made it at exactly the right time.

"Is this a bad time?" I ask her with humor clear in my voice.

She jumps and holds in the gasp that was about to escape her throat by holding her hand over her mouth. She shakes her head and removes her hand to put it on her chest. I can see her chest rapidly rising and falling. Her voluptuous breasts bounce with her hard breathing and it instantly turns me on. This little vixen knows how to handle her body and it's been a while since I've had a good fuck. Her eyes roam over my solid body and a wicked grin takes over her face.

"No, this is not a bad time at all, Alasdair," she cries wickedly.

I have appeared to her in my true solid form. She prefers to look at me this way and it turns me on even more that she prefers my true body instead of someone else's. It's a shame I'm only using her for her connections to the royals. She could come in handy as my personal sex slave. I begin to walk toward her and she stares up and down my body with a ravenous look. I stand around six feet tall with long brown hair to my shoulders and grey-colored eyes. My face could pass for fae, but my ears aren't pointed like the fae's are.

I could, however, pass for any of the warriors with my strong build. My well-endowed body has always come in handy with the women, especially this vixen in front of me. I didn't bother to appear in clothes, because I knew this visit was going to be nothing but giving her the box I hold in my hands and a quick release. I do, however, have my wonderful bloodstone talisman with me which helps me siphon energy. Once I get all the power I need from the Four, I will no longer have to wear this thing all the time. The power will be permanently inside my body when the power of the Four merges into me.

Now that I have Calista's power flowing through my veins I can keep my solid form for way longer than before. I can enjoy the feelings of life in my own body, but it still takes less power to take over other people's forms. There still has to be a magic object on the person I inhabit such as a spelled ring, bracelet, necklace, or anything else I've put magic on to help me enter their bodies. I've had help from many of my minions in securing a place for these objects with certain fae. What's great is that they have no clue their bodies are being taken over during this time. I silently laugh thinking back to all of those momentous occasions where I have fooled my victims. I've been patient throughout these past five years, and I have enjoyed them immensely. Also with Calista's power, I have been given the necessary magic to penetrate through the shields of the royals. Once my magical objects are in place I'll be able to take over a royal's body without being detected. I could take over the king's body and no one would know it. Now that I have infiltrated the Winter Court, I should be able to get my plan in motion tonight.

I stand in front of the Winter vixen and she licks her lips enticingly before kneeling down on the floor in front of me. This greedy bitch was easy to sway with my charms. The promise of being my Dark Queen has poisoned her mind and she was quick to take the bait. All she is good for right now is satiating my needs with a good lay and to carry out the next stage in my plan to get Meliantha's power. Moaning, she takes my cock in her mouth and sucks generously up and down the shaft. My knees go a little weak with her tormenting me, so I grab a hold of the bedpost with one hand while the other holds the small box. I can feel the release demanding to burst forward, but I hold it back with great fervor.

I throw the box of secret contents on the bed while I pull the vixen up by her hair. She loves it when I get rough with her and she lets out a moan to prove it. I push her down on the bed and I point to the box.

"You do know what I want you to do with the things in the box, right?" I ask.

She licks her lips and tauntingly opens herself up to me. She nods her head up and down and breathlessly whispers, "Yes, I understand. I will do what you told me."

"Good, now turn over on your stomach. Now!" I command.

A gleam sparkles in her eyes and she excitedly complies. She turns over on her stomach and lifts her glorious and smooth backside up in the air. I enter her hard and fast to pound away the tension that's been building up for days. She gasps and tightens around me even more sending a flood of sensations down my shaft that has me aching to release. I clench my teeth and I hold on to her tighter leaving bruises on her ass from my grip. The release hits me hard sending shudders throughout my body and hers.

Breathless from exertion, I lie on top of her for a moment to catch my breath. I can feel her heart beating spastically through her back while mine is pounding hard as well. It feels so good to fuck long and hard, and with a body like hers, I could do it all day and night. I pull out leaving her breathless and moaning on the bed. She obviously doesn't get what she wants from her lover, but I think I fully make up for it.

I stand up from the bed and move back toward the shadows on the wall.

"It's been a pleasure, but I must be on my way," I announce.

She turns her head to give me a satiated smile and answers seductively, "I promise not to fail you. I will follow through with our plan."

At that, I disappear from my solid form back to my spirit form, and I decide to keep to the shadows. My presence needs to remain here for the time being, at least until the ball begins, so I can carry out my plans. Calista's power has given me such a major boost even though she weakened me there for a while. I can travel to and from any place in the Land of the Fae in a matter of minutes, and my ability to do certain spells has been magnified. My special objects of power have been placed throughout the Court to give me access to the unwilling victims. I'm drawn to the power of the objects, so it's easier to locate my targets. I can feel the pull to one of them, so I head in that direction, and it looks like I'm heading to the front of the palace.

This is good, I think to myself. The Summer Court should be arriving anytime, so I'll be able to get a front row view. Excellent.

Thinking back to when I captured Calista I can't believe how I almost screwed myself in the ass with how greedy I became with her. I wanted her power and her body in any way possible and it almost destroyed me. Not this time, though. My plan to get her sister's power doesn't involve me keeping her, but just retaining her power in any means possible. If I happen to keep her in my grasp, that will be a bonus, but my bed is not short of women, so I have no need to go through extra work to keep her with me. Thankfully, she hasn't bonded with her other half and spoiled my plans. Once the bond is complete I can no longer retain the power of the Four from that certain individual. Why? I don't know. That's just the irony of things. Taking the power was not meant to be easy. Thanks to my superb thinking, that bond will probably never happen from what I have been seeing. My work has been quite easy this go around. I thought I would have to work a little harder to dissuade Meliantha from Kalen, but she has surprised me and banished him from her life without my having to urge her more. It's been extremely gratifying watching them through their torment the last five years. My objects of power have come in handy and have made their way to the proper hands. Needless to say, they have no clue I have been around all this time, watching and waiting. All that's left to do is wait for the ball tonight and hope that my plan works out accordingly; although, in the meantime, I think I might try to have a little fun.

Chapter Four

Meliantha

"I can't believe we're going to the Winter Court. I bet it's going to be amazing for you to get away from here for the first time in five years," Elissa says excitedly. She pauses to look at the clothes I'm wearing and shakes her head. "You know the king and queen are not going to approve of you wearing that. I bet they won't let you leave the palace."

They'll have no choice, I think to myself. I make my own decisions now. I shrug my shoulders and turn back to continue my packing. I can hear Elissa shift behind me, but then she starts to sing and jump around my room excitedly. Her blond curls bounce up and down as she dances, and I envy her carefree attitude. I remember when I used to be like that.

Elissa is my age of twenty-five and we have been close friends since birth. Her father is on the Summer Court Council, and he's also a good friend of my parents. Elissa will be coming with me to the Solstice Ball per my request. She has also been forbidden to travel during these past five years, so I thought it was time she had a break as well.

"It's going to feel good to get out of the palace walls and travel," I say while looking at Elissa. "I know it will be good for you as well." I look down at my clothes and frown. "As far as what I'm wearing, this is who I am now and nothing is going to change that."

She stops bouncing around and looks at me with concern etching her angelic face. I happen to look down and notice that she's wearing the amethyst necklace I gave her five years ago. It's the necklace Kalen gave to me on that day of hell. It pains me to look at it, so I avert my eyes quickly and hope she doesn't notice my hesitation. The memories are not something I want to remember. She walks over to me and tilts her head so she can see into my face. She has asked me repeatedly to talk to her about my feelings, but I've always declined. It's no one's business but my own, and sometimes her persistence is out right annoying. I huff in exasperation and then I pointedly meet her eyes.

"I wish you would tell me what happened to you, Meliantha. The person you are now isn't the real you. You're not some cold-hearted bitch from the Winter Court," she says as she points at the window. "You don't even garden that much anymore now that you've become a warrior. There used to be a spark of life inside of you that could brighten a room, and now it's just...gone. I miss the old you so much, and I want her back." Her eyes soften and she reaches down to take my hands. Her words are the truth, but I am who I am for a reason. She doesn't understand that all I'm doing is protecting myself, and most of all, protecting my heart.

I let out an audible breath.

"People change, Elissa. I'm one of the Four which means my life is going to be in jeopardy while the dark sorcerer plots to take me. If Calista hadn't trained, she probably wouldn't have made it out alive. I have to be strong. I was a weak and timid little girl before, and I didn't know how to protect myself. You may not understand, but being the cold-hearted bitch may just save my life one day."

She nods her head and looks down at the floor.

"I know, Mel. I just wish things didn't have to be like this," she sighs. Her sadness makes my chest tighten with guilt and I feel bad for snapping at her. I give her a loving embrace and she hugs me back fiercely. I love her so much, and I wish that she understood the way my life is now. She sniffles and wipes away her tears. I smile at her, but I know it doesn't come close to looking authentic.

"I'm going to go fetch my things and I'll meet you downstairs, OK?" she says, trying to sound cheerful. I smile at her again before her retreating form leaves me to a room full of silence. Finally, I get a chance to have some peace and quiet before making this journey to the dreaded Winter Court. I look down at my packed clothes and for this trip I have traded my usual Summer clothes and replaced them with pants, long-sleeved shirts, and jackets. My gown for the ball, however, is not long-sleeved, so I'm sure I'll be freezing the whole time. I'm going for a daring look this year. I unzip the garment bag to take a look at the one thing that is going to set me apart from the others. The ball is supposed to be a black and white affair, but there is nothing white or black in my bag. My parents are going to be none too pleased to see what I have in store for the ball.

My dress is a bright, fire red with an empire waist. The top is formed in a halter top style that wraps around the back of my neck. Red rubies are fastened across the top half of the dress with gold threading. They stop midstomach where the dress then flows gracefully down to the floor. The top fits a little snug and pushes my breasts together showing off the cleavage I now have. This is definitely going to get everyone talking, and I can't wait to see their faces when I show up. Not even the people close to me know that I have this dress. With a big smile on my face, I begin zipping my dress back up in the garment bag when in walks Ashur, my Guardian.

He stops mid-step and stares at me wide-eyed.

"What do you think you are doing?" he exclaims in my mind.

I burst out laughing hearing his exasperation in my mind. I'm in my warrior leathers with my gold armor breastplate and greaves. I have my brown leather vambraces tightly secured around my forearms, and my thick, auburn hair is pulled into a tight braid that hangs down my back. My bow and arrows are strapped and secure on my back as well. Not only does Ashur carry our special Guardian dagger, but I also carry some special weapons of my own. My arrows have been fortified with both mine and Ashur's blood making them just as lethal as the dagger. I have planned to ride to the Winter Court on horseback instead of riding in a carriage. I have no intentions of letting anyone stop me from doing this, not even my guardian.

"What do you think?" I ask sarcastically.

"I think you need to change, Meliantha. You are a princess and you should act like one."

"Oh, by being the helpless pretty girl that relies on everyone to take care of her? No, thanks. I plan on changing into a gown before the ball, so get the sword out of your ass and calm down," I tease.

He lets out an annoyed breath and speaks aloud, "I do not have a sword up my ass, but it's my job to make sure you're protected, and by the way you're dressed, I'm assuming you plan on riding with the warriors?"

"That's the plan, and I promise to stay right by your side...Achilles," I laugh.

I give him a huge smile and he shakes his head and rolls his eyes. He hates it when I call him that, but he does look like the actor who played Achilles in the movie Troy. Calista and I had watched that movie in the mortal realm a while back. Ashur is very tall with his six-foot four frame and warrior body. His dark blond hair touches down below his shoulders and his eyes are the greenest I have ever seen, they're almost as bright as Calista's. He's a very good-looking man and I mean it as a compliment when I tell him he looks like Achilles. He happens to be over two centuries old, but his body only looks to be in his late twenties. That's one of the advantages to being a faerie. Thankfully, he has no romantic feelings for me, but I have seen in his mind how he feels about my friend, Elissa. Needless to say, I have seen my friend unclothed in his mind one too many times.

"You know I hate it when you call me Achilles," he groans.

"And I will keep calling you that until you give in to me. Either way, this is how I'm going to the Winter Court, end of discussion," I argue.

He throws his hands up in the air and relents, "Fine, Princess, but when the king decides to scold me I'll happily point him in your direction. Are we clear?"

I give Ashur a huge smile and say, "Thank you, and don't you worry, I can handle my father."

Ashur looks around at my bags and begins to pick them up. I help him with the remaining bags and we head down to the foyer of the palace where everyone will be waiting. On the way down, Ashur speaks silently, *"Are you going to be OK going to the Winter Court, Princess?"*

This stops me cold, and he must notice because he shifts around hesitantly before meeting my eyes. He continues, "I only ask because I've felt the torment inside of you all these years, but I've never said anything about it. I just want to know what Kalen did to you that made you close your heart. I know you're with Finn now, but you still keep your heart guarded."

"That's the thing, Ashur. Nothing happened between me and Kalen," I say aloud. He gives me a disbelieving look, so I continue more forcefully. "I'll be fine. I'm strong now and nothing and no one is going to hurt me anymore."

His eyes go gentle when he murmurs, "I know you're strong, but you are mine to protect, and I don't want to see you get hurt." Hearing his words softens my heart a little, and I can feel a slight burn behind my eyes; however, I quickly brush it away and smile. He'll make someone very happy someday, maybe even Elissa.

"Thank you, Ashur. Elissa would be very lucky to have you," I respond, waiting for a reaction.

He just smiles and shakes his head. I was expecting him to say something, but instead he leads me on our way. We make it to the grand staircase and I see everyone down below standing around waiting on me. I did take a little extra time in preparing for departure, but I'm not exactly in a hurry to get to the Winter Court. I look at each one individually as I make my way down the marble steps. I see Elissa giving Ashur a timid smile, and I sneak a peek to my side to see Ashur return it with one of his own.

"Do not say a word, Meliantha," he warns silently.

"I'm not Ashur, but I think you need to tell her how you feel."

His reply is a grunt so I just laugh and continue on down the steps. My sister, Ariella, is in her own world checking over her bags. Training with the warriors has changed her in a good way. She still likes to play her tricks and cause mischief, but the past five years have turned her from a self-centered girl to a woman. In a few months she will be twenty-one and everything will change for her once she gets her guardian. I know there are plenty of warriors that are dying for the chance to be her protector. I take my eyes away from my beautiful blonde sister to my brother Drake. His fire red eyebrows are raised and he's smirking at me with a quirk to his lip. I know he's not surprised to see me in my warrior attire, but I think he is waiting to see how I handle our parents. Finn is standing off to the side and he has a huge smile on his face. His glowing amber eyes are feasting on my body with pride and it makes me smile. He always says he loves me in my leathers and that the way it hugs my body turns him on. I normally just roll my eyes at him when he says stuff like that, but it's nice to be admired. I spent years with the warriors never noticing me, and now it's like they can't get enough. It's been very interesting the past couple of years. I take a deep breath before looking at my parents, and when I see them their shocked expressions are just what I am expecting. Leave it to my mother to make an outburst.

"Meliantha! Just where do you think you are going looking like that?" my mother, Queen Tatiana, argues.

I was expecting her hostility, but to avoid a screaming match, I say nonchalantly, "I'm going to the Winter Court and I'm going to ride with the warriors alongside Finn and Ashur. I'm no longer a child or a frilly little princess that has to hide inside of a carriage. I am proud to be who I am, and this is *my* decision."

My mother looks at Ashur and he gives her an apologetic look. She huffs in aggravation before walking out the front doors. Drake gives me a grin and a thumbs up before walking out after my mother. Ariella just shakes her head and smiles before leaving the room. Finn and Elissa decide to hang back with Ashur and me; meanwhile, my father comes up to me and takes my face in his hands.

"We're just worried about you, dear. The dark sorcerer will come after you one day and we need to be careful. This is the first time you're venturing out, so you can't blame us for wanting to keep you safe. You're an excellent fighter, but that doesn't mean you're invincible." He looks back and forth between Ashur and Finn and commands, "Watch her, both of you. I don't think you want to know what I'll do to you if something bad happens to her."

They both look like they're trying to swallow a brick and it takes everything in me to keep from smiling. They bow their heads and reply together, "Yes, Your Highness."

My father turns around and makes his way out the door. The servants are milling about gathering my family's things to load them into the carriages. Ashur gives a quick glance to Elissa and then turns to me.

"I am going to get your horse ready. I will see you out there," he says silently.

He nods to both Finn and Elissa and then strides

toward the front doors.

Elissa watches him saunter away and quickly exclaims, "I'm going to go, too. See you out there!" She runs off to catch up with Ashur and trails beside him on the way out the door. I can't help but smile as I watch. Ashur needs to find someone that will love him, and Elissa would be the perfect woman.

Finn leans down to kiss my cheek and whispers, "You look amazing, Mel. You and leather go together perfectly."

I smile and give him a wink while looking appreciatively down his body. He has his long hair pulled back and he's wearing his complete warrior gear. Tonight he'll be in a tuxedo and on my arm the whole night. He's my date for the evening so wearing his warrior gear will not be needed. Hopefully, he can keep my mind off of a certain Winter Prince.

I reach up to run his long, silky hair through my fingers before asking, "Will you wear your hair down for me tonight?"

He smiles and moves closer to me, "I will do whatever you wish for me to do, Mel." Giving me a wolfish grin he continues, "That way it'll already be down the way you like it when I take you to bed tonight."

He leans down to quickly kiss my lips before gathering his things to exit out the front doors. He's such a good man, and he deserves someone so much better than me. Thankfully, he's never told me he loves me, which I'm glad about. I want to keep our relationship uncomp-licated. He doesn't seem to mind the arrangement we have now. My family knows that I am seeing him, but they keep their thoughts silent from me. They know that once I find the one I am drawn to it'll be over between me and Finn. The thought makes my heart ache with the loss of one day losing him. He's been an amazing friend and a passionate lover to me for the past five years. I do have my heart guarded by a thick wall, but I still feel enough to know that I'll miss him when the time comes.

I guess my time of procrastinating is over since I'm now standing alone in the foyer. I walk to the front doors of the palace and I look around at the land that doesn't feel like a home to me anymore. The sense of belonging just isn't there, and I don't know where I belong. I really hope to figure it out someday.

- *Journey to the Winter Court* -

    I have never been to the Winter Court before, but I have been through parts of the Mystical Forest. My horse, Prince Ashe, has been my riding companion ever since I was a little girl. I remember being little and trying to tie a purple ribbon in his hair. He didn't like what I was doing and made sure to let me know by nipping my hand. It hurt and I remember crying like a baby. I never tried to tie ribbons in his hair again. Prince Ashe is a midnight black fae horse with sparkly silver eyes. He's a little bigger than a mortal horse and his life longevity is five times as long as one, too. He's all dark with his black saddle and reigns, and boots that are black as night with silver spikes. He looks like a menacing creature, but he is as gentle as can be.

    The creatures all flock to me when I go through the Mystical Forest, and needless to say, they do so today. The sprites of the forest are flying everywhere, sitting on my shoulders, playing with my braid, tickling my back, and flying all around me. I'm reminded of Snow White and how the animals followed her around and helped her do things. I guess I'm the faerie version of her. I actually do have three rambunctious sprites that help me with my gardening back in the Summer Court. They have agreed to do my gardening while I'm away and have been doing so for a lot longer than that. I hope someday my heart will find the joy in gardening like it used to. I look around at all the little furry animals milling about and following us, and I give them all a warm smile. Once I acknowledge them, they head out on their way.

We ride for a few minutes more and I begin to feel the wind changing course. The breeze is no longer the warm breeze of the Summer, but the crisp and cool breeze of the Fall. The trees up ahead are changing colors so I know we are close to passing through my sister's court. I'm pretty sure Calista and Ryder have left already to head to the Winter Court. Calista used to visit me a lot by using Nixie to port travel. Nixie helped save my sister in the Black Forest and she also has the ability to port travel anywhere in the Land of the Fae in a matter of seconds. The dark sorcerer held her captive until Calista came along and promised to keep Nixie and her family safe in return for her help. Nixie and her family live out in one of the forests here in the Fall Court, and from what I hear, they are enjoying it greatly.

The color of the leaves is so beautiful, and I can see why Calista fell in love with Fall. The leaves are swirling and dancing in the wind while the cool breeze caresses my hot Summer skin. I feel like I belong with the cooler air, but the Fall is not where I belong. I've grown apart from the Summer Court, and I ache to find my place in our realm. Even though I have my family and friends, sometimes the loneliness takes over, and it feels like I am drowning in it.

"I don't like where your thoughts are right now, Meliantha."

I jerk my head to look at Ashur and I give him a dark look. I don't need him searching through my mind right now, especially when my thoughts are going to be harder to shield once we make it to the Winter Court. His eyes hold concern, but that doesn't stop me from snapping at him.

"I'm fine Ashur. My thoughts are my own and I would greatly appreciate it if you would mind your own business and stay out of my head."

He nods, but the concern is still there.

"Very well, Princess. I'm sorry to have distressed you, but we're almost to the Winter Court. Would you like your coat? It's going to be a lot colder there than you are used to."

My head aches from stressing about this trip and I close my eyes hoping it'll ease off. I'm sure the bitter freeze of the Winter wind is going to feel like nails biting into my skin, but I shake my head, refusing the offer. I feel bad for snapping at him so angrily, but I'm confused and terrified about what lies ahead when we reach our destination. With him butting in, it didn't help matters.

"I'm sorry, Ashur, for snapping at you. I'm just a little tense right now. Thank you for offering my coat, but I will decline."

He gives me an amused expression and shakes his head, probably from me not wanting my coat. If the warriors can stand the bitter cold without protection, then I can. His eyes lock on something straight ahead and I turn to look at what he's staring at. Up ahead, the distinction between the Fall Court and the Winter Court is apparent. It's amazing how things change from mild to extreme. The dividing line between the courts is clear. On one side, the green grass and the colorful leaves of the trees are present. The sky is still blue with a mixture of clouds. On the other side, there are thick snow clouds and the snow is cascading down in abundance. I can already see from here that the land is beautifully covered in white powdery snow. It sparkles and glistens like diamonds. We are almost to the dividing line when the temperature starts to change. A shiver rolls down my spine and my traitorous mind says that maybe I should rethink putting on my coat. No, I chastise myself. I can't look weak.

My teeth are silently chattering and my hands begin to shake from gripping the reigns so tightly. I close my eyes from the chill of the wind because it's starting to make them water and burn. As soon as I open them, the Winter Palace comes into view. My throat tightens and I struggle to swallow. This is going to be a test for me, a test to see how strong I am. I take a deep breath and with determination, I steady my gaze at the palace. I will pass the test, and I will come out on top.

Chapter Five

Kalen

The meeting with my family and the warriors went as well as could be expected. Safety was discussed and it was decided where our guests will be staying for the night. I'm now in my bedroom looking in anticipation at the cottage next to my cabin on the right. I was told Meliantha and her guests will be staying in that cottage for their visit. Excitement and dread both spiked in my gut when I heard they assigned her to that lodging. I want to see her, but I fear of what I'm going to see. Ryder has his log cabin beside mine on the left, and he and Calista will be staying there with little Merrick when they arrive. These three houses are the only ones on the eastern side of the palace. Everyone else will be staying in other places scattered around the Winter grounds.

Being so close to Meliantha is going to kill me. I felt the connection we had years ago and I thought she did, too, but she denied me when I went to visit her. I had planned to tell her how I felt and to possibly see if I was the one to complete her, but the door was slammed in my face. I am hoping to get the chance to talk to her tonight to see what I did wrong. Being rejected by her devastated me. She's probably not going to want anything to do with me now once she finds out I am to marry another.

I look out the window and the fountain across the way is frozen. I send out my power to melt the water to get it flowing again. It would be nice to see running water around here instead of ice, and to also see some color scattered about like the flowers in the Summer Court. I'm starting to get tired of seeing nothing but white. I hear my front door opening and closing, and the sound of light steps running up the stairs.

"Uncle Kalen!"

My thoughts of Meliantha and a different land are thrust out of my mind when the high-pitched childlike voice of my nephew screams my name. Hearing him brings a much needed smile to my face. He bursts through my door and runs straight for my arms squealing and laughing the whole way. I laugh and scoop him up to twirl him around the room.

"Hey, little man, how is my favorite nephew doing?" I laugh.

I look over at the door as Ryder and Calista enter the room with smiles on their faces. They look so happy together. A spark of jealousy ignites in my gut, but I try to swallow it down. I envy their happiness; I want it for myself, also. I often dream of what my children will look like and every time they come out looking just like Meliantha with her silky, auburn red hair and amethyst eyes.

I hug Merrick one last time before I set him down. "I saw puppy, Kalen, I saw puppy," he shrieks excitedly.

He must be talking about Accalia. She's the pup of Aki and Larentia and they are part of my pack of white wolves. They consider me to be their alpha, so I make sure to spend a good deal of time with them. I remember speaking to Meliantha about them and how interested she was in learning more since one of her magical abilities is with animals. I was looking forward to having her meet my wolves.

Ryder walks over, scoops Merrick in his arms, and grins.

"I told you, son, that they're wolves... not puppies."

Merrick shakes his head and shrieks again, "Puppies!"

Ryder looks to me and whispers loudly, "He gets his stubbornness from his mother."

He bellows out a laugh and Calista walks over to smack him across the head. Calista wraps me in her arms and whispers, "Your brother has no clue what he's talking about." She releases me from the hug and winks at me. It feels good having my brother back here. I didn't realize how much I would miss him after he left.

"I'm so glad you all could make it. Have you settled in already?" I ask.

"Elvena is here, and she's getting our stuff unpacked. She's going to watch little Merrick tonight while we attend the ball," Calista answers.

Ryder walks over with Merrick in his arms and claps me on the shoulder.

"Congratulations on the engagement, brother," he announces. "You know, Calista and I both thought you and Meliantha would have hit it off by now. You seemed really interested in each other at our wedding."

I couldn't stop my smile from fading. A sense of longing rumbles in my gut and the hole that's been placed in my heart from before has just grown bigger. I shrug my shoulders slowly. and I look at Calista when I speak.

"I don't know what happened. I felt the connection the moment I saw her and I instantly fell for her. I went to visit her not long after your wedding to pursue her, but she denied me and told me never to come back."

Calista's eyes go wide and she places her hand over her chest. She's obviously shocked.

She shakes her head in disbelief and cries, "I wonder why she didn't tell me. I had no clue you went to see her." She looks away and whispers to herself, "Why wouldn't she tell me?"

Ryder places his hand on her shoulder and squeezes. "I don't know why she wouldn't tell you, love. Maybe you should ask her."

She nods her head and then turns to me with worried eyes. She hesitates before speaking. "There is something else you should know, Kalen," she warns. "Meliantha isn't the same anymore. She's not the same tender-hearted and shy girl that you knew years ago. I don't know what happened to her, but she isn't like that anymore." She looks down to fidget with her hands, and if Calista is fidgeting then that means the situation is serious and she's truly worried. A feeling of dread settles in the pit of my stomach. It's been five years now, and I can only imagine what all has changed.

"By your tone, you make it sound like she's changed in a really bad way. What do you mean exactly?" I ask, pleading.

They both look at each other and then back to me.

"Maybe you should see for yourself when she gets here," Ryder insists.

Calista grabs my hand and squeezes. "I'm going to

talk to her when she gets here. I want some answers, too."

"Thank you," I say, squeezing her hand in return.

Ryder nudges Calista in the side and says, "Alright, love, we need to go and get this little one to Elvena so we can get ready for the ball." He looks at me with serious eyes and his tone grows urgent.

"If you're only going through with this engagement because of Meliantha, you really need to back out of it. Please think before you jump into it, because once you say the sacred vow, you're bound for life."

I don't love Breena, but I don't want to hurt her either.

"I'll keep that in mind," I quickly reply.

Merrick reaches over from Ryder's arms to give me a hug goodbye.

"Bye, Uncle Kalen," he squeaks.

"Bye, little man. Maybe I'll show you the wolves later?" I ask. He squeals so loud I have to put my hands over my ears to keep them from bursting. I guess the squeal means yes.

"We'll see you tonight, Kalen," Calista says while taking the squealing Merrick with her out the door. Ryder waves goodbye as well and follows them. Again, I'm left alone with my thoughts until I hear the horn sounding off from the palace tower. The sounds of the horns make my chest tighten with anxiety because they signify there are people approaching. Since I'm the leader of the Winter Court Army, it is customary to meet all approaching guests. I don't mind in this case because I know I'll get to see Meliantha, but I'm nervous about seeing her.

I don't know what to expect, but I'm also glad she's here because she'll have no choice but to talk to me. It'll give me some closure if I understand her hostility toward me. I leave my room and head down the stairs. It's snowing like always, but the cold doesn't bother me as I step outside. The Winter fae are not affected by the cold, but the Summer fae will find it more difficult to handle. I walk along the path that heads to the back palace entrance. From there I'll walk through the palace to the front doors where our guests will be entering. As I'm walking through the main palace entryway something stops me mid-step. The hairs on the back of my neck stand up, and a strong uneasiness washes over my body. This is really odd. Why would I feel this way?

I try to get an idea where it could be coming from, but I don't find anything unusual. I look at both warriors standing guard, but nothing seems amiss other than the prickling of my scalp sending off warnings. I haven't had these feelings in a long time, not since everything started with Calista. A revelation comes to mind, and I can't believe the thoughts haven't been discussed before now. This would be the perfect time for the dark sorcerer to strike. We all know he will come again, but with it being five years, I think some people have lost their fear and moved on. I need to ask Calista if she has sensed anything since she's been here. She's had first-hand experience with the dark sorcerer, so I'm sure she would know. What are we going to do if he's here?

"Kalen."

I am brought out of my reverie at the sound of my father's voice calling my name. He walks toward me with my brother, Brayden, in tow.

Brayden is about two years younger than me making him twenty-four now, and he looks exactly like my father with his short, chocolate brown hair and dark brown eyes. Brayden looks at me with a serious expression just like he always does. That is one thing that makes me completely different from him. He's always serious, whereas I normally joke around. Unfortunately, I haven't been my usual self for a very long time. I can't remember the last time I've seen Brayden smile or myself for that matter.

When they reach me my father looks from Brayden to me and commands, "When the Summer fae get here we will greet them, and then you," he points to Brayden, "will take King Oberon and Queen Tatiana to where they'll be staying and I will let you," my father then looks at me, "escort the princesses to their quarters since they will be staying in the cottage beside your cabin."

My heart starts beating frantically with the thoughts of having to escort Meliantha to her cottage. I have no idea how our reunion is going to be, but I put on a smile and respond, "As you wish, Father." Brayden just nods his head in reply when my father looks at him.

He claps us on the shoulders and says happily, "Alright, boys, let's go meet our guests. The dwarves and the elves should arrive soon as well." My father has always loved to have a good party. It'll be very entertaining to see King Oberon and him carrying on and having a good time.

We walk out the front doors of the palace to await our arriving guests. We stand at the top of the steps with my father in the middle, my brother and I flanking him. In the distance, the Summer fae are heading through the palace gates. There's a contingent of warriors on their horses and four carriages, but they are still too far away to get a good look at them.

"Where, may I ask, is the Queen?" I ask my father sarcastically.

He clamps his lips together like he's trying to hold in a laugh and shakes his head.

"You know why she's not here, Kalen. Her direct quote was," he clears his throat and mimics my mother's voice when he continues, "'I don't want to have to spend any extra time with that Summer wench than I have to.'" I can't help but laugh at how well he mimics my mother. Brayden smirks and looks off into the distance at our oncoming guests. My mother and Queen Tatiana have never really gotten along, so hopefully there won't be too much drama between them tonight.

"That is definitely something she would say," I say to my father.

My thoughts are cut off quickly when the contingent of Summer fae come into full view. My fae vision is immaculate, but I can't be seeing what I think I'm seeing. That can't be Meliantha on the horse coming this way, can it? I close my eyes and blink them a few times because surely that's not her. My eyes have not deceived me…it is her. Her long, beautiful, auburn hair is pulled back in a tight braid and her clothes—she's wearing warrior gear with the leather and everything. Her upper arms are bare and I know she has to be cold. Surprisingly, she's actually showing no signs of discomfort. She hasn't looked at me yet and by the way her face is averted, I can see she is trying to avoid it for as long as possible. There is one thing I know for certain, I can't seem to take my eyes off of her. I feel mesmerized like I did all those years ago. The connection I felt then feels like it's igniting in my chest all over again. The feelings are too strong to ignore. She may be with another man, but I know she can't be happy, just like I'm not happy with Breena.

It feels like I'm defying all balances of nature with keeping my distance from her. I should have pursued her more and demanded to know what I did wrong all those years ago. I left like a coward and didn't listen to my heart. I don't plan on doing that anymore. Now all I need to figure out is what I'm going to do about Breena.

The carriages are pulling up and I see Meliantha in the back riding along with the warriors. I bet the King and Queen didn't like that at all. Her face is turned away, but I can see the tight grip she has on her reigns and the rigidness of her body as she sits regally atop her black faerie stallion. Even with the harsh expression on her face, she is still as beautiful as I remember her. She's riding in between her Guardian, Ashur, and her lover, Finn. I remember seeing them both fight Merrick during the Guardian Ceremony for Calista. I look at Ashur and he nods his head at me in greeting, but Finn just gives me a blank expression and remains stoic upon his horse. It doesn't look like we're going to be friends. I honestly don't give a damn if he likes me or not. If Meliantha is meant to be with me, then there is nothing he can do about it and neither could Breena for that matter. I can't stop my eyes from travelling back over to Meliantha. She's looking at her Guardian with a serious but pleading look. They must be having a silent conversation, and by the look on her face, she doesn't look happy. I notice that her face has lost the sharp angles it once had and has now filled out to be soft and full. Her lips are still as pouty as before, and I remember how I had longed to kiss them when I was in her presence. Her body has also changed from gangly to well-toned and curvy. She was always beautiful, but now she's breathtaking.

I heard that she's been training all these years and I see that it's definitely changed her both mentally and physically. She seems to be more confident and obviously stronger. Her bow and arrows are strapped securely on her back, and I can see the special arrows I've heard so much about. It was a good idea by the dwarves to not only make the guardian daggers but to also make other special weapons to be used as protection. Looking at her proud posture and arrogant expression I can tell that she's not the same Meliantha I knew before. She could almost belong here in the Winter Court with the ice-cold vibe I'm getting from her.

King Oberon and Queen Tatiana step out of the carriage and my father greets them with a welcoming smile.

"Greetings King Oberon and Queen Tatiana of the Summer Court. I hope your journey went well."

Queen Tatiana smiles at my father then at me and Brayden. King Oberon addresses my father and clasps his forearm in the warrior greeting.

"Yes, King Madoc, our journey went well, thank you. I look forward to enjoying the festivities with you tonight, my friend." He gives my father a wolfish smile and they both laugh.

"As do I," my father laughs. Those two together can be quite a show. The parties are never boring when my father and King Oberon get together.

My father puts a hand on Brayden's shoulder and says to King Oberon, "My son, Prince Brayden, will show you and the queen to your quarters." He looks over at me and continues, "And my son, Prince Kalen, will show the princesses to theirs."

I heard a hiss come from Meliantha, so I jerk my head to look at her. She closes her eyes for just a second and pulls her bottom lip between her teeth biting hard. I can tell she wants to object. Damn it, I wish I knew what the hell her problem is with me.

King Oberon nods his head at my father and turns to clasp Brayden's forearm.

"Thank you, Prince Brayden. It's been years since I have been here and I look forward to the tour."

Brayden bows his head and murmurs, "It is my pleasure, Your Highness. Feel free to venture anywhere you please. I'll show you to your quarters now so that you can rest up before the ball tonight."

King Oberon motions to the carriage and out comes two beautiful ladies. I recognize the curly blonde-headed one as being Meliantha's best friend, Elissa, and the other blonde hair beauty is Ariella, Meliantha's younger sister. Ariella turns in circles to look at the palace and its surroundings in awe. I've never seen a Summer fae so fascinated in the Winter Court before. She appears to be more at home here than me. I look over to see that Brayden appears to be fascinated by her actions as well. I narrow my eyes at him and study him for a moment. It's very odd because he never shows interest in the females— or anything for that matter— other than fighting. I sneak a glance at Ariella and she notices him staring at her. She gives him a flirty smile and the trance he was in seems to break in an instant. I need to remind myself to ask him what that was all about.

He clears his throat and turns away from Ariella to

look at King Oberon. He stammers at first but then regains his composure.

"This way, Your Highness. I'll show you the way," he insists.

"Thank you," King Oberon replies. He takes Queen Tatiana by the hand and motions with his other for their servants to help bring the luggage and follow them. The contingent of warriors follows in their wake as well because they will be staying close to the King and Queen's quarters. My father follows along after King Oberon, and I can hear their laughs echoing off the palace walls as they walk through.

I'm now left with the remaining Summer fae, which includes Meliantha, Ariella, Elissa, Ashur, and Finn. They are all looking at me for direction, except Meliantha who still has her head turned away from me. I really want to see her reaction when she looks at me. I want to see if I affect her as much as she affects me. Ariella and Elissa walk up the steps to wait on the others to dismount their horses.

Ashur dismounts first and comes over to clasp my arm in greeting.

"Thank you, Prince Kalen, for offering to guide us."

"It is my pleasure, Guardian Ashur," I offer.

I noticed Meliantha's body shivered when I spoke, and I also noticed that she shut her eyes tight. Could she be feeling the connection, too? My thoughts are put on hold as the uneasy feeling I had before they arrived returns in full force. I look around quickly to spot the danger, but again, nothing seems wrong until I look up at Finn. His eyes hold a deadly intent that wasn't there before. He dismounts his horse and walks over to help Meliantha down from hers. She gives him an odd look, and I can tell she feels something is wrong as well. He reaches for her waist and he slides her off her horse to the ground. Finn grabs her hand in a possessive grip and pulls her closer to him. She clearly doesn't like what he's doing from the frown appearing on her face. Well, hell, I don't like what he's doing, and I believe my reddened face is clear proof of that. The heat rising to my cheeks make them burn, and if I had my way, I would rip off his arms. I tear my anger-filled gaze away from Finn to look at Meliantha. I can see she's looking down at my clenched hands, Her pensive expression lets me know she can feel my anger.

She bites her lip, and then from out of nowhere she lifts her face slowly to meet mine. Her amethyst-colored eyes bore into mine, and my heart instantly stops. Her eyes go wide and she puts a hand over her chest before sucking in a sharp breath.

The blast from the connection has me weak in the knees, and I would have stumbled back if I didn't catch myself in time. She can't deny these feelings now because I know she feels them, too. I see it in her eyes. The look on her face goes from shock to confused, but then it changes to anger.

I'm taken aback; I don't understand why she would have hostility toward me. I've never done anything to her to make her react this way. I thought she would be happy to have this connection. I know her feelings in the past were growing for me each second she spent with me, and I felt the same feelings for her.

Finn's grip on Meliantha catches my attention. It looks hard and bruising, and what's really strange is that his expression is one of alarm, not anger. This guy is acting really weird and the vibes I'm getting aren't good ones at all. I honestly don't like him being around Meliantha and holding on to her so hard. I reach for her hand, but she quickly pulls away. My chest tightens with rejection.

I'm beginning to worry about her relationship with Finn. Why won't she let me touch her, and why is she letting Finn do this to her? I don't understand what's going on. If we are meant to be together, why is she fighting it? I take a couple of deep breaths to calm my nerves before turning my attention to the group of Summer fae before me.

"I believe it's time to show you to your quarters now. If you would follow me please," I announce.

I take them to the back entrance of the palace so we can take the path to where the cottage is located. I'm confused as hell and uncertain about this turn of events. What the hell am I going to do now? I'm engaged to another woman, but have loved someone else this whole time. Now, the one woman I had fallen in love with years ago has changed into a different person and is deeply involved with another man. How did things get so complicated?

I can feel the frustration building, so I quicken my pace to hopefully get the thoughts of killing someone out of my head. I would really love to beat the shit out of Finn right now, but I don't think that would be such a great idea. Imagining him and Meliantha together all these years make me livid. I know I have had Breena, but I never enjoyed sleeping with her. I shake my head and run my fingers through my hair.

I really don't need to think about it, and so I chastise myself. I decide to concentrate on figuring out a way to get

Meliantha alone, so I can speak to her privately. She has to hear what I have to say. The only sounds I hear as we walk along the path to their cottage are the sounds of their footsteps crunching on the path, and the sounds of the snow pattering on the ground.

Chapter Six

Meliantha

- Arriving at the Palace -

This can't be happening, I scream at myself. How can I be feeling this connection to Kalen after everything that's happened and after everything he's put me through? I can see Kalen's hands clench when Finn possessively wraps his arm around me I kept repeating to myself over and over that I can do this and keep my distance; however, some strong force is urging me to look up. I tell myself not to look him, but my eyes have a mind of their own and betray me. They search for his eyes and find them staring back intently at me. The pull to him is so strong it makes me weak in the knees. I thought hearing his voice earlier was a shock to my system, but nothing compares to this. My heart flutters at the sight of him, and I grab my chest hoping it'll stop. I don't want to feel this way for the man that broke my heart. I need to feel the anger. The anger has gotten me through the pain all these years, so I dig deep within my soul to bring it to the surface.

I look at Kalen defiantly and I lift my chin. I refuse to be swayed by his charms; however, there is something different about him now. He doesn't have the callous and evil looking eyes he had back when he broke my heart. He still looks like the same playful Kalen from before, but now he looks defeated and saddened.

Finn momentarily distracts me with the vice-like grip he has on my arm keeping me by his side. The look he's giving Kalen sends chills down my spine and it has me worried. Finn has never been the jealous type.. He has always been easy going and laid back. I can tell Kalen is starting to get angry with the way Finn is acting toward him and the way he is holding me. He reaches for my hand, but I quickly step back. My heart stops at the thought of him touching me, but my mind refuses to let me budge. He looks hurt at my rejection, but it quickly dissipates into anger when he looks down at Finn's heavy grip on my arm. In a clipped tone, he addresses the whole group and says for us to follow him to our quarters. His stride is quick and angry as he leads us out the back of the palace and back into the bitter cold.

Finn and I follow behind him while Elissa, Ashur, and Ariella trail along behind us. We're all silent as we make our way along the path. I can hear Ariella sighing behind me in amazement. She's always had a fascination with the Winter Court and I'm glad she's enjoying her time here. At least one of us is.

The white and snowy landscape is beautiful here, but the absence of flowers and greenery makes me feel empty. I could never live here and be happy seeing nothing but white for the rest of my life. I can see down the path and we're headed toward three different houses and a gorgeous water fountain. The water is actually flowing, which I find odd since the temperature is below freezing. Kalen must be working his water magic on it to get it flowing. The houses up ahead are two log cabins —one more luxurious than the other —and a little cottage nestled off to the side.

The cabins are simple with their basic log frames, but the cottage beside them looks quaint and elegant. It looks like a cottage in Italy surrounded by a vineyard. I can tell it's made from various varieties of gray stones with a steep gabled roof, which no doubt has been used to keep the weight of the snow off the cottage.

This place would be absolutely lovely surrounded by flowers. I can feel a twinge in my heart at the thought of flowers and gardens. I've neglected them recently and I know the land feels like I've abandoned it. I have promised it numerous times that I'll return, but deep down I am afraid that I'm already lost.

I try desperately to get the thoughts out of my mind and to concentrate on the task at hand. The snow crunches beneath my feet and the frosty air smells of pine as it burns its way down my lungs. I have the urge to cough, but I hold it back as best I can. I'm not used to the dry, crisp air of the Winter Court. My body definitely isn't either, especially my feet. I can feel the cold spreading its way through my body, giving me the chills. I clench my teeth down hard to keep the chattering from being heard. I'm silently cursing my stupidity as I look at Elissa admiring the palace grounds in her fluffy wool coat. Why was I trying to prove how strong I was by not wearing a coat?

Finn must have felt me shiver because he pulls me in closer to his body. I can feel his warmth and it does help, but my comfort is put on hold when I look up at his face. He gives me a wink and a sly grin, but it's not a look I have seen on Finn's face before. I think the chills I'm getting are not from the cold, but from him. I try to pull away from him slightly but his grip tightens on my arm keeping me in place. I have never been manhandled before, and it sure as hell isn't going to start now. I grit my teeth to keep my anger held back. To avoid causing a scene, I call out to Ashur silently.

"Don't look at me. Ashur, and don't acknowledge that I'm talking to you, but I need your help. Something is wrong with Finn and he won't let go of my arm when I try to pull away. I'm trying to keep everyone from noticing, but he's beginning to piss me off and I'm not far from losing my temper."

"Calm down and breathe, Princess. I could tell his mood switched from being pleasant to hostile in a matter of seconds. I was going to say something, but I didn't want to alarm you. Has he done this before?"Ashur inquires.

"Not to this extent, but there have been occasions when…" I pause, not wanting to tell him the rest. "Well, there have been times when he's been a little rough and not his usual gentle self, if that answers your question."

"No need to explain, Princess. I really don't want to know the details. Oh wait…look ahead, Meliantha. I think you have your way to escape."

I look ahead and, yes, I see my escape plan. Little Merrick, Calista, and Ryder are in front of the log cabins playing in the snow and having a snowball fight. They all look so happy together and I can't help but be envious of what they have. I honestly believed that Kalen was going to be the man I shared all of that with. Calista notices us first and then Merrick. The snow throwing stops and with a mischievous grin, Calista leans down to whisper in Merrick's ear pointing straight at us. If I didn't know any better, I would say Calista might be plotting a snow war. She's not the only one in the family who can throw things and always hit their target. Merrick bends down to grab a handful of snow and charges off screaming in my direction with a huge smile on his face.

"Mel, Mel, Mel!"

I know he plans to bombard me with his snowball so I use this chance to pull away from Finn to run to Merrick. Luckily, he lets me go easily, but if he hadn't we were going to have some serious problems. I'm running toward the squealing Merrick and I lunge for his legs. I scoop him up into my arms and over my shoulders. He squeals when I pick him up and he slams the snowball into my back, laughing and giggling the whole time. The coldness of the snow makes me cringe and now I can't stop the shivering. I laugh it off and swing Merrick around and around in circles watching his fluffy blond curls sway in the wind. He wraps his arms around my neck and latches on when he squeals, "Miss you, Mel!"

I hug him tight and whisper in his ear, "I know, sweetheart, and I've missed you just as much." I kiss his cheek and put him down. His eyes find Ariella, and he squeals while running off to her. Ariella beams at the sight of Merrick, and she kneels down to embrace him when he reaches her. She scoops him up just like I did and they laugh and giggle the whole time while running and playing in the snow. I steal a quick glance at Kalen and he still looks rigid and angry while Finn stands off to the side with a bored expression on his face. Elissa is staring at Ashur and is failing miserably to be nonchalant as she slowly migrates toward him. If I wasn't feeling so uneasy right now I would find the situation humorous. I can tell by Ashur's posture that he can feel the unease in my body. His body is tense and remains on full alert. My heart swells with pride, and I know that I couldn't have asked for a better guardian than Ashur.

"It's good to see you, Meliantha," Calista says, capturing my attention. I turn to look at her and confusion is written all over her face. I can tell by the determination in her eyes that she plans to find out once and for all what's going on with me. It quickly disappears as a new look crosses her face. Her body goes tense and she looks around the group hesitantly before settling her eyes on Finn.

The moment he meets her eyes everything around me changes. The chills prickling my spine ease and the menace I felt permeating the air earlier evaporates. It's as if a huge weight has been lifted off my chest and I can now breathe easier. I think the whole group notices the change as well.

A look of worry passes across Calista's face and she quickly peers over at Ryder. They nod their heads in some kind of silent agreement and then Ryder turns to Kalen.

"Let's go, brother. We need to give Calista some time alone with her kin. She can give them the tour of the cottage while we have us some mead before the ball," he says to Kalen.

I can tell Kalen is clenching his teeth by the tension of the muscles in his face.

"Very well," he replies to his brother.

He gives me one last look and then turns around to walk toward the larger cabin that is beside the cottage. I guess that is the one where he stays. Ryder walks alongside him and I can't stop my traitorous eyes from staring at Kalen's retreating form. I've watched him walk away before, but this time it feels different. My heart is demanding that I follow him and the pull in my stomach is making it hard for me to stay in place. It's as if I'm a magnet being drawn to him and the harder I fight it, the harder it is to stay away.

With a devilish grin, Kalen turns around while walking backward and has his eyes trained on Finn when he yells, "You might want to watch where you step. The ground can be quite…slippery!" Ryder rolls his eyes and grabs Kalen by the shirt to jerk him back around. Finn starts to move toward me when all of a sudden he slips on a patch of ice that miraculously appears under his feet. He goes down with a thud and lands hard on his back side. I can hear Kalen's deep laugh as he makes his way onto the porch of his cabin. I give Finn my hand and he grabs it to pull himself up. Kalen stands on his porch and gives Finn a stare of pure anger. Finn stares right back at him with one of his own.

"What the hell is his problem, and why is he looking at me like that?" Finn demands. I look into his eyes, and yes, they hold anger from being laughed at, but I can see no trace of evil in them at all. The look he gives me is full of love and devotion, but also of confusion. He brushes off his clothes and lifts his eyebrows at me waiting on an answer.

"You have no idea why Kalen would be the way that he is right now?" I ask. Looking back and forth from me to Calista, he shrugs his shoulders and shakes his head. Oh no! This is just like before when he would have his episodes of forgetting. It hasn't happened in a while, so I was beginning to think it was over. He stands there looking confused when all of a sudden Calista gasps and brings her hands up to cover her mouth.

Looking wide-eyed she warns wearily, "Mel, this

isn't right. I felt something evil here and I felt it in Finn. It reminds me of the evil I felt five years ago when I was captured by the dark sorcerer, but right now I don't feel it at all. I think we have a problem."

My heart sinks to the deepest levels of despair because if what she is suggesting is true, then the dark sorcerer was here and…in Finn's body. I close my eyes and wrap my arms around my stomach. Bile rises in my throat and I begin to feel disgusted to the core. This would explain the reason for Finn's blackouts.

I look at Calista and scream, "Damn it, Calista do you know what this means?"

She looks at me with sympathy and understanding. She says softly, "Yes, I know exactly what this means. I'm so sorry, Meliantha." She takes my hand and pulls me into her arms. She clutches me tight and whispers in my ear, "There has to be something on him that allows the dark sorcerer to enter his body."

I take a few deep, shaky breaths and I close my eyes while she rubs my back soothingly. "We'll find it, Mel, but we have to find it now and get rid of it. There's no telling when the dark sorcerer will make his move again. We need to let everyone in the court know the dark sorcerer is back."

Tears of anger and despair are pooling behind my closed eyes and when I open them they fall, leaving warm trails in their wake. All those strange nights when I thought I was giving myself to Finn I was actually giving myself to the dark sorcerer. My chest tightens in anger because all I can think about is how much of a fool I had been not knowing the dark sorcerer was screwing me over…literally. Being violated and deceived like that makes this whole situation a million times worse. My lungs tighten and I pull away from Calista gasping for air. Finn runs over to grab my face in between his hands and Elissa runs up behind me and starts rubbing my back. They both whisper soothing words in my ear. Ashur hangs back because I know he heard my inner turmoil and he's trying to give me space. He knows there is nothing he can do to help me. Spots cloud my vision and my legs begin to feel weak.

Finn lifts my chin for me to meet his golden amber eyes, and his voice is angelically soft when he speaks.

"You need to calm down, Mel. Breathe slower…in and out. Come on, you can do it."

I listen to his words and I do as he says. His soothing voice lulls me back down and he pulls me into his arms and holds me tight.

"That's it, Mel. You're doing well," he says while rubbing my back.

He looks at Calista and demands in an urgent tone, "I need to know what's going on. I can tell it involves me, and you need to tell me…now!"

My mind goes numb and I no longer hear their words when my guardian's voice enters my mind filled with concern.

"I heard your thoughts, Meliantha. Could it really be true?"Ashur asks.

"I believe so, Ashur. I feel so ashamed and violated. All those times when we…when we…" I can't seem to finish my sentence because the thought of voicing it makes my body cringe with anger and disgust. I can't believe I never said or did anything about Finn's blackout episodes.

"You don't need to say it, Meliantha. I'm sure Finn's

going to be extremely angry when he finds out."

I sigh, "I know, and that's what I'm afraid of."

Finn pulls back, hands on my face, and leans down to kiss my lips. His lips feel warm against mine, but I can't seem to feel any comfort in them. I break away from the kiss and he gives me a hesitant smile before wiping the tears from my face.

"All right everyone." Calista grabs our attention and looks back and forth among the four of us. "Go to the cottage while I get Ariella and Merrick. We have to figure everything out immediately." She turns to walk up the path in the direction Ariella and Merrick went while playing in the snow.

I know my voice is going to be shaky, but I speak anyway.

"OK, let's get out of the cold and figure out what's going on."

I grab Finn's hand and we only have to walk a few yards before we get to the cottage. We walk up the steps to the small front porch and Ashur opens the door to let us enter. The living room is warm and cozy making my body instantly relax, but that is not what catches my attention when I look around the room. The room smells amazing with the scents of faerie flowers. Everywhere in the room there are vases filled with the millions of different flowers we have in the Summer Court. I wonder who did it all.

"I believe Kalen did it, Princess."

I jerk my head around to glance at Ashur and he gives me a faint smile.

"How do you know that?" I ask.

"I just do."

Well, isn't that just cryptic? I roll my eyes at him and

I look out the window to see Calista carrying Merrick in her arms with Ariella following alongside her. I see them talking so Calista must be filling Ariella in on the events of what just happened.

"Are you going to be OK?" Elissa asks me while taking my hand.

She squeezes my hand tight and I squeeze hers back while giving her a gentle smile.

"Yes, Elissa, I'll be fine," I assure her. Why don't you and Ashur pick out a room and rest before the ball?"

She nods her head slowly and complies, "OK." Elissa kisses my cheek and heads off down the hallway to find a room. I don't know how many rooms are in the cottage, but I'm sure she will have plenty to choose from.

"Ashur, I want you to stay with Elissa while Calista and I sort this out," I insist while turning to acknowledge him. He bows his head and his lips tilt up slightly. I know he's happy about my request, but I can feel he's hesitant to leave me alone. He knows I don't want them to be in here when Calista and I speak with Finn.

The door opens and Ariella walks in first and heads straight for me. Her long, platinum blonde hair is soaked and her translucent blue eyes can't hide the fear and worry emanating from them. Her boots squeak across the wooden floors as she closes the distance. She gives Finn a long, hard look while wrapping me in her arms and whispering urgently in my ear, "He's after you this time, isn't he?"

The thought of it should terrify me, and it did in the beginning, but now all I feel is anger and disgust for being played like a fool. The dark sorcerer has already violated me one too many times, so what's the worse he can do now? I'll be ready for him when he makes his move.

I hold onto my younger sister and I can feel the power flowing through her body. She'll be twenty-one in another few months and there's no telling how much her power will grow then. I hate keeping the secret of my healing capabilities away from them, but now that I know the dark sorcerer has been spying on me it's a good thing I haven't said a word. I look over Ariella's shoulder at Calista and she motions with her hand for me to hurry up. She's holding Merrick in her arms and the poor little thing looks tuckered out. I let go of Ariella so I can look at her face.

"Yes, he's after me this time, but I don't want you to worry about me. I'll be fine," I encourage her. "Can you take Merrick into another room while Calista and I speak?"

"Of course," Ariella says while nodding her head. She walks over to Calista, takes the sleepy Merrick into her arms, and ventures off down the hall.

Finn is impatiently tapping his foot up and down on the floor waiting on Ariella to leave the room. Once she is gone, he looks back and forth from Calista to me expectantly.

"Alright, we're alone now. What the hell is going on?" Finn demands.

"There's something on your body that is laced with black magic and we have to find it, now!" Calista answers urgently.

Finn's eyes go wide as he takes in a sharp breath. I think he realizes the dire situation we are in. He backs up slowly and lowers his gaze. He looks distraught and it makes my heart ache for him. I can't imagine how it would feel to know my body was being taken over and used in a sick game of charades. There are so many emotions flowing through me that I don't know which one to hold on to. If the dark sorcerer fooled us all these years, there's no telling what things he has done without our knowledge.

Finn is shaking and clenching his hands into tight fists of fury. I take a couple of slow steps toward him, but he abruptly turns around to put his back to me.

"I'm so sorry, Mel," he whispers. "Did I ever do anything to hurt you when he was in my body?"

Thinking back there were times when he did get a little rough during our intimate moments, but telling him that would just send him over the edge. I don't want to hurt him like that.

"No, Finn. You never hurt me," I whisper back.

We need to find the magical object and get rid of it. That way the dark sorcerer can never take over his body again. The dark sorcerer can imitate him, but with all of our powers combined in one place, I don't think he'll be able to fool us. Being around my sister feels like it's magnified my power to a whole other level.

I could feel the dark sorcerer's presence more when Calista was around. I'm starting to think that we're more powerful together than apart. This concept is definitely something we need to discuss.

Finn gently pulls away and turns around to face me. He looks down at me with his sensual amber eyes and draws me tight against his body. I wrap my arms around his waist and I lay my head on his chest.

I can hear the deep rumble of his voice when he asks Calista, "What could I possibly have on my body that would have been spelled by the dark sorcerer?" He lifts the arm that has his golden band circling his bicep and continues, "I'm not wearing anything other than my clothes and this golden band I received as a gift from Durin, the dwarf leader when Mel's arrows were delivered."

I stand back abruptly to take a look at his gold cuff. It was supposed to be a gift from Durin, but Durin didn't deliver it, one of his people did. I knew I found it odd that Finn would receive such a gift. It never made sense, but now that can only mean one thing...there's a traitor in the dwarf kingdom!

"It's the cuff! Finn, take the cuff off!" I yell apprehensively. As long as he has it on his body, the dark sorcerer can take him over. He slides it off quickly and it falls to the floor with a heavy thump. We all freeze in place and stare at the gold band lying helplessly on the floor. I want to take it and rip it to shreds, but I have no idea how to destroy it.

"Finn, would you mind getting me something to wrap it in?" Calista asks.

"Yes, Your Highness," he says and quickly sets off in search of something to use. When he's out of sight Calista grabs both my arms in desperation.

"Mel, this is really bad news. He's played games with you for five years now. He could have taken you multiple times. Why would he do that?" she asks, confused.

"I don't know, but I could tell earlier that Kalen could feel that something was wrong around us, and when *you* came in sight the feelings intensified. I think with us together it makes us stronger. You felt how fast the evil disappeared when you looked at Finn the way you did. I'm beginning to believe the dark sorcerer wasn't expecting us to be stronger together," I state.

At my mention of Kalen, she furrows her brows and purses her lips.

"Speaking of Kalen, what happened between you two? I thought things were going great for you at the wedding. One minute you look like you're in love and the next you turn into Xena the warrior princess with a heart of ice." She pauses and then continues to look at me skeptically when she continues, "The reason why I'm asking is because I'm concerned for you, and Kalen has wanted to know for years why you denied him."

What? Kalen wants to know why I denied him? That doesn't make any sense. He's the one that turned me down.

"When did you talk to Kalen?" I snap.

"Right before you arrived he told me he came to visit you and you denied his visit. Why would you do that when you were obviously in love with him and him with you?" she retorts back.

I guess I can't keep the past hidden forever. I didn't want to have to tell anyone of that horrid visit, but I know Calista will understand. I close my eyes and take a deep breath. When I open my eyes Calista's gaze is filled with wisdom and sorrow. She's known pain and loss. I can't believe I was too afraid to confide in the one person that's always been by my side.

"Kalen came to visit me right after your wedding and said some real terrible things to me. He said I was too timid for his tastes. He broke my heart into a million pieces, and I vowed to never fall for a man like that ever again. I don't know what he told you, but that's what happened and that's what fueled my persistence to change."

She looks at me confused and shakes her head.

"He never said anything about talking to you." She bites her lip and looks around the room mumbling, "Something doesn't feel right about this. If the dark sorcerer fooled you once, who's to say he hasn't done it before, maybe with...Kalen?"

Thinking back to that day, things did feel a little odd and detached with the way Kalen was acting. Could it have been the dark sorcerer who visited me that day? He can't take over any of the royal's bodies, or at least he used to not be able to. Now that he has Calista's power we're not sure what capabilities he has. If it *was* the dark sorcerer being Kalen that day, then that would mean the *real* Kalen wasn't the one who denied me. How could I have been so stupid? I should have known something was wrong that day.

"Do you really think it could have been the dark sorcerer impersonating Kalen?" I ask Calista, hopeful.

She looks at me like I'm crazy and rolls her eyes when she says, "Mel, the dark sorcerer has been screwing around with you for years. Hell yeah, I think it was him. Kalen would never have done that to you."

"What am I going to do now? I've spent the last five years hating him for nothing," I cried. Feeling weak, I find the closest chair I can and fall into it. Resting my elbows on my knees, I cover my face with my hands in hopes of being able to think.

Calista kneels in front of me, takes my hands away from my face, and holds them in my lap.

"You're going to talk to Kalen, that's what you are going to do," she answers.

I can hear Finn fumbling around in a room down the

hall, so I take the chance to quickly confess to my sister. I whisper quietly, "I felt the connection, Calista. As soon as I saw Kalen, I felt it and I know he did, too. It blasted through my body with such force that I could barely stand. It feels the same way you said your connection with Ryder felt like."

She closes her eyes and sighs while hanging her head. This wasn't the reaction I was hoping for.

"Why are you acting like this? What's going on?" I demand.

She lifts her head with a sad look in her eyes. I can tell she's keeping something from me, but what? My hands start to sweat and I can feel my heart pounding. I'm beginning to get frustrated with all the secrets and lies being flown my way.

"There's something you should know," she begins, but stops when Finn enters the room carrying a thick black towel. Damn it, why couldn't he take a few minutes longer? I need to know what Calista was going to say.

"Do you think this towel will work?" Finn asks Calista while holding it out to her.

She gets to her feet and accepts the towel.

"Yes, Finn, this will work. Thank you." He bows his head in reply and comes to stand by my chair. Calista walks over to the gold band lying on the floor and picks it up using the towel making sure her skin doesn't touch it. I know I've touched it before and I've often wondered why the metal always stayed frigidly cold even after being on Finn's warm skin all day. It never made sense until today. The cuff is filled with the essence of black magic and there is nothing warm about that.

"I'm going to get Ryder and Kalen and tell them

everything. We need to inform King Madoc and Queen Mab as well as our parents to let them know we need to be on our guard tonight." She looks directly at me and commands, "You stay here with Finn and Ashur. I don't want you going anywhere by yourself, understand?"

She's treating me like the scared Meliantha from the past. I'm not that girl anymore and to be treated like it infuriates me.

"You don't need to treat me like a baby, Calista. I can take care of myself now if you haven't noticed," I say angrily. Her face falls at my outburst, so I soften the next words I speak. "I appreciate your concern, Calista, but I'm not stupid. I know to stay here with Finn and Ashur, and I didn't need you to have to tell me. What I need you to do is stop underestimating me. Can you do that?" I don't want to be mean to her, but I need her to be fully aware that I can take care of myself. The dark sorcerer is after my power this time, and I plan on being ready.

Calista looks back and forth between Finn and me, and with the band wrapped up and in her hands, she turns to head down the hall. A few minutes later she's back with a sleeping Merrick in her arms and Ariella following in her wake.

"What about the ball tonight, Calista? What are we going to do about that?" I ask quickly. If the dark sorcerer is here, he's bound to try something malicious.

She gives me a faint smile and answers hesitantly, "The ball is still going to happen and as long as you're not alone, you will be safe. Rest for now, sister, and I'll see you tonight."

Dealing with the dark sorcerer can't be easy for her. I know it's been five years, but the traumatic events she went through during her capture are bound to leave scars on her soul. I may not have been captured and watched my best friend die, but knowing the dark sorcerer has had his way with me intimately has left some deep wounds on my essence as well.

Calista and Ariella leave quickly and I'm left alone with Finn. My time with him may be coming to a close if what I suspect is true about Kalen. If he's the one I'm supposed to be with, then I have to let Finn go. Standing before me, Finn's face displays an array of emotions making it hard for me to tell what he's truly feeling.

He takes my face in his hands and sighs heavily before pleading, "Mel, I can't begin to express how sorry I am. You know I would never hurt you. Please don't let this come between us." He takes a deep breath and leans his forehead against mine.

I can hear the anger rumbling in his chest when he adds, "If the dark sorcerer ever, ever lays a hand on you again, I promise I'll do everything in my power to make him regret it." Finn is a very strong warrior, but I don't think his ability for air and wind is going to damage the dark sorcerer. I'll never tell him that, but it warms my soul to know that he'll risk his life to go up against the dark sorcerer to protect me. I would also do the same for him. I may not be in love with Finn, but the thought of being without him or losing him to death will be an extreme agony.

I kiss his cheek softly and I look at him with sheer determination.

"I know you would do that Finn, but if the dark sorcerer tries this again, it will be *me* that makes him regret it. He's toyed with me for far too long."

He tilts his lips up in a slow smile and chuckles.

"Of course you would, Mel. Why don't we rest for a while before getting ready for the ball?" He looks down my body and his eyes take on a lusty glow when he adds, "I can't wait to see you in your dress tonight. I bet you're going to have all the men demanding to dance with you."

My eyes go wide at the thought of my dress. I'm sure everyone's going to have something to say about it. I wonder if Kalen is going to be one of those men to ask for a dance, and if he is, what am I going to say to him? I have a few hours until the ball, so I'll worry about that when the time comes.

I smile sweetly at Finn and tease, "I'm pretty sure I'll be dancing with you most of the night. You are, after all, my date." His eyes sparkle and I laugh. "Come on, let's go find a room and relax. I'm sure tonight is going to be eventful and we're going to need our rest because of the long journey here."

We walk through the kitchen and down the hallway to find a room. There are so many to choose from, so I pick the first door I come to. I open the door and inside is an immaculate king size bed with a light purple comforter. Actually, everything in this room is purple, and there are flowers everywhere. Did Kalen do this for me, too? If he did, I think he went a little overboard with the purple. It is still beautiful, though. Finn walks past me into the room and begins to take off his warrior armor; however, he doesn't stop there. When he's done taking his clothes off, he lies down on the bed naked and pats the area beside him.

My stomach is in knots while I slowly remove the breastplate from my chest and then the vambraces from my arms. I don't want to give him the wrong impression by taking off all my clothes. He's very understanding, so I'm sure he'll understand if I don't want this to go further at the moment. I give him a faint smile and I know my eyes are conveying to him that I'm not in the mood. He smiles and shakes his head while patting the bed again. I leave my leathers on and I climb onto the bed beside his naked body. I honestly don't think sleep is going to come easily for me.

Finn moves closer to me from behind and presses his warm body against my back. He wraps his arm around my waist, and he snuggles closer as I lay my arm over his. We entwine our fingers and I grip his tightly. Finn has always been a comfort to me, but I don't think anything is going to calm and relax my rapidly beating heart. The terrible warnings from my soul are screaming at me saying that something terrible is going to happen tonight. All I know is that whatever it is, I'll be ready.

Chapter Seven

ALASDAIR

- Dark Sorcerer -

I left the warrior's body quickly as soon as I became discovered. I stick to the shadows as I make my way through the palace. I should have known that bitch Calista would sense me around, and what's worse is that when Meliantha got near I could feel their power intensify. Their other sister was there, too, and I could see the light shining inside of her, meaning that the power of the Four is growing. Her power will be ready for the taking very soon, but it's not her time yet. All I need to do now is keep the girls separated so their power can't track me as well.

By now Meliantha has probably figured out that it wasn't the real Kalen that betrayed her before. She may have turned her heart into stone all these years, but with this revelation she'll probably go running after the Prince like a bitch in heat. That works out just fine with my plan. It'll make everything that much better when she's forced to kill her one true love. Not only will I get her power, but it'll ruin all chances of their union once he's dead. The Land of the Fae will be closer to being mine.

Poor Meliantha will be useless when I take everything away from her. I silently laugh to myself thinking back to all the times I fucked her and she didn't even realize it was me. I might just have to find a way to get back between her legs somehow. She had a fiery temper in the bed, and I know I lost control on several occasions. Her fool of a lover had no clue I was using his body to have my way with the princess.

I arrive at my destination and appear on the other side of the door in my true form. I notice the box I brought earlier is on the bedside table and my vixen is already dressed for the ball. She's standing motionless by one of the windows with a blank expression on her face. Her eyes go wide as she sees my reflection in the window. She turns around abruptly.

"Alasdair," she says. "I wasn't expecting you so soon."

"Neither was I, but I came to inform you of the recent developments," I add, agitated. She furrows her brows and waits for me to continue. "The Summer fae know I'm here and I'm sure they are going to spread the word. Meliantha most likely knows already that it wasn't Kalen that broke her heart over five years ago."

Her eyes go wide and she puts her hand over her mouth.

"What's the plan now?" she asks. Her voice sounds muffled coming from behind her hand.

"Act like nothing is wrong when Kalen finds you and warns you of my presence. Give him his gift as soon as you can. Now that they know I'm here they will expect me to go after Meliantha. Their focus will be on her, so they'll never believe I would go after the prince."

She nods her head and agrees.

"OK, I will give him the gift as soon as I see him. Is there anything else I need to do?"

"Yes, I need you to give Kalen and Meliantha a little

time together to speak before our plan goes down tonight. Do what you have to, but make sure they get together. As soon as Meliantha and the prince talk to one another, they'll realize the past five years were wasted on false betrayals. He'll most likely call off the engagement once he finds out and that will put Meliantha exactly where I need her."

Breena goes completely still and clenches her jaw until she's red in the face. Her anger strikes me as odd. I'm beginning to wonder if she has developed feelings for the Winter Prince. How could she be so stupid to fall for the man she has been hell bent on destroying?

"He's never loved you, Breena," I snap. "No matter what you say or do he'll always love Meliantha. After tonight your prince will be dead, so get the hell over it. He's used you all these years, and I would think you would want payback for that."

She lifts her chin defiantly and wails, "I do want payback, and the reason I'm mad is that I hate being second best. What does that Summer bitch have that I don't?"

A million things for starters, I think to myself. Her attitude is starting to seriously infuriate me. I can feel the heat of my anger rising to my face, and if I didn't need her in one piece, I would put her in her place right now. Her petty little jealousies are not going to ruin my plans. I use my power to force her down on her knees.

"First off, you worthless bitch, Meliantha has fifty times more power than you will ever have, and she's also one of the Four which makes her valuable beyond belief. Second, you have no redeeming qualities other than being a filthy whore that will sleep with anyone and anything to get power, and third, she's much better in bed than you."

She's crying uncontrollably now and I bend down to grab her chin hard between my fingers. I jerk her face up to where she's looking me straight in the eyes.

"I've been patient with you all these years, and I didn't wait this long for you to fuck it up over an adolescent jealousy." I grip her chin tighter and she hisses in pain. "We are almost at our goal and if you screw this up, I'm going to make sure you join your precious prince in the Hereafter once all things are said and done. Are we clear?"

The tears run down her cheeks in rivulets and her body shakes uncontrollably. Her voice catches when she replies, "Yes, Master."

"Good."

I stand up and move away toward the door. I'm going to hang back during the ball and try to make some appearances. As long as the Four are not together, I'm sure I can have a little fun. I've worked too long for my plan to fail now.

Chapter Eight
Kalen

It took everything I had to walk away from
Meliantha. The pull drawing me to her refused to budge,
so I went against all instinct and moved my feet in the
opposite direction. Thankfully, Ryder was with me, and it
made things somewhat easier. I thought I was going to die
with laughter when I saw Meliantha's warrior fall flat on
his ass. Ryder scolded me, like the older brother he is,
when we made it inside my cabin. I flipped him off and
said some distinctively aggressive words back to him.

He left me to raid my kitchen cabinets in search of
my famous mead. I can brew a mighty good mead and I
make it potent as hell. Two tumblers will put a man on his
hands and knees. I've been that way plenty of times and
with the Solstice Ball being tonight, it might not be such a
good idea to get drunk. I decide against going to the
kitchen, so I can stay and watch Meliantha through the
window. I notice there's something strange going on, but I
can't tell what.

I can see both Meliantha and Calista look stressed by
their worried postures and the frowns upon their faces. If
something is wrong with Meliantha, I have to know. I
make my way to the door, but Ryder steps in my path.

"What the hell, Ryder, get out of my way. Something is wrong out there and I need to find out what it is!" I roar.

He shakes his head and puts his hands on my shoulders.

His voice sounds distressed when he speaks, "She's not your concern, Kalen. Have you forgotten that you're engaged to be married?"

I take a step back and hang my head. Why did I ever agree to marry Breena? I was so mad over the news of Meliantha and Finn that I did the most drastic thing possible. One of my downfalls is acting before I think and I think it just bit me in the ass.

I step away from Ryder because I don't want him to see the shame in my eyes when I confess, "I don't love Breena, brother. I never have and I never will. I fell in love with Meliantha the moment I saw her, and as soon as I saw her today, those feelings magnified ten-fold."

I hear Ryder chuckle behind me and he grabs my shoulder to turn me around.

"Are you saying what I think you're saying?" he asks, delighted.

I look him in the eyes and say the only word that manages to escape my lips. "Yes."

Ryder slowly smiles and looks up at the wooden beams of the ceiling.

He chuckles before looking back down at me and points out, "How you manage to get into the worst pile of shit every time a woman is involved I will never know. You cause more trouble than you're worth, you know that?"

I smile genuinely at him before tearing my gaze away to look out the window. It looks like everyone has gone inside the cottage since there's no one in sight. I don't know how I'm going to handle this evening with the engagement announcement. I don't want to embarrass Breena with refusing her, but I know I don't want to marry her. I need to find a way to talk to Meliantha and explain before anything happens tonight. Recalling what Ryder just said, I do believe I am a magnet for trouble.

"I think trouble follows me, brother," I claim whole-heartedly.

Ryder slaps me on the shoulder and coaxes me toward the kitchen.

"Come on, little brother, I think you need a drink. You have a busy night ahead of you with breaking a certain Winter fae's heart. I would say you need to relax."

My heart aches with the thought of hurting Breena, but I know it's for the best. I'm sure she will find someone that will love her completely. I nod my head in agreement at Ryder, but I honestly think that one drink needs to be ten. We're in the kitchen, so I take a seat at the table and I pour myself a tumbler full of mead. While we're retelling epic stories of our childhood adventures, Calista barges through the door with Ariella behind her holding Merrick. Ryder is up in a flash and hurrying his way to his queen. She's holding a bundle in her hands which looks like a towel and her face is flushed with trepidation.

"Calista, what's wrong?" Ryder implores anxiously.

She looks straight at me with anguish in her eyes before she begins, "It's Meliantha." My eyes go wide and I know my heart has stopped. What does she mean by that?

She holds out the towel and continues, "Apparently the dark sorcerer has been deceiving her for the past five years. What I have in this towel is something Finn believed was a gift from Durin when actually it had been spelled with black magic."

Oh no! If what she's saying is true, then that would mean...I take a deep breath before I finish the thought. That would mean the dark sorcerer has been taking over Finn's body. I shake my head back and forth and I clasp my eyes shut. I don't want to think about all the things that bastard has done to her and *with* her over the past five years.

My hands shake with anger and Calista rushes over to me quickly and takes my cold hands into her warm ones. My eyes see nothing but red, and all I can think about is how I want to do every vile thing possible to make the dark sorcerer suffer.

Calista squeezes my hands and shakes them.

"Hey, Kalen! Snap out of it! She's fine and every-one's fine. She just found out the dark sorcerer has been taking over Finn's body, and she's miraculously handling it very well. There's nothing anyone can do about it now."

"You don't understand. That bastard has touched her and done who knows what to her, and you say everything is fine!" I scream. "She's not fine!"

She lets go of my hands and takes a step back.

"That's not all, Kalen. I need to ask you a question and I want you to be honest with me." She hesitates before asking, "When you visited Meliantha all those years ago, did you ever see her before that time you spoke of?"

Why would she ask that? Of course I didn't see her before then.

I shake my head and reply, "No, I haven't spoken to her since the wedding."

"I didn't think so," she points out.

"What are you saying, Calista? Why did you ask me that?" I ask curiously. Although, I have a sinking feeling in my stomach that I'm not going to like what she has to say.

"Meliantha had a visitor just a few short days before you came and she thought that visitor was you."

"WHAT?" I roar.

Before I can yell every obscenity in my mind, Calista cuts me off.

"It was the dark sorcerer, Kalen. He pretended to be you and he said some terrible things to her that broke her heart. She's hated you ever since."

So that's why she has hated me all these years. If I would have pursued her more instead of cowering back to the Winter Court, I could have solved this problem years ago. How could she think I would break her heart like that? I head for the door because the need to speak with her has me bursting at the seams. My heart belongs with hers and she has to know how sorry I am, and...that I love her. Calista screaming my name stops me from my pursuit, and I turn around impatiently to see what she wants.

"What, Calista? I need to speak to Meliantha and tell her the truth."

"I know, Kalen, but she's with Finn right now getting some rest before the ball. She already knows that it wasn't you, and I told her she should talk to you, but right now is not the right time. So many things have happened and she needs a break from it all. You'll be able to talk to her tonight." She hesitates before speaking again, "One other thing, she doesn't know you're engaged. I'm afraid that when she finds out it's going to break her heart even more, but she did tell me about the connection she felt with you earlier."

I admit whole-heartedly, "I felt it, too. It's the strongest feeling I have ever felt, and separating from her felt like I was defying all bounds of nature. I know she's the one, Calista."

"Have you ever touched her or seen a vision like Ryder and I had?" she asks.

I shake my head no and say, "No, I have not touched her yet. I tried earlier today, but she backed away from me like I had the plague."

Calista gives me a faint smile and shakes her head.

"I'm sure it won't be like that tonight. Try to talk to her if you can and tell her how you feel. Finn's not going to be too happy, but there's nothing he can do about it now."

Thinking of Finn infuriates me to all levels of rage. He's enjoyed *my* Meliantha for five years now while I've been miserable here in the Winter Court. Not anymore. Tonight I will make her mine and break a few hearts in the process.

"What are we going to do with that?" I ask Calista while pointing at the towel. The spelled cuff is in there, and it's too dangerous to keep it lying around.

"I don't know yet. I think I should take it to Durin when he gets here and ask him how to destroy it. We can't let anyone get near it or put it on. We also need to inform our families about this as well and have everyone warned. The dark sorcerer is here and it looks like he's after Meliantha this time. We need to do everything possible to keep her safe," she commands.

I nod my head in agreement while Ryder cuts in and advises, "Well in that case, we need to head to the palace and speak to my parents. I know they will still have the ball tonight, but we need to be on guard. There's no telling how many traitors we have in our midst." He looks around the room at us all and settles his protective gaze on Merrick.

Fear and concern splay across his face, but he quickly shakes it off and says, "Alright everyone, let's go to the palace and call a meeting."

We leave the cabin and I can't stop myself from staring at the cottage beside me. Meliantha is in there alone with her warrior, and I pray that she waits for me to explain everything before jumping back in bed with him. I ache to talk to her, but I know the urgency of our situation. We need to warn the Court about the dark sorcerer, and the evil that has been taking place.

The meeting lasted about an hour, and now I'm back in my cabin getting ready for the Solstice Ball that will be taking place in a matter of minutes. I run my fingers through my hair and then down to slip the last button of my black dress shirt in place before layering on my tuxedo jacket. I know it's a bold move, but I take the purple rose lying on the table, and I pin it to the lapel of my jacket. It's the same color as Meliantha's eyes. I haven't seen her leave the cottage yet, but I did just get back from the meeting. Breena had stopped me on the way to meet my parents saying she had a gift for me, but I was in a hurry and told her I would have to accept it later. She looked hesitant and angry when I walked away, but there were more important matters that needed to be dealt with.

The meeting consisted of my parents, King Madoc and Queen Mab, the Summer King and Queen, Durin of the dwarves, and Aelfric of the Elvish Kingdom. Once everyone was situated, Calista, Ryder, and I took the floor and explained the recent events. Gasps of hysteria and outrage filled the room. My parents were livid while King Oberon and Queen Tatiana were overtaken with fear. We explained to Durin that it was said he was the one who made the golden cuff for Finn, and that it was delivered with Meliantha's arrows.

Durin was angered by our information and informed us that he made no such gift, and the only way to destroy it is by the magical fires of the elves. It's strange how items made by the dwarves can only be destroyed by the elves. We were also informed that the messenger he sent to deliver Meliantha's arrows had recently gone missing. I think we can all assume his messenger had gone traitor. Finn's golden band was secured and will be taken to the Elvish Kingdom by Aelfric to be destroyed.

Knowing the dark sorcerer is here and plotting to take Meliantha wasn't settling well with anyone, especially me. I vowed to protect her with my life and I meant it when I announced it in the meeting. My parent's vigilant expressions were clear; they understood my intentions. I met with them in private and told them of my feelings for Meliantha and about calling off the engagement to Breena. They offered to withdraw making the announcement at the ball. It's like the weight of the world was lifted off my shoulders. Now all I have to do is break the news to

Breena.

I walk over to one of the windows in my bedroom, and I glimpse two of my warriors standing guard outside the cottage doors. Being the leader of the Winter Army, I delegated more warriors to shadow Meliantha to make sure she's safe at all times. Each warrior has been thoroughly searched to insure no magical objects were placed on them. I know I should trust my men, but this is Meliantha we're guarding and I can't afford to take any chances. I can't have her taken away from me when I'm about to get her back…hopefully.

The time has now come for the ball to begin. I thought if I took my time, I would be able to escort Meliantha up to the palace. I stare out the window for another minute and decide it's probably a better idea if I don't wait on her. I know I'll see her tonight.

I head down the stairs to my front door, and I saunter out into the frosty cold air. The minute I'm outside I am met with the whimpering sounds of a baby pup. I peer down to see Accalia pawing at Aki's ears vying for her father's attention while Larentia, her mother, watches in amusement. All three of them are a stunning breed of white wolves and are part of my pack. I have eight more of them, and I know they are somewhere around here causing mischief. I laugh at Accalia and reach down to pick her up. Her fur is fluffy and white reminding me of a giant ball of cotton.

"Hey, girl, I see you like irritating your father," I say while hiding my smile behind her fur so Aki can't see it. I scratch her head and she licks my hand. I whisper in her ear, "Don't worry, most women find it amusing to pester the men." I know Aki heard me and he lets out a loud huff in response. I set Accalia down so I can look into Aki's eyes.

"I need to tell you something, Aki. Something bad is going on around here and I need you to keep your eyes vigilant and aware. I want you to guard Princess Meliantha any way you can and keep her safe," I demand. Aki is a faithful and loyal wolf, and I know he would do anything I asked of him. The same goes for my other wolves, but Aki is the one I spend the most time with. He huffs again and I know that is his way of saying he'll do as I ask.

"Thank you, Aki." I walk down the front steps and I stroll my way to the palace. The air feels frostier than normal for some reason. I'm usually not affected by the coldness of our court, but chills reverberate through my body and I shudder. My senses go on hyper alert and I know this can only mean one thing. The dark sorcerer must be near and I have a sinking suspicion he's going to use this night to play his sick and twisted game.

I grumble amongst the wind, "Bring it, you worthless bastard."

Chapter Nine

 *Meliantha*

I'm standing before the full-length mirror looking down at my ruby-colored evening gown. I have my tawny red hair hanging down in soft waves flowing down my bare back. It at least covers up some skin. The silky quality of my dress feels smooth and soft as I run my hands down the fabric. The shoes I'm wearing look amazing with it as well. Let's just hope I don't fall and break my neck walking in the snow in these shoes.

The gloves I'm wearing match the color of my dress. I usually don't wear gloves with my evening gowns, but knowing I was going to be in the Winter Court I opted to wear them. They are long gloves stretching up to my elbows where only my upper arms and shoulders are left bare. I figured they might keep me somewhat warmer than if I went without.

"Mel, hurry up or we're going to be late," Finn yells from outside the bedroom door. My heart jumps and it feels like it's in my throat from being startled unexpectedly. Maybe my heart feels like that because I'm nervous, who knows?

I grab my bow and arrows from the floor and my black cloak that is splayed out across the bed. The cloak will cover my dress until one of the servants will no doubt take it from me. I wonder what Kalen is going to say when he sees me.

I stop at the bedroom door and I take a deep breath. Here I go, I say to myself. I open the door to step out into the hall and I peer around the corner. Finn has done what I asked and has worn his long, white-blond hair down. His black tuxedo is very elegant. He looks ethereal with his appearance, but also devilish wearing black. It's not long before they all notice me staring at them from around the corner. I am met with three sets of bulging eyes the minute I step into view.

Finn snaps out of it first and gives me an enticing grin when he calls out, "Meliantha, you look amazing." I can't help but laugh, and I soak up the compliment by twirling around in my dress to give them the full view. Finn marches over to take my cloak and holds it open for me to slide into.

"You do realize this is a black and white affair, Princess?" Ashur utters silently.

I glance over at him and he's shaking his head in disbelief. I shrug my shoulders at him and taunt back sarcastically, *"I guess I didn't see that on the invitation, Ashur."* I put my hand over my mouth, *"Whoops."*

"You know you're getting just as bad as Ariella with breaking the rules."

Thinking about it, this would be something she would do. The thought brings a smile to my face and Ashur quickly pipes in, *"Laugh about it now, Princess, but we will see who is laughing when they throw you out of the ballroom."*

I wave him off and turn our conversation vocal.

"They will do no such thing," I tease.

I see Elissa waiting by the door looking ravishing in a black jewel-encrusted gown. She smiles as I approach.

"Ashur giving you a hard time?" she asks.

"Doesn't he always?" I reply back.

"You look beautiful, Meliantha." She looks down at my hand and sees the bow and arrows I have clutched in my grasp. "Do you really think you will need those tonight?" she asks dubiously. I hope not, but with the way things are going, I probably will.

I shrug my shoulders at her and confess softly, "You never know, Elissa. That's one thing I've learned…you never know." I give her a warm smile. "You look amazing tonight." She blushes and waves me off.

She doesn't seem frightened at all about the dark sorcerer being around and for some reason that bothers me. She could easily be a target just like Ashur and Finn could be. We all saw how easy it was for the dark sorcerer to infiltrate his way into Finn's body.

"Come on ladies, we need to go," Finn urges while gently pushing me toward the door.

"OK, OK, let's go," I give in.

Ashur opens the door and a blast of cold wind comes rushing in sending shivers racing down my body. I grit my teeth to keep them from chattering. I hate the cold weather. I notice two warriors stationed outside the door on both sides and I kindly give them both a nod. They bow their heads before preparing to escort us to the palace. I appreciate the added security, but I also hate it because it makes me look helpless. There's nothing they can do against the dark sorcerer, or any of us for that matter, because unfortunately no one has figured out how to destroy him.

Finn takes my arm and walks me down the steps. I take a quick peek over at Kalen's cabin and it looks eerily dark and quiet. He must have already left. The back veranda of the palace is swarming with people, and they are all milling about and smiling like they have no other care in the world.

Twinkling lights are floating all around and it reminds me of my sprites back home. I really miss them and the times I would spend with them in my gardens. As soon as I get home, I plan to devote all my extra time with them. The twinkling lights also remind me of the mortal realm at Christmas time. We don't celebrate mortal holidays here, but I guess you could say this ball is our Christmas celebration, minus all the presents. This is more of a Winter Court celebration that we are obligated to take part in.

Walking in the snow in high heeled sandals may not have been the best idea. My toes are numb and they'll probably fall off from frostbite. My temperature runs naturally hot, but the cold still affects me. It only takes a few minutes to reach the veranda at the back of the palace. Now that Kalen is the leader of the Winter Court Army, he must have ordered extra security for the ball tonight. The place is swarming with warriors.

We enter through the doors and are motioned toward what I can only assume is the ballroom. I can't really see because of the huge mass of people scattered about. There's a long line of guests waiting to enter, and I can hear the booming voice of an announcer calling out each individual's names. I silently groan and squeeze Finn's arm to grab his attention.

"This is going to take forever," I whisper to him.

He just smiles and elbows me in the ribs lightly.

"Look at it this way, Cinderella, at least you get to make your grand entrance with that beautiful gown of yours." He lifts my hand to his lips and kisses it softly. "I'm honored to be by your side tonight."

But for how long, I think to myself.

"I heard that," Ashur says, interrupting my inner turmoil.

I peek over my shoulder to steal a glance at him. He's holding onto Elissa's arm escorting her just like Finn is doing with me.

"Kalen wasn't the one that broke my heart, Ashur. I've hated him for nothing, and because of what the dark sorcerer did, I closed off my heart and soul to the people that cared about me the most. I've missed out on so much."

I turn my head forward and we continue our slow pace to the entryway of the ballroom. Ashur's voice comes back full force inside my head.

"You may have closed off your heart during the past five years, but I feel it beginning to open up again, and I love the feeling. For the first time since I've been your Guardian, I can feel that spark of happiness trying to come back into your life. The dark sorcerer made a mistake when he played you for a fool. I hate to say this, but this experience has opened your eyes and made you a stronger and smarter woman."

My eyes begin to burn, but I fight it off.

"I hope so, Ashur. I truly hope so."

We eventually make our way to the ballroom doors and the announcer obviously recognizes me.

"Good evening, Your Highness." He bows his head

and lifts his gentle eyes at Finn and then back to me. "Who, may I ask, is your escort for the evening?"

"His name is Finn, and he's a warrior of the Summer Court," I kindly respond back.

The announcer is a short, pudgy man wearing a white tunic and white pants. His rich, black hair and black beard contrasts greatly with his pale features and white clothes. He gives me a warm smile as one of the servants approaches me to help me out of my cloak. I hand over my bow and arrows to Ashur so that I know they are safe while we attend the ball.

The announcer's eyes grow wide at the sight of my dress and it takes him a few seconds to gain his composure before announcing in his deep booming voice, "I give you Princess Meliantha, and her escort, Warrior Finn, from the Summer Court."

Everything goes in slow motion while I'm met with hundreds of different pairs of eyes all trained on me. Some are smiling, some are gaping, and some of them are giving me hostile looks. I look around, but I can't see Kalen anywhere. I can tell he is near because the pull tugging on my soul is demanding I go to him.

We walk down the steps and into the crowd. The room is immaculate with white draperies hanging from the ceiling and glimmering in the light. Clear glass windows surround the room making it feel as if we are in the midst of falling snow. The twinkling lights from outside are also in the ballroom giving off the illusion of falling snowflakes. I find it amazingly beautiful because the illusion of snow is a whole hell of a lot better than freezing in the real snow.

"Would you like to dance?" Finn asks.

I look up at him and smile.

"I would love to dance with you." Guilt tightens my chest because even though Finn is my date and I love dancing with him, I secretly have been hoping to dance with Kalen as well.

Finn takes my hand and leads me onto the dance floor. He places his other hand on the middle of my back and moves his body a little closer to mine. He smiles at me with a longing passion and begins to sway to the soft flow of the music taking me with him. We dance together, lost in the melodies of the music, when I notice Elissa dancing with a Winter Court fae. He is a very handsome man, but I wonder what happened to Ashur. I glance around the ballroom for him until I finally see him scowling in the corner.

"Calm down, Ashur. I know she cares about you, so stop looking at them like that."

"Well, it doesn't look like that to me, Princess. Why do women always do this?"

His anger-filled gaze finds me and I give him a scowl of my own.

"Men aren't innocent either, dear Guardian. Just hang in there. She can't dance with you all night, now can she?"

His shoulders sag at my declaration and his eyes become weary.

"I know she can't dance with me all night, but it doesn't make it any easier to see her ogling another man."

"She's not ogling." I turn my eyes from Ashur to take a look at Elissa again. She actually happens to be staring at her partner with an evil glint in her eye instead of ogling. I've never seen her look that way before. She takes the man by the hand and starts to lead him out of the ballroom.

I don't know where they are going, but I know I don't want her traipsing about by herself.

"Please follow her, Ashur. Something doesn't feel right with the way she's acting."

"I will, Princess. Will you be OK in here?"

I give him an incredulous look.

"Ashur, I'm surrounded by people and I have Finn in here with me. I don't think anything is going to happen to me around this many people."

He nods his head and then searches the crowd for Elissa. We have lost sight of her, so he quickly exits the ballroom in search of her. I hope he catches up to her. The sick feeling in my stomach feels like warning bells ringing throughout my body telling me something is wrong. I've had this feeling a lot today and I know it's just a matter of time before something awful happens.

"Is everything OK?" Finn asks. I look into his worried amber eyes and I plaster on a fake smile.

"I hope so, Finn. I'm just a little concerned for Elissa, but Ashur is going to check up on her," I say, concerned.

"I'm sure she'll be fine. Ashur isn't going to let anything happen to her. He's in love with her. He has been for years," he informs. Yes, I know he's in love with her. I think I knew before he did that he was in love with her from the feel of his emotions being heightened every time she came near.

Finn pulls me closer to his warm body and starts to hum along to the tunes of the sweet melody in my ear. I get the feeling someone is watching me, so I search the crowd until I am stopped by the piercing ice blue eyes of a certain Winter Prince. Finn is oblivious to the man staring daggers at him. I can feel the heat of Kalen's penetrating stare, so I decide it might be best if I take a break from dancing. I don't want any trouble involving men fighting over me. I fan myself to make it look like I'm hot, and I casually lay my hand over my throat.

"It's so hot in here. Do you mind if we go and get a drink?" I ask Finn. He nods his head and takes my hand. The bar is set in the corner of the ballroom, and, unfortunately, we have to walk through the massive crowd to get there. Finn orders me a drink and I sip it slowly. Faerie wine is the best liquid I have ever tasted in my life and nothing compares to it. It feels amazing as it glides down my throat, instantly working its magic through my body and making me feel toasty and warm. People in the mortal realm would freak out at the sight of faerie wine. It's bright blue in color and gives off a glow as soon as it's poured out of the bottle. It sparkles in the glass and glitters when swirled around. I have always been fascinated by it. The wine is also very potent, just like any other substance in the Land of the Fae.

I'm taking a sip of my wine and I almost choke at the sound of my mother hissing in my ear, "What the hell are you wearing? Are you trying to embarrass us?"

I turn around to spit out something sarcastic when an unexpected voice spears back at my mother.

"I think the red dress looks lovely on the beautiful Meliantha."

I stand frozen at the sight of Queen Mab giving my mom a lethal look. It's never been a secret that the two women don't like each other. I've been waiting for the day they let all sentiments of manners fly out the window and have it out in front of the other guests. My mother snarls at Queen Mab and then focuses back on me.

"We'll talk about this later," she snaps. She doesn't give me time to respond because she quickly turns around and walks the other way. I release a heavy sigh while Queen Mab doubles over laughing. She runs a finger underneath her eyes to catch the tears that were escaping from her laughter.

"Your mother doesn't know how to loosen up, does she?" she says while still trying to contain her laughter.

I bow my head to her.

"No, your Highness, she does not. Thank you for the compliment."

"It was my pleasure, Princess Meliantha. It gives me great joy to torment your mother." This makes Finn and I both laugh and the Queen smiles warmly at us both.

"Do you mind if I have a word with you, Princess?"

I look at Finn and he nods his head.

"I'll be here by the bar, so don't worry about me." He winks. "I'll keep my eyes on you."

I turn back to the queen and coyly reply, "I am all yours, Queen Mab."

She takes her cold hand and gently grabs mine to place it on her forearm. Even though I am wearing gloves I can still feel the coldness of her skin.

"I meant it when I said you looked lovely in your dress. I did not just say it to aggravate your mother."

"Thank you, Your Highness," I murmur appreciatively.

"You are very welcome," she responds thoughtfully. We walk over to a quiet corner and she continues to speak. "I'm sorry, dear, about what's been happening and what you went through. We had an emergency meeting today and Queen Calista filled us in on everything."

I drop my eyes from her warm gaze and I grit my teeth. I don't think I will ever get over the anger I feel at what the dark sorcerer has done. I take a calming breath before responding.

"Yes, it has been a tragic misfortune," I confess.

"Well, I believe you will be in capable hands here. Kalen will no doubt do everything in his power to keep you safe." A twinkle sparkles in her eye when she says, "I believe you have bewitched him, Meliantha. He offered to be your personal bodyguard for the rest of your visit here."

I stare transfixed and stunned at the queen for what felt like an eternity. A small laugh escapes her lips breaking me out of my stupor. My heart feels like it's going to pound out of my chest, so I take a few deep breaths. Why did I suddenly get this light-headed feeling?

The queen gives me a sly smile and I notice a hint of curiosity in her voice when she asks, "Have you not spoken to Kalen yet?"

I take in a quick shallow breath.

"No, Your Highness, we have not spoken yet."

Her smile turns into a huge grin and then her eyes move away from mine to focus on something or *someone* behind me.

"I believe now is your chance, dear."

My eyes go wide and I quickly turn around. The moment I do I am met with the hypnotic blue-eyed prince that has inhabited my dreams for the past five years. So that is the reason why I was beginning to feel light-headed. He must have been standing behind me and my body had been responding to his presence. The smile Kalen gives me is the same smile I fell in love with years ago. I hold back my gasp when I see the light purple rose pinned to the lapel of his coat. It's the same color as my eyes. I haven't seen any of the other Winter fae wearing flowers on their coats. I wonder if he did it for me. He looks down at my hand and the corners of his mouth slowly turn down into a slight frown. He meets my eyes again and in his deep, sensual voice he greets me softly.

"Good evening, Meliantha."

He reaches down and hesitates before clutching my hand to bring it to his lips for a gentle kiss. He kisses my gloved hand and keeps his steely gaze on me the entire time. Oh, I wish I could feel his lips on my bare skin. His black hair falls forward as he leans down and I ache to touch the soft tendrils as they tickle my wrist. My pulse jumps with his touch and I know he can hear the loud drumming of my heart. The fiery blast of our connection is smoldering in my veins making my body feel heated and on fire. I wish I could feel the coolness of his skin on my body, cooling me down from this internal inferno. From the smoldering look in his eyes, I can tell he's just as entranced by our connection as I am. We have never actually touched bare skin to bare skin, and now that I'm wearing gloves his touch will not bring about the vision. He appears disappointed about my gloved hands, and honestly so am I.

I thought five years ago it was him I touched in the gardens. I remember my heart deflating when the vision didn't come. It's hard to believe I found out just a few short hours ago that it was all a lie, and that the dark sorcerer did that to me so I would feel betrayed by the one man I loved. Through hell or the Hereafter, I will spend the rest of my life making the dark sorcerer pay for what he has done.

93

"Good evening to you as well, Kalen," I say while bowing my head ever so slightly.

He's still holding my hand in the gentlest of touches when he asks in a low voice, "Will you do me the honor of dancing with me, Princess?"

I can't stop the smile from forming on my lips.

"I would love to," I reply breathlessly.

He walks me to the dance floor and keeps a respectable distance between our bodies when he pulls me in for the dance. I regret my decision for wearing gloves because it would feel amazing to touch his skin. His skin has the perfect complexion, as do all fae, but there's something about his creamy smooth skin that makes me want to touch every square inch of it. I groan in silence. I wish I could smack myself in the head to keep the thoughts from plaguing my mind. It feels like every single lustful thought that I had of Kalen years ago is resurfacing. I'd kept the thoughts locked away in my brain, but now I can't stop imagining all the things we could do together. I never thought I could go from hating someone with a vengeful passion to having feelings for them in a matter of a day. The feelings were always there from the very beginning. My heart is screaming at me to take my walls down, but my mind keeps telling me to stay guarded. How am I supposed to know what to do when my heart tells me one thing and my mind tells me another?

I look around the dance floor and I see my parents talking to King Madoc. My mother likes King Madoc and enjoys talking to him. It's the Queen she cannot stand. Ariella is off making the rounds through the ballroom and speaking to everyone she can. She is a very charismatic woman, and I know one day she will make a great leader.

It appears I wasn't the only one who has changed over the years.

My eyes land on my brother, Drake, next. He seems to be mesmerized by something across the room. I follow his gaze to a dark-haired Winter beauty who happens to be on the dance floor with another man. I recognize the lovely fae and I know her as being Sorcha, Winter Court Princess, and also Kalen's sister. Interesting. I wonder if there will be another love in the making.

I notice Calista and Ryder dancing closely together and the love that shows in their eyes could make even the saintly souls jealous. They look magical as they stare at each other longingly in the eyes, and even though I envy her, I have never been happier for them.

I turn my attention back to Kalen and I am instantly hypnotized by the swirling pools of endless blue in his eyes.

I feel lost in their depths when his deep voice whispers in my ear, "We need to talk, Meliantha. There are so many things we need to catch up on." He intently searches my face, like he's trying to memorize every square inch. He almost looks scared, like he's afraid to let me go.

I smile warmly at him and reply, "We do have a lot to talk about, and I want to start with saying how sorry…"

"There you are, lover."

Gritting my teeth, I politely look over to see who the interrupter is. What I find is a beautiful brown-haired Winter Fae looking up at Kalen with adoring eyes. I somehow find her expression at him forced, but then she turns to look at me with absolute contempt and I know for a fact this one is genuine. I narrow my eyes at her and return the look. Kalen notices the hostile exchange and gives the other faerie a lethal stare.

"Breena, what are you doing?" he hisses.

She bats her eyes and her voice takes on a faux innocent tone when she pleads, "When you left in such a hurry earlier I couldn't give you your *engagement* gift. I think right now would be the perfect time to announce it." She says the last part while looking straight at me. My heart stops beating and I know my face has gone pale. Did she just say the word 'engagement'?

I quickly let go of Kalen's hand and step back. He gives the Winter bitch a scowl and turns his gentle blue eyes to me. Could my night get any worse? The moment I think things are looking up is the moment it all falls apart. I refuse to cry, and I refuse to show how angry I am. If the Winter wretch wants to see me upset, then that is the last thing she's going to get. I can tell by the smug look on her face that she's doing it on purpose; however, it still doesn't change the fact that Kalen is *engaged.*

I look at them both, mainly at Kalen, and I ignore his pleading look.

In a flat tone I say, "Congratulations." I turn my gaze to Breena and I politely point out, "If you will excuse me, I need some fresh air. For some reason the air in here just turned rancid."

Breena's smug expression turned into one of shock, then outright hate. I would love to call her every foul name I can think of and use her as a practice partner for my brutal training, but that wouldn't look good for my court. I really do need some fresh air so I turn around slowly and start to walk out of the stuffy ballroom. If I could, I would be running as fast as my body would allow me toward the nearest exit, but that would give away my true feelings on how upset I really am.

Kalen quickly calls out, "Meliantha, wait! You have to let me explain!"

At this point we have drawn everyone's attention, so I keep a steady pace as I head out of the ballroom and cleverly sneak past the Winter Court warriors stationed on the back veranda. I don't need them following me everywhere I go even if Kalen did order them to.

Ashur never returned to the ballroom, so I assume he is still out searching for Elissa. I hope everything is all right. He still has my bow and arrows and I can't help but feel lost without them. Next time, no matter what the occasion is or what I am wearing, I will keep my bow and arrows with me at all times. The snow is rapidly beginning to fall and the flakes melt the instant they hit my warm skin. I refuse to walk back inside the palace, so I head down the path to the cottage. I can see the fountain up ahead, sitting frozen and lonely in the midst of the cabins and the cottage. The fountain would look absolutely breathtaking with running water spraying out of the spouts and flowers decorating the outer edge.

I sweep a mound of snow off the ledge of the fountain, and I take a seat. I wrap my arms around myself hoping to bring in some warmth. I do know of one way to send warmth through my body. I bend down on my knees and I cringe as the cold snow soaks into the fabric of my dress. I don't plan on going back to the ball so ruining my dress now is of no consequence. I lay my hands on the cold, snowy ground and I close my eyes. I concentrate on the very core of my magic, summoning it to do my will. The power of the magic warms me with its gentle caress and it spreads all around the fountain and deep into the land. I breathe a sigh of relief. I haven't felt this good in a really long time. The first thing I'm going to do when I go home is spend plenty of time in my gardens. The rush of using magic is intoxicating.

As the power begins to fade, I start to feel something cold and wet nuzzling my hand, and I open my eyes quickly to find a huge white wolf lying down on his belly in front of me. This must be one of Kalen's wolves! I remember talking to him about them at Calista's Guardian Ceremony and how much I would love to meet them. Having a magical ability pertaining to animals always draws them close to me and I love spending time with them.

Communicating with them also comes with my ability. They may not speak words, but I hear them all the same through images. With a simple touch, they can tell me everything. I reach over with both hands and I cup the wolf's face to bring it level with mine. His fur is soft and feels like the fluffy fabric of cotton. His eyes glow a bright green making the snow on the ground give off a faint emerald glow. He is one magnificent creature.

"Why hello there, boy. What, may I ask, is your name?"

Still holding onto him, I close my eyes to concentrate on his thoughts. It starts off jumbled and not clear, but then the thoughts come together in a slow procession.

"Ah, so your name is Aki, right?" He huffs and licks my hand. I laugh and rub my face against his. He smells like the freshness of a winter snow and his fur is icy cold when I rub my cheek against it. He sends images cascading through my mind and what I see is absolutely amazing.

I can see his mate and his pup frolicking in the snow, and I can see an image of the pack resting together in their den. The image is breathtaking — I can see the whole pack together. I wish I could see them now.

"You have a beautiful pack, Aki." He huffs again, pushing me to look further so I delve deeper into his thoughts. The next images are of Kalen. He looks forlorn and lost in all of them and it breaks my heart to see him so defeated.

"Was he this distraught over the past five years?" I ask the wolf.

He nods his head up and down with a painful set to his glowing green eyes. I shake my head.

"I don't understand, why has he chosen to marry someone else then?" As soon as I ask, I can see the scene play out in my mind just as Aki had witnessed it. Kalen is training with the warriors when one of them mentions they heard one of the princesses of the Summer Court was dating one of their warriors.

Kalen approaches the warrior immediately and demands to know which princess. When he finds out it is me, his face turns crimson with anger, and he throws his sword half way across the training grounds and storms off. I never knew he had been living in pain and loss just as I have.

"Oh, Aki, it was all a misunderstanding. I had no idea he was that upset over the situation. We were tricked by the dark sorcerer and have been living in lies for the past five years."

Aki abruptly stands up and guards me with his body, instantly on full alert. I snap to attention, but then calmly breathe a sigh of relief when I see who approaches. The

99

thought of Aki protecting me is endearing, but it's only Finn approaching, and I know he means me no harm. He's carrying my cloak with him, and I can't stop the excitement of knowing I will be warm in a matter of seconds.

"He's a friend, Aki. You don't have to protect me from him." I rub behind his ear one good time and then I walk toward Finn with anticipation in each step. I really want my cloak. He opens it for me and the soft, velvety material slides over my cold body and begins to warm me instantly.

"The flowers are beautiful, Meliantha. I always loved what you could do with a garden."

"Thank you, Finn. I haven't used my magic in a long time and it felt good to use it." I wrap the cloak tightly around my body while looking at my creation around the fountain. It's a shame the flowers won't last long once I leave.

Finn comes closer to me and takes my hands. I can feel the sadness in him rolling off in waves, and I hesitate a few seconds before lifting my face. I know what he's about to say and it hurts my heart to feel this pain coming from him. I look into his watery gaze and my eyes burn with the unshed tears that are beginning to surface.

His voice is sad when he asks, "Is this the end for us, Princess?"

My heart lurches at his words and I know there is no way I can stop the tears from flowing. I pull him closer and I rest my head against his chest. I haven't cried in a really long time, but knowing that I'm going to lose and hurt him is too overwhelming to hold the feelings inside.

I can't bring myself to look at his face, so I sob

against his chest.

"Finn, I don't want to lose you, but my heart is with *him*."

He blows out a loud breath, "I know, Mel. I've always known you would find your heart. It still doesn't make it any easier. I have enjoyed every minute with you, and I want to know that you felt the same way with me."

Tears stain my cheeks, but I look up at Finn anyway.

"Of course I have enjoyed every minute with you. You were my lover and best friend, Finn. I will always hold a special place for you in my heart." I reach up to cup his face and I lay a gentle kiss across his lips. I taste the saltiness of his tears and it just makes me cry even more. I hold him tight, and for however long, I do not know. I break apart from him at the sound of someone clearing their throat. I look over to see that Kalen is staring at us with a scowl on his face and his arms crossed over his chest. Aki leaves my side to run over to his alpha.

Kalen looks at us, but keeps his gaze on mine when he speaks, "I really need to talk to you, Meliantha."

He looks over at Ashur and in a firm voice he commands, "Alone."

I give Finn an apologetic look and he nods his head.

"I'll see you back at the cottage," he says softly. I wonder how the sleeping arrangements will be now. I assume he'll find another room to sleep in. He takes my hand and squeezes it before walking over to Kalen. Please don't let them fight, I say to myself.

I'm a few feet away, so I can't hear the words that come out of Finn's mouth. All I know is they are not friendly words by the way he glares at Kalen. Kalen smirks and says something back. Finn stares fiercely at him for a few extra seconds and then turns away to walk toward the cabin. He never looks back.

When Finn was out of earshot, Kalen walks toward me with impatient steps.

"Meliantha, you never gave me time to explain. You have to know what's going on," he says quickly.

"Oh, the part where you're getting married to a raging bitch? Yeah, I think I know what's going on," I storm back.

His shoulders sag in defeat and he shakes his head.

"No, you don't. I told my parents during the meeting that I wanted to call off the engagement. With everything that's been happening I haven't had time to tell Breena. I told her as soon as you walked away." He takes a couple steps closer to where we're only a foot apart. I can tell he's contemplating his next words.

Hesitant, he takes in a deep breath and asks, "Do you love him?"

I look toward the cottage where Finn has just entered and Kalen follows my gaze. I sneak a side-long glance at him and his jaw is rigid and clenching. I guess it's about time to put him out of his misery. He looks back at me, jealousy clear across his face, and I reach up with my glove-covered hand to place it against his cheek.

"He's special to me, Kalen, but I had never been in love with him. There is only one man I can say that has taken that place in my heart."

The anger slowly leaves him and now the man staring at me is the loving and playful Kalen I fell in love with years ago. I reach my other hand up to where I'm holding his face between my hands. I pull him closer and whisper across his lips.

"You, Kalen, are the *only* man that I will always and forever be in love with."

In a rush of passion, he closes the distance and merges his soft lips with mine. The second our lips touch, the world falls away and we are thrust into the vision we have longed to see.

The Vision

We are lying on the ground in a sea of flowers. They surround our naked bodies while we bask in the pleasure of our love and our land. The smell of rain vastly approaches and it fuels my hunger for Kalen to a whole new level. It feels like we have done this a million times in the rain before. He gazes down upon me as he settles himself between my legs. I can tell he plans to tease me by the lustful smirk on his face. His skin is no longer pale, but the light golden complexion of what the Fall fae look like. His body also feels warm on top of mine and no longer cool like he would have been if he was still a Winter fae. We're not in the Fall Court so we must belong to somewhere else in the Land of the Fae. Everything falls into place as I look around at the flowers and up at the man about to make love to me. How could I not have known?

The rain begins to fall making our bodies slick and wet with desire. It feels cool against my heated skin and Kalen takes this time to enter me hard and deep. I scream out in pleasure which only fuels his appetite to deepen his thrusts. The orgasm sends shudders through my body while Kalen holds onto me tighter releasing his own pleasure inside my body. We lay spent on the ground, enjoying the feel of our bodies together, while being bathed in the purity of the rain. I can feel the life growing in this land, and the magic making it strong beneath me. I can also feel the beginnings of a new life growing in my womb and becoming strong. This is my home and my court. The Spring has begun.

Chapter Ten

ALASDAIR

- Dark Sorcerer -

Keeping to the shadows and skulking around the palace is degrading. It's as if I'm cowering like a spineless dog. I should be the one these people bow down to and worship.

I look down at the talisman and it glows the blood red color it normally does after getting a dose of energy. It's warm as it touches my chest from the unsuspecting victims I laid claim to just moments ago. No one at the palace is going to notice some worthless servants that have gone missing. Taking their power is energizing, but it is minor at best. I need someone with a little more power before I make my move tonight. I look around the ballroom at the hundreds of fae striding around and having a splendid time. They have no clue I'm here, watching and waiting. To make a bold statement, I need to find someone of importance that I can take away. Making a statement will no longer be necessary once I gain all the power of the Four. Being the ruler of the Land of the Fae will be the grandest of statements. Soon, I think to myself.

I spot the perfect candidate for tonight and he appears important enough standing with the nobles. I would say he is the son of a council member by the arrogance in his stance. That's good enough for me. Now I need to find the person I have come here to take over. I could tell she was wearing the magical object because of the strong pull urging me toward it. I can see my target across the room and there lying between her breasts is the magical purple stone dangling from a silver chain.

I only have to wait for a few minutes before my chance to take over her body suddenly appears. As she's sauntering away by herself, I take the opportunity to plunge into her body and take it as my own. With my enhanced power, she will have no idea that her body has been taken over. That is one of the factors that will make tonight even more enjoyable.

I have never taken over a woman's body and being in one is awkward and uncomfortable. How can they wear this shit? The dress is tight as hell and I can barely breathe. I find the Winter fae I am to pursue and I sashay as best I can in these worthless contraptions women call shoes.

"Would you like to dance?" I ask him. I cringe at the sound of a female's voice coming from my throat. It is awkward, but I have to do what is necessary to get what I want.

He looks this body up and down and bites his lip. The look he gives my host is pure animalistic. I groan in silence. This is going to be harder than I thought. He bows his head and holds out his hand.

"I would love to dance with a Summer beauty." Not for long, I think to myself.

I grab his hand firmly and I pull him to the dance floor. He seems to like how I take control. He's delighted, so I plaster on a seductive smile and continue. How pathetic can someone be? I can sense his power is stronger than the servants, but it in no way matches one of the royals. Calista's power was unimaginable when I took it, and when I take Meliantha's it will be just as strong and enticing. Time is wasting, so I decide to move along.

With a faux politeness I ask, "May I have the pleasure of your name?"

He responds snobbishly, "My name is Darius. My father is on the Winter Court Council and highly respected among the Winter Court fae." I was right. He is a noble and too arrogant for his own good. I wouldn't tolerate people like this in my army. They all know their place and to act in this manner would mean death.

I'll be detected if I linger much longer.

To speed things up I say, "After the dance, how about we take a walk and get to know each other better?"

He raises his eyebrows with a glint in his eye.

"That sounds like a perfect idea," he answers with a malicious grin. Yeah, I bet it does. I look around the ballroom and I see Calista and Meliantha dancing on the floor with their escorts. They give no notice of me, so I'm safe for now. However, Meliantha's guardian is looking at me with suspicion. I need to make sure my departure goes unnoticed by his prying eyes.

The song ends and I quickly drag the Winter fae out of the ballroom and into the bitter frost of the night. I'm glad I planned ahead and hid my iron dagger in the snow on the west side of the palace. I spelled it so no one could see it or detect it. Darius grabs the hand of the body I have overtaken and loops my arm through his. Being this close to him makes me want to kill him at once, but I try to keep in mind that this isn't my body and that I am pretending to be a helpless Summer fae maiden. One thing is certain…never again will I take over a female's body.

I pull him in the westward direction and we set off in a brisk pace away from the palace. He must be eager to get a taste of this Summer apple, but I'm afraid he is going to be sorely disappointed. We are nearing the western courtyard where I have hidden the dagger. It is nestled under a canopy of snow by the base of the giant birch tree.

"How do you like the Winter Court palace, my lady?" he asks.

I shrug my shoulders, "I don't like the cold, but I like that it's dark."

He's still smiling, but he looks confused when he asks, "But you're a Summer fae. I thought the Summer maidens usually danced in the sunlight naked, and enjoyed the light…or at least that's what I have dreamed." I should have ripped his tongue out earlier. He deserves to die because of the ridiculous shit he's babbling off.

I give him a malevolent grin and the menacing tone in my voice has him panicked when I sneer, "Most of us like it sunny, but not me. I like it dark and violent with the smell of death."

His eyes go wide and he nervously takes a step back.

"It's getting late, maybe we should head back."

I bend down to the ground and I remove the spell from the iron dagger. I reach down to grab it from its resting place.

I leer back at the quivering fae and tease, "But I thought you wanted to have some fun?" I notice his body is physically shaking, and I can tell his flight response is about to kick in. I heave magic at his feet to keep him rooted in place.

"Tsk, tsk, Darius. That isn't very gentlemanly of you to leave a lady out here all by herself," I taunt.

"Whatever you are, you are no lady."

Underneath the skin of my borrowed body is the talisman ready to be brought forth. I wear it around my neck inside of my host's body. To get it to the outside I have to will it. I make the talisman appear around the host's neck and I pull it off to place around the Winter fae. We are far enough away that if he screams, I'll be finished before anyone even gets here. Once the talisman is securely placed, what do you know…he screams.

"You are *so* pathetic. You're nothing but a worthless pussy," I hiss. "This right here is why I'm glad I am not one of you."

The bloodstone of the talisman glows a faint red color letting me know that it's satisfied. I take it off quickly and place it around my neck. It absorbs through the body to mine underneath, perfectly hidden from fae eyes. The screaming stops and the Winter fae looks at me with dead, empty eyes. The power I absorbed is flowing through my body and it's expanding through every cell of my being. I wish I could lay back and enjoy the ride, but there is work that still needs to be done.

The Winter fae is swaying on his feet, so I retrieve the dagger from the ground and hold it tightly in my borrowed hands. The iron dagger is poisonous to the fae and as soon as I pick it up with the fae's hand it instantly starts to sizzle and burn. I can feel the poison taking away the skin, so I move swiftly to make the killing blow. The dagger is about twelve inches in length and sharper than any blade imaginable. I swipe the blade across the Winter fae's chest, gutting him where he stands. Blood sprays all over this body and all over the ground making the scene look horrific. It is a shame no one will see what I have done.

When everyone gets here they will see nothing but the ashes of the worthless fae I killed. I drop the dagger to the ground and the sizzling stops immediately. The pain is excruciating, but it will not be my pain much longer.

Movement up ahead catches my attention and I see Meliantha's guardian racing toward my host. He approaches cautiously and looks down at the Winter fae slowly drifting away into ashes while I stand there smiling.

"What the hell have you done?" he asks.

I shake my head and laugh, "I was just having a little fun, Guardian. Give Meliantha my best and tell her I will see her soon."

I exit my host's body, laughing the whole way. I drift off into the shadows of the night and I stare down humorously at the warrior cradling the host's body in his arms. Once she wakes up, she will be in the most agonizing pain and not to mention she won't remember a single thing about killing the Winter fae.

I wonder if Meliantha will realize how I was able to take over the Summer fae's body. All I know is that she's going to have a hell of a time getting her friend out of this one, and it's going to be a pleasure to watch.

Chapter Eleven

Kalen

The moment the vision stopped I gasped for air. Meliantha is breathing hard and gripping onto my arms with a strength I didn't know her body could possess. What really caught my eye are the changes in her body. The transformation has already begun to happen, just like it did with Calista and Ryder. I knew it would happen, so it's not that much of a shock, but I guess I didn't expect it so soon. Meliantha's eyes go wide at the sight of me as well, and a huge grin takes over her face.

The vision was so intense and so real that I could take her right here and now with how turned on I am. I know she can feel me pressing up against her stomach and it appears as if she doesn't mind because she's rubbing her body against me.

Breathless, she whispers, "That had to be the most amazing vision ever. It felt so real, and I say that literally."

I groan loudly. Why did she have to say that? I push my groin into her stomach harder and tease, "Well, I'm sure you can feel what the vision did to me." She laughs and I laugh along with her. It feels so good to be able to be like this with her. I look around the fountain and I almost forget to compliment her on the flowers. Between the confrontation with Finn and the vision, I haven't had time to tell her how amazing they are.

"The flowers are beautiful, Meliantha, but I don't think they will last very long here."

I send my magic to the frozen water of the fountain and I make it flow again. She walks over to it and splashes her hands back and forth through the spouting water.

Her voice is wistful when she speaks.

"They may not last here, but they will in *our* court."

I grab her arm to pull her into a tight embrace and I kiss her fiercely one more time. Her lips are smooth and taste like the sweetness of a summer apple. Oh, how I have longed to hold her in my arms.

"You know what this means, don't you?" I tease.

I can feel her nodding her head underneath my chin and she laughs.

"Yes...you're going to have to learn to live with warmth and flowers."

I shake my head and sigh, "No…it means I get to keep you forever." I lean in to give her another kiss when out of nowhere she pulls back abruptly with a look of horror on her face. She looks like she's concentrating on something and I can only assume she is talking to her guardian.

Anxious, I grab her hands and ask hastily, "Meliantha, what's wrong?" Her eyes are wide and terrified. Before she has a chance to answer, I hear the most bone-chilling scream echoing in the cold, frosty wind.

"It's Elissa! We have to help her, now! Come on!" Meliantha urges, raising her voice.

We race up the path toward the west side of the

palace. The sick feeling in my stomach warns me that what I am about to witness isn't going to be good. Aki races ahead of us and is nothing but a white blur as he speeds across the snow. He will make it there long before we will. I wish she would tell me what's going on.

"What did Ashur say? You need to tell me what is going on," I demand.

"He told me what he saw. He believes the dark sorcerer got to Elissa and made her kill someone," she stammers hastily. We move as fast as we can to the sound of the scream.

By the time we reach our destination, there are about twenty of my warriors surrounding something *or someone* up ahead. Ashur comes running toward Meliantha and falls down to his knees at her feet, pleading.

"She killed someone, Princess, or at least her body did. I know for a fact it wasn't actually her that did it. You have to help her!"

He gets to his feet and turns to me, "She would never hurt anyone, Prince Kalen. It wasn't her that did it, and I know this because…"

"Kalen!" I turn to see Breena running toward us and she throws herself in my arms. Aki growls at my feet and bares his teeth while snapping at her.

"Stop it, Aki!" I hiss.

I gently push her away and her eyes go wide and she gasps in bewilderment. She looks angry and shocked when she surveys my newly changed body.

The moment is over quickly and she screams loudly, "She killed Darius! That heartless Summer bitch killed him and I saw it. I saw everything!" Meliantha starts toward Breena looking angry and ready to kill, so I hold my arm out to hold her back. Her face is blazing red and I know that if I let Meliantha have her way with Breena there is no way she would come out alive.

I whisper softly to Meliantha, "Calm down, my love." She's breathing hard, but my soft words catch her attention. She gazes into my eyes and eventually nods in compliance. I can tell it's taking a great effort for her to back away. It looks like she has grown quite a temper in the last five years.

I recall Ashur never finishing what he said. so I turn to him and ask curiously, "What were you saying, Ashur, when you were interrupted? You said you think what?"

Ashur looks at Breena with a hate-filled gaze and then back to me.

"I said I don't think it was Elissa that killed your fae. The reason why I know this is because she said something before she collapsed, or might I say the dark sorcerer said something before he left her body. His exact words were 'I was just having a little fun, Guardian. Give Meliantha my best and tell her I will see her soon.' I know that isn't something Elissa would say." Ashur pauses and then continues, "She was also holding an iron dagger."

Meliantha grabs my hand and squeezes.

"I believe him, Kalen. I saw her earlier dancing with a young man and her eyes didn't look right. They looked…evil. It had to have been him in her body the whole time."

"Well, then you're just as guilty for this murder as she is," Breena hisses while pointing in the direction where, I assume, Elissa is being held.

"You were too busy being a whore and stealing my prince to care about anything or anyone else, right?"

Everything happens so quickly and I couldn't have stopped it if I tried. Meliantha's fist flies hard and swift, connecting with Breena's face in a loud sounding crunch. By the sound of the hit, I would have to say Breena's nose is broken along with other bones in her face. Her blood sprays across the white snow and she lands hard in a heap on the ground. She deserves it, and I don't feel a shred of sympathy for her either.

I grab the closest warrior to give him orders.

"Take Breena to her quarters. I want her packed and gone by morning."

Breena jumps to her feet, blood running down her face, and wails, "But she's the one who hit *me*! This is all her fault, and she needs to be locked up with her friend and executed."

Silence has descended upon the crowd and they're all looking at me. I have had enough of her mouth, and if she wasn't a female, she would already be laid out on the ground preparing for punishment.

I clench my hands into fists and through gritted teeth I hiss, "If you don't shut the hell up right now, I'm going to send you out of the palace immediately. Be thankful your father is on the council or else you would have already been gone. Do me a favor and get the hell out of my sight."

I nod my head at the warrior, and with a firm grip he takes hold of Breena's arm and prepares to haul her toward the palace. Her look is menacing as she stares back and forth from Meliantha to me.

Her voice sounds hateful when she sneers, "You're going to pay for this...both of you."

The warrior drags her away and I watch as she is

escorted to the palace. The laugh she expels makes the hair on the back of my neck stand straight up. Something isn't right about her and it hasn't been for a very long time. I just never could figure out what it was.

I command the warriors to step aside, and once Elissa comes into view, Meliantha runs straight to her. She is still passed out on the ground and not moving. Her hand looks misshapen and deformed from the poison of the iron dagger. In time it will heal, but her hand will remain badly scarred. I walk over to Meliantha and I kneel down on the ground beside her. She takes off her red, silky gloves and places them on the ground beside Elissa. I wonder what she plans on doing. I look her in the eyes and she brings her finger to her lips as a silent gesture for me to stay quiet. I nod my head in compliance and she closes her eyes. She picks up a fallen glove and begins wrapping Elissa's hand in it. Each second she's touching Elissa's bare hand I see the tissues forming back together and healing before my eyes. How can this be? I have never heard of a fae having healing capabilities like this.

By the time she's finished wrapping Elissa's hand, her skin is completely back to normal and not misshapen at all. But why would she keep this a secret? As soon as we are alone, I plan to ask her.

"I need to take her with me, Meliantha. I'm going to have Heylfred, our advisor, take a look at her. He's very powerful and he will be able to help her and figure out what happened."

She looks up at me, and although her expression is strong, I can still see the quiver in her lip when she asks, "Are you going to lock her up?" My chest tightens at the thought of her friend being punished for something she didn't consciously do, but I have to take her with me to make sure she is secured. I don't want to cause Meliantha more pain, but it's looking like the dark sorcerer plans to continuously cause it. I really hope one day we will find a way to destroy the bastard.

I take Meliantha's hand and I lightly kiss her palm.

"She's not going to the dungeons, if that's what you are asking. I'll have her safely secured in a nice room until we figure it all out. She killed a noble, Meliantha. Dark sorcerer or not, Darius is still gone, and we have to prove her innocence to the court." I tilt her chin to look up at me. "I am *so* sorry, my love."

She nods her head and gets to her feet. Her eyes look tired, but she's holding her body strong. I admire her for her loyalty and courage, and best of all, I love that she is mine. I pick Elissa up off the ground and I cradle her in my arms. Ashur and Meliantha both place gentle kisses on her head before stepping back.

"I'm going to take good care of her," I say to both of them.

Then to Meliantha I say, "After I get Elissa settled and Heylfred sent to her, I'll come see you first thing in the morning. We haven't finished talking yet." She nods her head and kisses me tenderly on the lips.

"Please keep her safe," she whispers. I watch her walk away with her guardian by her side. She looks back once before disappearing down the path.

"Alright, warriors, let's go."

Last night was the best and worst night of my life. Having the vision with Meliantha was the best, but having to take away her best friend was the worst. Not to mention, the dark sorcerer is trying to wreak havoc in Meliantha's path. After I left her last night, I secured Elissa in a private room where she remained unconscious throughout the night until early this morning. I sat with her the whole time Heylfred performed his magic and found the solution. The necklace Elissa had been wearing was spelled with dark magic and that is how the dark sorcerer gained his entry. I wonder where she got the necklace. It is now with Aelfric to be taken back to the Elvish Kingdom where it can be destroyed in the magical fires, along with Finn's gold cuff.

After Elissa woke up, she was confused and lethargic. I gave her a few minutes to herself before explaining to her what happened. She was hysterical at first, but later calmed down slightly when I promised to bring Meliantha and Ashur to come see her before the trial. It is tragic that we lost one of our own, but the devastation and heartache Elissa is going through right now is a punishment in its own. I wish I could console her, but I know there is nothing that could make the events of the past night easier on her. Meliantha will know what to do to help.

I couldn't get my mind off Meliantha last night. Knowing she was in the cottage alone with her past lover had me on edge. Finn seems like an honorable warrior, but if he tries to seduce her in my absence, I'm going to kick his ass all the way back to the Summer Court. If I wasn't busy handling this travesty, I would have liked her to stay with me...alone.

I'm beginning to understand how the twisted mind of the dark sorcerer works. He's doing everything possible to keep Meliantha and me apart. If we're separated, we can't fulfill our destiny. He's succeeded at it for five years so he could...damn it! He's been laughing at us the entire time while fucking with Meliantha physically and emotionally. Just thinking about it makes my body shake in fury. He's had his hands all over her and done who knows what to her out of his sick and twisted enjoyment. I know Meliantha is strong, and she has me to help her, but how long is it going to before she breaks from the sorcerer's perverted pleasures?

My eyes are heavy and they feel like a bag of salt has been poured into them. I think I may have gotten about an hour of sleep during the whole ordeal. I plan to spend the morning with Meliantha and take her somewhere special before Elissa's trial today. I don't know when she plans on leaving, but I know she has to go back to the Summer Court to get everything arranged before forming our court. The pull to the land has grown stronger since last night and I know it's telling me to come claim it. I am sure Meliantha is feeling the same way. I can't wait to say the sacred words and be bound to her for all eternity. I plan to make the announcement of our bonding after the trial.

I rub my eyes and stretch to get the kinks out of my muscles. It's snowing outside, like usual, but for once I don't dread the day. I quickly get out of bed and into the shower. Once I'm out, I towel dry and comb my hair. I have to be prepared if I'm to protect Meliantha, so I put on my full warrior gear. My breast plate is in place and I have everything strapped and laced. My sword is heavy hanging from the holster on my hip, but it's a welcome weight that I find great comfort in.

It's still early, but I can't wait a moment longer to see her. Before walking out of my cabin, I see my reflection in the window. After taking a shower earlier, I can't believe I didn't take the time to notice my newly changed body. It's amazing how different my skin looks and feels. My heart finally feels like it belongs somewhere — it belongs with Meliantha, and in *our* court.

I walk out the front door and Aki is waiting for me on the porch.

"Come on, Aki, let's go get our princess."

He huffs and runs around me once before bolting away to the cottage. His enthusiasm and excitement brings a smile to my face and joy to my heart. I know Meliantha has an affinity for animals, but I think Aki would have been drawn to her anyway, affinity or not. He is wagging his tail and staring at the cottage door as I approach. I knock firmly on the door and wait patiently for someone to answer. A few seconds later Meliantha opens the door and looks at me and Aki with the most beautiful smile. Her eyes look a little sad, most likely from the situation with Elissa, but it doesn't take anything away from the lovely features of her face.

Her auburn red hair is down and she's wearing a knitted cream-colored cap that hugs the top of her head and over her ears. She's also wearing a cream-colored snow jacket with cream-colored snow pants to match. I know she can't be comfortable in all that, being from the Summer Court and all, but she looks absolutely amazing.

After being stunned into silence by her beauty, I finally find my voice.

"I have a surprise for you," I say with enthusiasm as I hold out my hand for her to take. She gazes at me with excitement and quickly grabs my hand. Seeing her elation fuels mine, so I pull her hurriedly out the door and into my arms.

"Come on, let's go."

Chapter Twelve

Meliantha

- Night of the Attack -

My mind feels like it's in complete shock. I think it's a combination of everything that is taking over my body. I am angry, tired, hungry, devastated, frustrated, and every other terrible emotion you can think of. The list could go on forever, and it still wouldn't touch the way I truly feel. How many of my loved ones is the dark sorcerer going to use to torment me? First Kalen, then Finn, and now Elissa. Who knows what's going to happen to Elissa at the trial?

The walk back to the cottage with Ashur is not easy. He was the one who witnessed the horrid display and I know he fears what will happen to her, and also for me. He cares for Elissa in a deeper way, so his feelings go way beyond just fear. While we were with Kalen and the warriors, Ashur told us what the dark sorcerer said while he was in Elissa's body. He said he will see me soon, and deep in my gut I know it is the truth. He will come for me because I know his time is running out. But when will he make his move?

My home will not be long in the Summer Court now that the transformation has begun. Kalen and I will form our new court as soon as possible, I hope. I can feel the land calling to me. It's pulling me with an invisible force, demanding I claim it and make it mine. I'm deeply honored by this gift, and as soon as I leave this Winter haven I'll be one step closer.

"Soon," I whisper among the wind.

In order for the dark sorcerer to get my magic, he has to get it before Kalen and I bond. Once I combine my power with Kalen's, the dark sorcerer will no longer be able to use it because it will no longer be pure. By the way things are going, it might be best to complete the bond tonight. My heart races at the thought of making Kalen mine tonight, and being able to make love to him. I wonder what he would say about completing the bond tonight. I shake my head and silently laugh at myself, I'm sure he wouldn't mind in the least.

When we made it to the cottage and walked inside, Finn was nowhere to be found. I wonder if he's in my room or in another one. I'm sure I am about to find out.

"Get some rest, Princess, we have a long day tomorrow."

Ashur looks worn and defeated, so I walk over to him and put my arms around him, holding him close. He grips me tight and all his sorrow and all his heartache pours into me in a huge rush. His pain runs deep like a knife being shoved in my gut. It's deeper than I could ever imagine, so I do the only thing I know of to help. With him holding me tight, I release my power, sending it through every ache and every pain in his body. I mainly send it to his heart because that is where he needs it most.

His grip lessens, and he pulls back, startled and wide-eyed.

"What did you do?"

I take his face in my hands and I answer silently, "I'm

taking care of my Guardian for once. The pain was too much for you to bear, so I took it from you, but you must not speak of this to anyone. I don't want anyone to know what I can do yet."

He closes his eyes and bows his head.

"Thank you, Princess."

I kiss his forehead and release him.

"You are most certainly welcome, Guardian."

He nods his head and slowly walks away toward his room. Once I hear his door shut, I make my way to my room. The door is shut and I hesitate for a second before turning the knob. I turn it slowly and open the door. I look around the room and Finn is nowhere to be seen. I'm relieved, but I also feel guilty. I open the door to the room beside mine, and there he is. His white-blonde hair is fanned out across the pillow and his steady breathing lets me know he's in a deep sleep. Knowing I'll be leaving him and the Summer Court sends a twinge of guilt sparking through my chest. I will miss his companionship greatly.

I close the door quietly and I walk back to my room. It's late in the evening and my body is worn from the long journey here and the stress of the recent events. I unfasten my dress and slide it off. A nice, hot shower is what I need before I go to sleep for the night. Maybe it'll wash away all the evil I feel surrounding me. The bathroom smells of lavender and everything is laid out in all shades of purple. I need to make it a point tomorrow to ask Kalen what the obsession is with the color purple; although, I think I already know the answer.

The hot water relaxes my body, and I sag against the wall of the shower. I can't wait to see Kalen tomorrow so we can figure out everything with Elissa and also talk about our future plans. I am going to mention to him about my earlier ideas of completing the bond as soon as we can.

The bathroom is steamy with the smell of lavender and fresh cut flowers. I dry off quickly and I take the bathrobe hanging on the back of the door and wrap it snugly around my body. It's soft and cool making my heated body feel sensational underneath its silky covering. The bed looks comforting and it takes every ounce of energy I have to make it there. I lie on the bed, sinking into its comforting embrace, but I can't help but feel like something is missing. It only takes one quick second to realize this will be the first night I have spent alone in years. The silence is lonesome, but the fear of being alone doesn't come. Soon I'll be in Kalen's arms every night for the rest of my life.

I can feel my eyelids getting heavier by the minute. I blink a few times, but then I quickly fall into the labyrinth of sleep. All I see as I close my eyes are the colorful array of flowers in the field from the vision, and the ice blue eyes of the man beside me holding me tight.

I wake to the sound of light knocking on the bedroom door. I wait for the person to enter, but the door never opens.

"Come in," I call out.

The door opens and Finn walks in carrying a tray of food and a steaming cup of something that smells absolutely wonderful. My stomach is growling so loud I know he can hear it as he makes his way into the room. A smile takes over his face and it instantly makes me smile. After everything that's happened, he is still trying to take care of me. He truly has a heart of gold. He walks over to the side of the bed and his smile slightly falters when he sees me up close. I completely forgot that he would be seeing me in a new light now. Finn never saw me again last night after the change from the vision, so seeing me now has to be hard for him.

I open my mouth to explain, but he cuts me off before I get my first word out.

"You don't have to explain, Mel." He sets the tray down in front of me and takes a seat on the bed beside me. I wish he would let me explain so I can tell him how sorry I am and that I don't want him to hurt. I hold back the tears as best I can. The burn makes me want to blink, but if I blink they will fall.

He continues, "I knew what I was getting into when we became lovers, and I'm fine with that. I'm not going to lie to you, but it does hurt to see you like this." His eyes are sad and full of longing when he meets mine. "I hate knowing that I will never be with you again." He reaches over to grab my hand, squeezing it tight. I guess it's safe to assume he will not be following me to the Spring Court. I know it's for the best, but I can't help feeling the twinge of disappointment in my chest.

"So you'll be staying in the Summer Court, I presume?" I ask to confirm my assumption.

He nods in affirmation, "I would love to follow you, Mel, but I don't think it would be a great idea." He pauses for a few minutes in thought, and then his lip starts to tilt up into a mischievous smirk when he teases, "As much as I would like to torment your prince, I don't think he would enjoy seeing your ex-lover every day." His smirk grows into a full out grin and the laughter he bellows eases the tension in my chest.

I lean over to kiss his cheek and when I pull back, I give him a warm smile. He stands up and motions to the food he brought in for me.

"You need to eat something, Princess. Elissa will need you to be strong for her today." Yes, she will, and I plan on doing everything possible to get her out of this mess.

I take a sip of the warm, chocolaty drink that's in the cup and it tastes like heaven as it glides down my throat. I can taste the touch of cinnamon that's been sprinkled on top of the cream making the mixture absolutely sinful. Finn looks from me to the covered dish in amusement so I lift the cover curiously. My eyes go wide at the sight of . My mouth is watering and I can't wait to taste the masterpiece of the food. I thought I was going to have to forgo having my favorite breakfast on this trip. I'm starving, so I will probably eat everything on the plate and then some. I beam at Finn to show my appreciation.

What lies before me is a loaf of pumpkin bread with crumb topping that's been sliced into thick slices and is surrounded by an assortment of fae berries. It's my favorite breakfast and Finn knows it. He has been with me every morning for years and has seen me eat the same thing over and over. We have grown to know each other well. What's strange is that Finn knows more about what I like than Kalen does. I guess I will need to remedy that.

"Thank you so much for this, Finn. How did you

come across pumpkin bread here?" I ask curiously.

He shakes his head and laughs, "You think the Winter fae would have this stuff here? No. I packed it, along with the berries, when we loaded up to come here. I knew you would miss it if you didn't have it. Besides, I didn't want you to go through withdrawals. You've eaten your pumpkin bread every morning since I've been with you."

The clenching in my stomach starts up again because it's another reminder of losing him.

"I'm going to miss you so much," I say. He was headed for the door but stops at the sound of my voice.

He looks at me over his shoulder and gives me a tender smile. I can hear the sadness in his voice when he replies, "And I you, Meliantha."

He opens the door and quietly shuts it back when he leaves. I need to eat and get ready for the day. I'm sure our departure has been delayed because of the incident with Elissa. She is most likely going to have a trial today to prove her innocence, and I know she will need my support. Kalen said he'll be here first thing in the morning and it is now morning. I relax to enjoy my pumpkin bread and berries before looking through my things to find something warm to wear. I have never had to wear winter clothes, so it'll be different having so much clothing on my body. There is one thing I know for sure: I am not going to be freezing cold today.

I decide on the cream-colored snow jacket and pants to match. I put on the outfit and I look in the mirror. I groan at the figure looking back at me. I look like a snow cone with a cherry on top.

"Your prince is coming, Meliantha," Ashur relays silently.

I guess this will have to do. Even though I am upset about everything going on, I can't stop the excitement bubbling in my chest at the thought of being with Kalen. I search around frantically for a pair of boots.

"I'm almost ready. I'll be there in one minute," I hastily reply to Ashur.

I find my boots and slide them on. I run to the bathroom to brush my teeth and wash my face. I take a brush to my bundle of red hair and I can honestly say it doesn't look too bad today. I put my winter cap on, and before exiting my room, I strap my bow and arrows to my back. Ashur is in the kitchen eating a bowl of fruit and he points at the window. My heart jumps at the sight of Kalen walking toward the cottage, and I can see Aki bounding down ahead of him.

"Where is Finn?" I ask silently, looking at Ashur.

"He didn't want to be in here when Prince Kalen came to call on you. I thought you might also like to know that we will be here for probably an extra day since the incident with Elissa."

I thought that would be the case. I knew there was no way I was going to leave without her. As far as Finn is concerned, I understand completely why he feels like that; however, it still makes me feel guilty.

"How are you holding up?"

Ashur shrugs his shoulders and continues to eat his fruit. He chews his food for a few seconds and then slams his fork down making a loud clatter. He voices his concern out loud this time.

"I don't know, Princess. Coming here has been one huge disaster after another. The dark sorcerer is coming after you and there is no way to keep you safe. I'm happy you and Prince Kalen could work everything out, but it's too dangerous for you to be here or anywhere for that matter. I hate what happened to Elissa, and all I want is to get her back."

I take his hand and look straight into his bright green eyes.

"I know, and we will. She'll be OK, I promise. I'm not going to let anything else happen to her," I vow.

"Thank you," he replies softly.

The firm knocks on the door startle me and I turn from Ashur to stare at the door. I check over my clothes to make sure I look all right before grabbing the door handle. I take a deep breath and open the door. Kalen is there in full warrior mode and so is Aki standing dutifully beside him. His eyes go wide at the sight of me and he gazes over my body with a huge grin on his face. I guess I look fine in these ridiculous clothes, but at least I'll be warm.

It seems as though Kalen has lost his voice, but after a few seconds, it looks like he's found it.

He holds out his hand and sounds excited when he says, "I have a surprise for you." My eyes light up and I know I have a goofy grin on my face, but I don't care. I instantly grab his hand and he pulls me out the door. "Come on, let's go," he insists.

We begin walking away from the palace and to the woods beyond. I am so used to forests of colors and greenery. Looking at one that is covered in ice is just unusual, but in a good way. It is very beautiful here, but I wouldn't give up my plants for any of it. I can feel the cold wind against my cheeks, and I'm thankful that I dressed warmly today. Aki walks beside me rubbing against my legs, and I know that he's happy to be coming along to wherever we are going.

Kalen squeezes my hand and I look up at him.

"Did you rest OK?" he asks curiously. There's a look on his face that I can't decipher, but I can sense a hidden meaning for his question. But what?

"I did rest well, thank you. I was worried about Elissa, but I knew you would take care of her. I think I was exhausted after everything that happened yesterday."

He nods his head, "I did take care of her, and I have so much to tell you, but first..."

I look at him with a smile and I raise my eyebrows at him to prompt him to continue. When he doesn't I decide to ask him myself.

"What is it Kalen? What were you going to say?" I can tell he wants to ask or say something, but he's holding back.

He takes a deep breath and sighs. I detect a hint of jealousy when he speaks, "I didn't like you being alone with Finn last night, OK. I wanted you with me and it killed me knowing that he was here alone with you and I wasn't. If it wasn't for the tragedy with Elissa, I was going to spend the whole evening alone with you in my cabin."

I can only imagine what would have happened if we had that alone time. The bond would most likely have been completed and things would have been set right. I also can't believe he was worried about me being alone with Finn. In a way I'm flattered by his jealousy, but I am also perturbed by his lack of faith in me. I can just picture him pacing and wondering if Finn was having his way with me. I know he was worried, but he needs to know that he can trust me.

"Kalen, you have nothing to worry about. I was alone

all night. Finn would never do anything like that anyway. He knows and understands that our bond is what's meant to be. He knew I would have to fulfill my part of the prophecy and he was prepared for that. He's not going to cause any problems, trust me."

He breathes a sigh of relief.

"Good, I didn't want to have to kick his ass."

I roll my eyes and shake my head.

"Men," I huff.

He finally laughs and pulls my arm around his waist and secures his arm around my shoulders.

He looks at my bow and arrows and asks, "So how good are you with your bow?"

"I never miss my target," I boast while lifting my chin.

"That's amazing," he admits. "Maybe you could teach me how to aim straight. I could always use the help."

"I would love to. Maybe you could help me with my sword fighting skills."

He nods his head, "It's a deal."

We have entered the forest, and Aki bounds swiftly through the trees. We follow his tracks while heading farther into the woods. I know it's time to hear the verdict on Elissa, so I come right out and inquire.

"Now tell me about Elissa."

"She had a necklace on that was spelled with dark magic. That's how the dark sorcerer was able to enter her body."

Oh no! Why didn't I think of that before? I stop Kalen abruptly and I look at him with a horrified expression. This is my fault.

"Was it a necklace with a purple stone?" I ask,

hesitant. A sick feeling is tearing away at my stomach because I know deep down the answer is going to be what I don't want to hear.

"Yes, why?" He looks at me skeptically.

I pull away from his body and I turn my back to him.

My shoulders sag when I confess, "I gave her the necklace, Kalen."

He pulls me around by the shoulders and captures my face in between his hands.

"What? Where did you get it from?" he exclaims.

I played right into the dark sorcerer's hands on this one. He knew I wouldn't get rid of the necklace; therefore, leaving another entryway for him to take over the people that I love. Damn it! How could I be so stupid? I think back to that dreaded day when the dark sorcerer laid out the beginnings of his twisted game. I didn't know at the time that I was the main player, and unfortunately I still am.

I look into Kalen's eyes and sheepishly admit, "That day, five years ago when I thought it was you visiting, he gave me a necklace as a parting gift. I couldn't bring myself to get rid of a gift from you, so I gave it to Elissa. Everything that has happened is my fault."

"No! It's not your fault!" he demands, shaking my shoulders. "You had no idea it was the dark sorcerer that day. No one is to blame."

"Will Elissa be able to go free?" I ask, hopeful.

"I have no doubt. Heylfred, our advisor, is extremely powerful and once he gives his testimony, my court will have no choice but to release her."

He pulls me into his arms and I sag in relief. This is the best news yet. Maybe I will be able to enjoy my time here with Kalen after all. Whatever happens, I am not going to let the dark sorcerer win this game.

"Thank you," I whisper against his chest.

He moves back and takes my hand.

"We are almost there."

We walk for a few minutes longer and up ahead I see a cave of huge boulders with a large opening for an entrance. I recognize this place from searching through Aki's mind. This is the pack's den. I'm so excited that I pick up the pace dragging Kalen along behind me. Aki is standing at the entrance patiently waiting on us.

"You must know where we are going judging by your enthusiasm," Kalen jokes.

"Of course I know!" I exclaim. "Aki showed me this place in his mind and I have been dying to see his family."

Kalen laughs and picks up his pace to match mine. Aki comes forward to bow his head in front of Kalen before circling me and rubbing against my legs. I enter the cavern and walk a little ways into the heart of it when I notice the mound of white wolves lying in a heap on the ground. I stare at all of them excitedly while they sleep. The white wolf is a majestic creature and to be able to see a whole pack of them is amazing.

I can see the little one cuddled with her mother, but she opens her eyes at the sound of Aki entering the cavern. Once she fully opens her eyes, she notices me at a first glance. She topples over the other wolves as she races to reach me. I can't stop the giggle from escaping my throat as I watch her charge through the other wolves to get to me. I bend down on my knees and I open my arms wide to catch her when she bounds. She jumps into my arms and licks my face over and over until I beg her to stop. By touching her, I already know everything about her from her name to what she's done today. It seems she has missed her father greatly.

"You are such a beautiful girl, Accalia." I rub behind her ears and she licks my hand. I set her down and she runs straight for Aki.

I peer over at Kalen and he's looking at me with admiration in his eyes.

"They are amazing, Kalen. I can see why you love them so much," I whisper.

"I thought you would say that." He gapes lovingly at the wolves and then back to me. "They have truly been a family to me. I don't know what I would have done without them."

I could hear the melancholy in his voice, but he quickly perks up and takes my hand.

"There's something else I want to show you." He tugs on my hand, and the light shining in his eyes sparks my curiosity as we make our way through the cavern and tunnels. I wonder where we're going. The air gets colder the farther we go into the tunnels and the smell of fresh earth and moss overtake my senses. I have to lower my head to walk through the small tunnels, but it's not long before it opens up to…

The gasp I let out echoes in the enclosure, and I stand frozen in awe as I take in the immaculate scene. The ceiling is high and there are white draperies hanging down from all sides, flowing delicately down the cavern walls. Plush white carpets adorn the cavern floors and an enormous bed takes up the center of the room.

"I have never brought anyone here," Kalen admits as he walks up behind me. "This is my special place, and I never wanted to share it with anyone until now." I'm flattered he never brought anyone here, but I wonder what he's up to bringing me here. Does he want to complete the bond now?

"Thank you for sharing your special place with me," I say while looking around the room. My eyes settle on the bed, and I spy him looking at me through the corner of my eye.

He shakes his head and laughs, "I didn't bring you here to seduce you, Meliantha. Although, I *would* love more than anything to have your naked body under my own; however, there are things I wanted to talk to you about, and I didn't want to be at the palace when I said them."

I don't want to rush things, but I couldn't help feeling the slightest bit of disappointment when he told me of his intentions not to seduce me. I have some things I would like to discuss with him as well, but I'm curious to know what he has to say. He takes my hands and pulls me over to the bed where he gently urges me to sit. He kneels in front of me and grazes his lips across my hands before lifting his eyes to find mine.

"I know you came back into my life just yesterday, but in my heart you have always been there. I love you, Meliantha, and I want to know if you will complete the marriage bond with me tonight?"

Hearing those words come out of his mouth takes my breath away, and makes my heart soar to the stars above. I take his face gently in my hands and I brush his lips softly with mine. I pull back slightly to whisper against his lips.

"I would love nothing more than to be your wife…and your queen."

He moves closer to my body and groans against my mouth.

"Then you shall get your wish."

He takes my lips in a fierce embrace with his own. His kiss tastes different from last night and I realized this is the first time I am kissing him since our change. His scent is like the intoxicating aromas of exotic flowers and his taste reminds me of the sweet perfection of honey.

We all have a unique scent that distinguishes us between courts, so this must be the way the Spring fae will smell. The Summer fae have their own smell just like the Winter and Fall fae do. Kalen's masculine scent is intoxicating and it's driving my body crazy.

"If you're not planning to seduce me, I think we need to get out of here. If we stay here a moment longer, we're going to be on that bed and not leaving for several days."

His eyes take on a lustful glow, and I can see his control slipping away inch by inch.

"Well then...let's stay here," he taunts seductively.

His lips press harder on mine and the heat of it makes my body scorch in my thick clothes. His hands begin to unbutton my coat, and the will power I thought I had slowly begins to slip away. I want nothing more than to make love to him and feel his body meld with mine.

My coat falls to the floor, and he begins to lift my shirt. He has the gentlest of touches as he reaches underneath and caresses my back sending shivers running up and down my body. He moves me slowly back toward the bed and lowers me down to the soft, fluffy bedding below. Kalen steps back to remove his weapons while I kick my shoes off and fling them across the room where they land on the floor with a loud thud. Once his weapons are gone, he starts to take off his armor.

My body grows desperate with need at the sight of his muscular chest and his chiseled arms as he takes off the armor on his upper body. His eyes roam over me seductively like he can't wait to devour me, and I bite my lip in return to entice him. I decide to help him along by slowly removing my shirt in a teasing way. I guess we're not going to wait and make things official after all. That's perfectly fine by me because I am ready for him to have me here and now.

"What happened to waiting?" I say, breathless.

He climbs on the bed and pulls me on top of him.

"I say we complete it now," he growls. I straddle his waist and I can feel his groin hard and stiff between my legs. If we finish this now, not only will I have Kalen bonded to me, but I'll be untouchable to the dark sorcerer. I lean down to kiss him and I sway my body up and down against his growing erection. He moans loudly and grips my hips moving me harder.

"How about we take these off?" he says while tug-ging on my pants.

I lie down beside him and he reaches over to unbutton my pants. He slides them down my legs along with my underwear, and as he does, he kisses my skin the whole way down until my pants have been hastily discarded on the floor. I am naked and bared to him on his bed for the taking. Watching the way his muscles move makes my body clench in pleasure. I stare at the lower half of his body waiting on him to remove the last bit of clothing, but he stalls for a second, grinning at me wickedly. His smile tells me he is enjoying my torment. He lets the rest of his clothes fall from his body and onto the floor. I am left staring wide-eyed and speechless at the masterpiece of his form before me. I motion for him to join me on the bed and he happily complies. This is it! So many things will change after this. I breathe a sigh of relief and longing as he settles himself between my legs. Before we get any further, we are interrupted by the sound of growling and massive paws echoing up the tunnel in our direction.

Kalen groans and looks toward the doorway. No more than a couple of seconds later, in comes Accalia, followed by Aki and Larentia chasing after her. I know they are just wolves, but I cover myself with a blanket and look over at Kalen. He looks angry and amused all in one, but shakes his head as he looks at his wolves.

"I knew there was a reason I didn't want to do this here," he admits to me.

As much as I want to finish what we started, it is kind of funny they interrupted us at that exact moment.

"What reason could that be?" I ask humorously. "No doors, or the fact that you have a pack of wolves demanding your attention when you're here?"

"Both, my love. Accalia likes to sneak in here when I'm sleeping and snuggle with me. Aki and Larentia usually let her, but given that you are here with me it looks like they were trying to stop her." He kisses me sweetly on the lips and helps me off the bed. He looks disappointed, and honestly, I feel disappointed too, but at least I know we will finish the bonding tonight. The pull to the unclaimed land is strong and I know it wants us to complete the bond there, but unfortunately, we need to complete it as soon as possible. I begin to put my clothes back on and Kalen does the same. He looks at me and sighs.

"I'm so sorry, Meliantha. I guess this is our sign that we need to do things right."

I shrug my shoulders and smile.

"It's OK. At least now I know what I'll be getting tonight." I look down at his groin and I wiggle my eyebrows. He laughs and throws my shirt at me.

Aki is impatiently whining by the door and he sounds frantic. Something must be wrong. I walk over to him and I search into his glowing green eyes for answers. He needs to tell me something and it's important. I lay my hand on top of his head and I concentrate on what he wants me to see. He was out scouting for game when he noticed a dark shadow moving swiftly through the trees. The dark shadow swoops down and strikes one of the other wolves that are hunting with Aki. I can see the shadow clearly and it's not just a shadow. My heart slams in my chest and my adrenaline levels surge to new heights. I grab my bow and arrow off the floor and I strap it to my back. I expand my senses to see if I can feel the spirit of the wolf, but I sense nothing. No!

"Damn it! Kalen, the dark sorcerer is out there. I thought the wolves might have been playing with each other, but they were growling because he attacked one of your wolves. We have to get out there, now!" I yell.

Kalen's eyes go wide and he quickly gets the rest of his gear put in place. I start to walk out of the room, but Kalen stops me with a firm grip on my arm. He better not think I'm going to stay in here like the damsel in distress and do nothing. The playful Kalen is gone and now in his place is a full-blown warrior.

"I don't want you going out there, Meliantha. I'm not going to let him take you or harm you in any way. I will die before I let him have you." I have no doubt he would die trying to protect me, but it's my job to make sure that doesn't happen and to take care of myself. No matter what happens, I *am* going to fight out there alongside him. The last five years were hard enough on my heart without him.

The wolves join us outside as we make our way to the fallen wolf. Kalen walks close to me and keeps his hand hovering over his sword. Tears burn my eyes because I know it's too late to save the wolf with my healing magic. There was no way I could have gotten there in time. My heart aches for his mate as I watch her by his side nuzzling him with her nose. Fire burns in my chest and my vision becomes clouded over with all shades of red. The longer the dark sorcerer toys with me, the more hate fills my body. It is consuming me to the core and all I want is for him to pay for everything he has taken from me. Some way or another, whether it be now or ten years from now, I will be a part of his demise. I *will* be there the day he is destroyed.

"Meliantha, are you OK? I can feel your distress," Ashur demands. It's amazing how he can feel my emotions even though we are miles apart.

"I'll be fine, Ashur. We're headed back to the palace, and as soon as I get there, I will tell you everything. Don't worry about me, I'll be OK." I assure him.

"Please don't shut me out. I need to make sure you are safe at all times. Oh, and by the way, there's a surprise for you here when you get back. Be safe, Mel, and I will see you when you get back."

"Thank you, my Guardian."

I can't sense any black magic around, but I'm starting to believe the dark sorcerer is keeping his eyes everywhere on us. He must have known what Kalen and I were about to do and decided to cause a distraction. All I know is that he's going to pay for it. I can feel the heat of Kalen's anger as he looks down at the fallen wolf. His hands are shaking when he sinks to the ground beside him, and I can hear his whispered words of love and passing to the wolf in the Old Fae language, bidding him a safe journey to the Hereafter.

He is silent for a few minutes before his gravelly voice takes on a menacing edge.

"I'm going to fucking kill him!" he roars. Kalen stands and clenches his hands into fists. The air around him is intense with rage, and the scream that explodes from his body is filled with both fury and heartbreak. He collapses to his knees on the ground and puts his head in his hands. I walk over slowly and sink to my knees before him. I wrap my arms around his neck and I pull him closer and gently guide his head to my shoulder. He instantly folds his arms around my waist and pulls me in tighter.

"I am *so* sorry, Kalen," I whisper in his ear. I know I can help him with his pain, and I almost use my magic on him unintentionally, but I don't want to do it against his will. "Do you want me to take the pain away?" I ask softly.

He shakes his head strongly and keeps his head down when he replies, "No, I have to remember the way I feel." He then looks up at me with watery eyes and a determination that sends chills down my spine. "I *need* to remember the way I feel because if you take that anger and rage away," he pauses to take a deep breath and starts over. "I need to have that rage so I can rip his fucking head off when I see him." I nod my head, and I wait there silently while he gets his anger under control.

We make our way back to the palace quickly. Now that the dark sorcerer knows how close Kalen and I are I have a feeling he's going to become desperate to make his move as soon as possible. Kalen is going to inform his parents of the recent attack and of the urgency of our bonding. I plan to tell my parents as soon as we get back as well. Having a big ceremony means nothing to me, so I wonder if Kalen would object to completing the bond alone and not having a ceremony. The ceremony itself isn't the important part, but the words that are spoken are. I think I'll wait until we get back to the palace to voice my idea. The anger is still pouring off of him in waves, and I can tell he is in no mood to talk.

We pick up our pace and my feet are pounding against the snow as we run the last mile to the palace. Deep down I can't seem to shake the dreaded feeling in my stomach telling me we have already run out of time.

Chapter Thirteen

ALASDAIR

- Dark Sorcerer -

I followed Meliantha and the prince to the wolf pack's den. I expected them to be out in a few short minutes, but what I didn't expect was for them to try and complete their bond so soon. I could smell the scents of lust and sex wafting out from the cavern and I almost charged in there myself to put a stop to it, but if I did, it would ruin all chances of my master plan. I see one of the wolves race out of the cavern and into the woods. It only takes me a second to decide what my next move is. My smile is chilling as I stare at my reflection in the dagger.

"This is for you, Prince Kalen."

The wolf is on the hunt for prey not knowing that he'll become the prey himself. I sweep low and gut the wolf from end to end. He only had time to give a small yelp before death took him. The yelp was not loud at all, but I could hear the slight echo reaching the cavern. The pack's hearing will no doubt hear the last call of their fellow pack member, and then they will alert Meliantha and their precious alpha. Unfortunately, after this ordeal they will push harder to get bonded. I'll just have to work quickly after this.

I wait for a few minutes longer to see if the word has spread yet, and I believe it has when I see Meliantha and

Kalen running out of the cave followed by the rest of the wolves. My distraction has worked, and in return, I bask in the glorious taste of anger and rage floating in the wind. The sound of Kalen's roar fuels my enjoyment, and I revel in the sounds of his torment as I glide across the wind and back to the palace.

Breena is packing her clothes and throwing things across the room when I enter. I could hear her ranting from across the palace grounds. The more attention she draws the less my plan will work from her idiocy. Other than fucking her, she has been nothing more than a pain in my ass.

"What the hell are you doing?"

She looks up at me and I hiss at the sight of her face. Meliantha really damaged it when she hit her. Her nose is swollen and her eyes are black and blue underneath. I'm surprised she hasn't healed yet. The princess must have used some powerful magic and force behind that blow.

Breena scowls at me and hisses, "I'm packing if you must know. I've been kicked out of the palace and I'm supposed to be gone this morning."

No, she will not, I think to myself. My game is about to reach its finale and I need her help. I look at her and smile, "You are not going anywhere. We're going to make them *think* you have left, but you're actually going to still be here."

She looks at me confused, "I don't understand. How can we do that?"

"I will tell you in a minute, but first, where is the box with Kalen's gift?" I ask. She bends down to reach under the bed and pulls out the box.

"Excellent," I say as I reach out to take the box. "We have to move fast tonight. Your precious prince and Meliantha almost bonded today, but I intervened by killing one of his wolves."

She gasps and puts her hand over her mouth in shock.

"You killed one of his wolves?" she asks in a shaky voice.

"I needed a distraction and the wolf presented itself to me, so I took the opportunity. I gutted it for all of them to see. It was actually a glorious sight," I boast.

Her mouth is still hanging open in shock, but she shakes out of it. "He's going to have your head for that. One way or another, he is going to come after you. His wolves are dear to him."

I just shrug and smile.

"He can try, but no magic or weapon has been discovered that can kill me. I'm invincible." Unfortunately, I know I'm not fully invincible, but no one knows of the magic that can kill me and I plan to keep it that way. Calista's dagger wounded me when she stabbed me with it or actually when she stabbed Avery with it with me in his body. It took a lot out of me, but I soon recovered. There's something about the mixture of magic and fae blood in the daggers that can hurt me.

No one knows I have the scrolls with the ancient text transcribed on them that states how to destroy my people. My family had secured them before the legendary battle took place that killed them all. We tried to destroy them, but we were unsuccessful. Apparently, the scrolls can't be destroyed. Only a few of the fae knew about the magical scrolls, and of course they were the ones who wrote them. No one knows how they received the knowledge of how to defeat us. Before they were able to share them with the courts, my people had them hunted down and slaughtered. As far as I know, there has never been a mention of them since then. I have them hidden away in a safe location. As long as I have them secured, there's no way they can figure out how to defeat me. It's best they think I cannot be killed.

Breena is done with her packing and I should have told her it was a waste of time because she's not going to be taking any of that with her where we're going.

"Are you ready to see how you're going to disappear? The next step of our game happens now," I prompt.

I hold out my hand and she takes it enthusiastically. The gleam in her eyes lets me know she is ready.

"Of course I'm ready. I am ready to pay that bitch back for fucking up my face," she snaps. I laugh at her words because there is no way she could ever get Meliantha back for screwing up her face. I'm surprised the princess didn't kill her last night. I would have. I pull Breena to me and I spread the darkness around my body to expand over hers. We are now one with the shadows, so I float us through the palace and out into the night beyond. I take us to the place where we will begin the next stage in the game.

Chapter Fourteen

Kalen

Seeing my wolf butchered on the ground was the most agonizing thing I have ever seen. His name was Malachi and he was one of the best hunters in the pack. He and Aki always accompanied me when I took my adventures in the forest as a child. The loss of him has left a permanent scar on my heart and it is not something I will ever forget. Meliantha offered to help me heal, but I refused. I love her for offering to help, but I need to remember the pain I felt in the moment.

Meliantha and I are in the throne room with my parents, King Madoc and Queen Mab, and also her parents, King Oberon and Queen Tatiana. We have explained the events of the afternoon and what we propose as a solution. They all glance from Meliantha to me and then at each other.

My father speaks first.

"If you want to complete the bond on your terms, your mother and I fully support your decision, son."

I bow my head and reply, "Thank you, Father." I knew my parents would be supportive and honor my proposal.

We have one family down and one to go. I smile at

Meliantha and she smiles back. I love to see her smile. It's one of the loveliest things about her face, other than her magnificent amethyst eyes. Her strength will help me get through my loss.

We are sitting at the council table side by side while both sets of our parents are seated opposite us. King Oberon looks over at Meliantha and raises his eyebrows in question. Meliantha smiles and nods her head in a silent agreement of sorts. I guess she can understand what's going on in her parent's mind. The King smiles lovingly back at her and turns to me in all seriousness.

"Queen Tatiana and I will support your decision as well," King Oberon states. He tells Meliantha, "We know this is your path and we want you to embrace it. If bonding tonight keeps you safe, then that is all that matters."

"Thank you," Meliantha cries.

We all stand up to say our goodbyes and I lead Meliantha out of the throne room and out of the palace. I loop her arm through mine while we make our way down to the cottage. Her long, red hair is beautiful blowing in the wind and her eyes sparkle with a magnificent intensity when she stares into mine. My groin instantly hardens at remembering the sight of her naked body on my bed ready for the taking. I sigh to myself. I just have to wait a little longer. I wish I could scoop her up in my arms and demand she come with me right this minute to finish what we started earlier. Unfortunately, I'm not going to do that because our first time together deserves to be special.

"Listen, I am going to take you to the cottage to retrieve some of your things so you can bring them over to my cabin tonight. I'm going to get things ready for you while you get your things together. I want Ashur to escort you to my cabin in an hour."

She raises her eyebrows at me and asks, "What are *you* going to be doing during this hour?"

"I can't tell you, my love." I place my hand on the back of her neck and I bring her forward to press my lips against hers in a deep embrace. I caress her tongue with mine and the taste of honey envelopes my senses. I groan into her mouth and she groans back. I bet every part of her body tastes this good. I press my hardening groin up against her stomach and she reluctantly pulls apart from me, breathless.

"We better stop or we will be making love out here on the ground," she jokes.

I look at the ground and I wiggle my eyebrows. I would gladly comply with that request if she asked. She playfully hits my arm and laughs.

"That is *not* going to happen. I'll end up with frostbite on my ass." We are both laughing now, and it feels good to be able to laugh after the kind of day we've had.

I look down at the cottage and Aki is waiting for us on the porch along with Ashur who happens to be pacing. When he sees Meliantha he bursts forward. "Are you okay?" he asks her.

"Yes, I'm fine. I told you I would be," she says.

She must have talked to him silently during my breakdown. He could probably feel her distress and wanted to make sure she was alright and out of danger. I don't think she will ever be out of danger until we bond ourselves together. He narrows his eyes at her and nods his head.

"I told you there would be a surprise for you inside when you got back. I think you need to come see it," he says with a grin. I bet I know what he's talking about and I'm sure Meliantha will be pleased.

She looks up at me and I nod my head.

"Have fun and I will see you in an hour." I kiss her gently across the lips and I look at Ashur and say, "I would like for you to escort her to my cabin when the hour is up. She doesn't need to be alone, and I want Aki with you as well."

"I will, Your Highness," Ashur responds firmly.

"Thank you."

I leave Meliantha to walk to my cabin. The water has frozen in the fountain, so I send my magic to make it flow again. I look down at the ground and Meliantha's flowers have all withered away during the night from the cold. Her flowers have always been so beautiful, and I look forward to seeing what our land is going to look like after she gets through with it. There's going to be flowers everywhere, all full of vibrant colors and perfumes. I can only imagine what it would be like to take her body amidst them.

I open the door to my cabin and my instincts quickly become alert, warning me of danger. The evil is so potent in the air that I can taste the bitterness of it going down the back of my throat. I grasp my sword and I draw it out of the holster on my waist. I glance around the room, searching the lower level of my cabin thoroughly, but find nothing. I make my way to the stairs and climb each one of them as quietly as I can. The hairs on the back of my neck stand straight up and my heart begins to race. The stench of black magic is coming from my bedroom. I hastily make my way to the door. I'm sick of being played for a fool by the dark sorcerer, and one way or another, these games are going to end tonight.

I open the door slowly, sword in hand, and charge into the room. What I find is not what I was expecting. I have to blink my eyes twice to clear my vision because I can't be seeing what I think I am seeing. Anger boils in my gut at the sight of Breena lying naked and lounging on my bed like she belongs there. Her face looks like shit from where Meliantha hit her.

"What the hell are you doing here?" I ask furiously.

Her mouth folds down into a pout and she lifts up on her knees.

"Well, good evening to you too, lover," she croons.

Not only is she supposed to be off the palace grounds, but I am afraid I'm also going to have to banish her from the Winter Court altogether. Why would she do this to me? If Meliantha shows up, this situation is going to turn ugly real fast.

"I'm not your lover, not anymore. I'm going to give you ten seconds to get dressed and get the hell out of here before I throw your ass out myself. Believe me, that's the last thing you want!" I yell venomously.

I am caught off guard as I hear a voice speak out behind me, "Oh, I think she will be staying, and for that matter, I think I will, too."

I am frozen in place because the voice isn't from someone I know, and by the way the magic feels in the room, there is only one person it could be. The anger and rage from before intensifies and the sword in my hand shakes along with the rest of my body. This bastard is going to pay for what he has taken from me.

I turn around slowly, vision turning red with rage, and stare disdainfully at the one creature that has tormented and destroyed the lives of those I hold dear, including my own. The dark sorcerer appears as nothing but a shadow until his form starts to ripple and he takes on the shape of a man before me.

I stand bewildered as I look upon my own reflection before me. So this is what he looked like when Meliantha thought it was me five years ago. With my sword held tightly in my hands, and with the speed of lightning, I slice my sword down into an arc across his body. It sinks right through him as if he was air, not damaging him at all.

The dark sorcerer laughs and shakes his head.

"Now, now, Prince Kalen. I don't think that was a proper greeting."

"Fuck you," I snap. I scan the room to find something, anything, I can use to distract him, but what can be used to distract a being that can't be killed?

"I wouldn't bother if I were you. There's nothing in here that will protect you from me," he smirks.

"What do you want?" I ask, even though I already know the answer. I have to find a way to warn Meliantha, but how? The dreaded feeling in my stomach warns me that I'm too late and there's nothing I can do. We should have just completed the bond instead of wasting our time in the palace. I wish I could kick myself in the ass for being so stupid. The dark sorcerer approaches me and I stand my ground firmly. I refuse to cower and bow down to this man. I match his sadistic glare with one of my own, and it seems to amuse him which infuriates me more.

"I think you know what I want," he taunts darkly.

"You can't have her!" I yell into his face.

He takes a step back and laughs while his appearance begins to blur and takes on the shape of another man. I stare transfixed as the transformation comes to a close.

There's a dark cloud surrounding him, and the stench of black magic permeates the room making it smell dank and rancid. This must be what the dark sorcerer looks like in his true form.

He smirks at me with his evil smile and brags, "Oh, I have already had her, Your Highness. Many times as a matter of fact. Her fiery temper in bed was something to behold, and I look forward to fucking her again."

Without a moment's thought, the anger boils over and I lunge straight for him, only to see him disappear before I make contact.

"You son of a bitch! I will kill you before you touch her again," I roar. My lungs are on fire and not being able to hurt him angers me more. The rage surging through my veins demands action. I take all the anger and all the hate inside me and I put them into words.

"No matter what you do, Meliantha will always be smarter than you. You can play your twisted games, but in the end we will all see you as what you truly are...a fucking coward that hides in the shadows."

The dark sorcerer's smile fades and he clenches his jaw. I smile because I know that was a devastating blow and it struck a nerve. After a few seconds his frown changes to a mischievous grin.

"Yes, well, it's just a shame you won't be here for the ending. I would have preferred for you to see what I do to your precious princess."

The warnings in my body instantly sound off, and I am about to make my move to escape when something hard and cold wraps around my arm. The room begins to fade and it feels like my inner soul is disappearing and being replaced by something malevolent and evil. The last things I hear as I fade out of my body are the sounds of Breena laughing and the taunting words of the dark sorcerer.

"Don't worry, Prince Kalen. I will be sure to show Meliantha a good time when you're gone."

Meliantha…

Chapter Fifteen

Meliantha

I watch Kalen walk away and Ashur picks this time to elbow me in the ribs playfully.

"Come on, Princess. You can't stare at him all night." I look at him and smile. He looks extremely happy and I wonder where it's coming from.

"Why are you so happy?" I ask, excited and curious.

He takes my hand and pulls me toward the cottage.

"I'll show you." We walk up the steps and onto the porch. Aki runs in as soon as Ashur opens the door and when I look inside I finally understand where his happiness is coming from. Sitting in the middle of the room talking to Finn is Elissa. I let go of Ashur's hand to dash through the room toward her. She startles at the sound of me bursting through the door and stands up only to be crushed by my arms as I hold her tight. It feels so good to have my best friend back and out of harm's way. Everything that has happened to her is all because of me and my ties to the dark sorcerer. I hope she can forgive me.

"I'm so sorry, Elissa," I cry. I let the tears flow because not only am I torn, but I can feel the torment inside of her as well. The knowledge of what she has done is taking a toll on her emotional state. It weighs heavily on her heart and the guilt is eating away at her. She holds me tight and sobs against my shoulder. "Please forgive me. I should never have given you that necklace."

"I don't blame you, Mel," she whispers. It feels good to hear those words, but I know I will always carry the blame no matter what she says. She lets me go and the pain I see in her eyes makes my heart ache for her even more. With tears streaming down her face, her eyes search mine frantically.

"How am I going to get through this? I killed someone, and I have to live with that for the rest of my life. How can I bear it when it's consuming me inside?"

Ashur comes over and pulls her into his arms. He looks me straight in the eyes when he speaks soothingly to her.

"We are all here to help you through it. *I* will help you through it." Her crying stops and she sniffles while peering up at Ashur. He wipes her tears away and then he leans down to kiss her lips. She melts in his arms and returns the kiss passionately. I hate that it took something this drastic to make them realize how much they need each other.

Finn turns his head away from their display and looks at me. His smile is weak, but he tries his best to make it strong. He gets up from his seat and disappears down the hallway until I hear the door to his room shut lightly. I hope with all my heart that he finds someone to love who will love him back.

Ashur and Elissa are still kissing, and I know his love for her will help her through anything she has to face. They break apart, but are still in each other's arms when Ashur pleads to me silently, *"Please help her, Meliantha. I am begging you to help take some of this guilt away. As much as I hate to say this, she is not strong enough to handle it, even with our help."*

The moment I saw her I wanted to take the pain away, but messing with people's emotions is not something I want to make a habit of. I know what happened to her is my fault, so I will do anything in my power to help her. I come up behind Elissa and I place my hand on her shoulder. I can feel the electric current of my magic leaving my hand and entering her body. The tingling sensation feels good as it comes alive in my body. I can sense it taking away the pain and guilt in Elissa and leaving only a dull ache in its place until there is no more.

Her body sags in Ashur's arms, most likely from my magic and exhaustion, so he scoops her up and cradles her against his body. Knowing that Elissa will be fine and safe releases the heavy burden that's been building on my chest.

"Thank you," he whispers to me. "I'm going to lay her down to rest for a while, and I believe it is time for you to get ready for tonight."

My insides scream with joy and I nod my head vivaciously at Ashur before going to my room. I open the door letting Aki follow me in and I lean against it to take a calming breath. So far things are going in the right direction, I think to myself. Let's just hope it stays that way. I have Elissa back and now her heart will be healed so she can move forward. Also, in just a few short minutes I will be on my way to being bonded to the man I love.

I take off my bow and arrows and the cream-colored winter jacket and pants I wore throughout the day. I take the white, silky bathrobe I wore last night and I wrap it around my body. I need to find a suitable dress to wear for my special night with Kalen. I look through my things and I sigh in disappointment. None of the dresses I brought are catching my eye. I sink to the floor and I lean against the trunk filled with my clothes. I know it shouldn't matter since the dress won't be on long anyway, but I still want to look amazing for him.

Aki comes over and nuzzles my cheek. I know he can sense my angst and he's trying to make me feel better. I nuzzle him back and sigh, "Oh, Aki, I just want this night to be perfect, and nothing I brought will be suitable." He lies on the ground beside me and whines his understanding.

I wonder what will happen to the wolves when Kalen and I leave the Winter Court. Will they come with us or stay here?

"You have a visitor, Meliantha," Ashur informs me through our connection. I'm not expecting anyone so I wonder who it could be. A knock sounds at the door, so I walk over to open it. On the other side of the door is a dark-haired Winter beauty with the most amazing green eyes I have ever seen. I remember meeting her years ago at Calista's wedding and how unique her eyes looked. It is rare for a Winter fae to have green eyes just like it's rare for a Summer fae to have purple eyes. We are unique and I know it's most likely because we are part of the powerful Four, which means we are also the ones that are supposed to save the Land of the Fae.

"Come in," I say while motioning her inside. She's carrying a garment bag and I'm curious to know why.

"Thank you, Meliantha. I'm sure you remember meeting me at your sister's wedding to my brother."

I nod my head, "Of course I remember you, Sorcha. I could never forget those green eyes of yours."

She laughs and lays the garment bag down on the bed.

"Yeah, most people can't forget, just like no one can forget yours." She looks around the room and shakes her head. "It looks like someone else couldn't forget them either by the looks of this room."

"What do you mean?" I ask curiously.

I've had my speculations about who decorated the room, but I want to hear for sure if it was Kalen or not. I meant to comment about it earlier to him, but never got around to it. Sorcha grins while motioning her hand all throughout the interior of the room.

"This is all my brother's doing. He did it for you, can't you tell? Everything in here is almost the exact shade of your eyes." She shrugs her shoulders. "I guess he thought you would like it."

"I do," I reply.

She breaks her eye contact and looks down at the floor.

"You know, I hated you for the past five years," she admits. I snap to attention and stare at her wide-eyed even though she hasn't taken her eyes from the floor yet. I am about to ask why when she lifts her hand and quickly continues, "I don't anymore, Meliantha, not after hearing about the real reason you and Kalen never got together. He became a different person after you turned him down. He never joked anymore or had the spark of life that made him who he was. I hated you for being the cause of that." She lifts her gaze to meet mine and she takes a deep breath, looking concerned. "I am the one who pushed

Kalen to date Breena, and I'm sorry for that. I didn't realize the trouble she would cause. Do you forgive me?"

"There is nothing to forgive, Sorcha. I wish things could have been different, but the dark sorcerer screwed us all over and led us down that wretched path. Not anymore, though. Tonight we turn the tables in our direction."

Her face brightens up and then she grabs the garment bag off the bed.

"Hence, the reason I am here. I brought a dress that would look wonderful on you for the bonding tonight. I didn't think you had come prepared, so I thought I would show this to you."

"Thank you, Sorcha. I was just sitting here trying to decide what to wear when you showed up. Let's see the dress," I say, ecstatic.

She unzips the bag and in it lays the most exquisite dress I have ever seen. The color of the dress matches my amethyst eyes and it sparkles in the light from the crystals adorned in the fabric. I couldn't have asked for a more perfect dress. It's a strapless gown that will hug at my waist and then flow down gracefully to the floor. The fabric feels silky to the touch as I run my hands over its shiny material.

"It's beautiful, Sorcha. I don't know how to thank you."

She lays the dress on the bed and reaches for my hand when she approaches me. "Just make my brother happy. That is all the thanks I need."

"I will take care of him for the rest of my life. You have nothing to worry about," I assure her. She kisses my cheek and leaves the room shutting the door behind her. I take a deep breath while staring at the dress. It's a shame it won't be on long enough to enjoy it. Shivers take over my body in anticipation of the evening, and soon Kalen will take those chills away by warming me up with his own body in a long night filled with passionate love making for the first time. The making of our bond will also begin our court, and the Land of the Fae will be one step closer to defeating the evil. So many things are going to change tonight.

I am dressed and ready to go in my lovely bonding dress along with my bow and arrows and my cloak. Bonding or not, I will always carry around my bow. Ashur is waiting for me by the door and Aki is following behind me.

"Are you ready, Princess?" Ashur asks, smiling.

I take a deep breath.

"Yes, I'm ready." Ashur opens the door and we step out into the cold, wintry night. We walk up the path to Kalen's cabin and my teeth are chattering along the way. I can't decipher if it's from the coldness of the night or from being nervous. I stand frozen on the porch while trying to calm my rapidly beating heart by taking in some deep breaths.

"It's OK to feel nervous, Princess."

"I have had sex before, Ashur. I am not nervous about that."

"I know, and that's not what I am talking about." I

look over at him and furrow my brows. What is he talking about then? I do not want to be viewed as weak by being nervous.

"You are about to be the queen of your own court. There is a lot of responsibility involved in that, and it's normal to feel nervous. You are not weak, Meliantha. You never were."

I narrow my eyes at him, but in a playful way. He's the only man that will ever know my deepest and darkest secrets. I kiss his cheek and bid him farewell.

"I will see you in the morning," I say aloud.

He starts to walk away and hollers over his shoulder, "Have fun tonight!" I laugh at his candor and watch him walk away.

Aki is staring up at me so I take one last deep breath before opening the door. "Wish me luck," I say to Aki.

As soon as I open the door, the hair on the back of my neck stands straight up. My mind is telling me to run quick and fast away from here. Aki is outside growling and scratching on the door to get in, but I couldn't bear it if anything happened to him so I leave him outside. I walk up the steps cautiously, and the evil is growing thicker the closer I get to the top. I can see a flicker of candlelight emanating from the room the evil is coming from. I approach it slowly and guarded.

"Kalen!" I call out.

There is no response other than the giggling sound of a female coming from the inside of the room. What the hell is this? Anger envelops my body and I rear back giving the door a powerful kick. It explodes off its hinges and flies across the room. The smell of black magic engulfs me, but I fight through it and storm into the room.

I look toward the bed and Breena is lying there naked with a smug smile on her face while Kalen is next to her running his hands all over her body. It only takes one good look at him to know he is not *my* Kalen. I still feel a twinge in my gut at watching him all over Breena, but I keep repeating to myself that it's not really him. I can't believe I was off taking my time getting ready while Kalen was here facing off with the dark sorcerer by himself. He needed me and I wasn't here. My throat tightens up at the thought that Kalen might be gone from me forever. Whatever I do, I can't show weakness. I hesitantly look around the room for ashes and thankfully I see none.

"I am so glad you came to join us," the dark sorcerer says. The voice is the same as Kalen's, but this one is full of evil and malice. I recognize the same tone from five years ago.

"Go to hell," I spit. "Where is Kalen?"

I wonder how long it would take Ashur to get help if I called out to him. I have my bow and arrow but they are strapped underneath my cloak. There is no way I could get to them in time. Next time, I need to make sure they are out in the open and ready to fire, but for now I have to suck it up and deal with this myself. He gets off the bed and stalks towards me. He's wearing the same warrior gear that Kalen was wearing earlier. He looks exactly like Kalen, but the eyes give him away.

He motions down his body and answers, "Your prince is right here, Princess, and I'll kill him right where we stand if you even think about calling out to your guardian to come rescue you."

"I don't understand. How can you take over a royal's body? You've never been able to do so before," I state.

He steps closer and I take a step back. This bastard has touched me way too many times, and I am *not* going to let it happen again.

"Oh Meliantha, so many things have changed over the years. There are lots of things I can do now that I couldn't do before." I look over Kalen's body and I notice a silver cuff wrapped around his forearm. It looks exactly like Finn's did, except his was gold. The dark sorcerer looks at his borrowed arm and then back to me. "Smart girl," he says. "Kalen spouted off how smart you were right before I took him. I also let him know how much I enjoyed you during those nights I fucked you. He didn't seem to like that at all." I flinch at his candor and he laughs at my response.

"What do you want, sorcerer?" I demand.

He looks my body up and down and licks his lips. Seeing him in Kalen's body looking at me like that is odd and wrong in so many ways.

"First, I want you to call me Alasdair. I think we are close enough now to be on a first name basis."

"You make me sick, you twisted bastard," I storm.

I know he wants my power, but I have to find a way to get him out of Kalen's body. The only ways to do that is if the sorcerer leaves his body or if Kalen dies, but the latter is not an option. He moves forward and I continue to step back. The wall is closing in behind me and he smirks because he knows that I have nowhere else to go. He reaches out his hand and I smack it away.

"Feisty, just like I remember," he laughs.

"Ugh, don't remind me," I hiss back. I look over at Breena and I can tell she's getting angry at our interaction. She's breathing hard and fuming while looking back and forth between the sorcerer and me. Her face still hasn't healed and I find great enjoyment in that because she seems like a woman who values her vanity above all else. I regret not killing her when I had the chance. Breena secured her death the moment she sided with the dark sorcerer.

The dark sorcerer looks from me to her with Kalen's eyes and dismisses her like a piece of trash, "Leave us, Breena. I want to be alone with the princess."

Her temper spikes with jealousy making her scream, "No! I don't want you alone with her." His whole demeanor changes in that instant from menacing to outright violent. The look he gives her makes her cower in fear and she fumbles while trying to leave the room quickly. The air in the room has drastically changed and it begins to make fear crawl through my veins as well.

Once Breena leaves, the dark sorcerer turns his attention back to me. It hurts to see Kalen used this way, and I'm beginning to think this is just the beginning to the cruel game. "Now, where were we?" He furrows his brows and then continues, "Oh, right, I remember now. We were discussing what I want from you."

He abruptly pushes me up against the wall pinning my arms to the side. It catches me off guard and I gasp in surprise. My breath is knocked out of my lungs from the hit, so I quickly suck in a much needed ragged breath.

His breath is hot against my skin as he trails his tongue up my neck to my ear.

"I want your power, Princess, and I *am* going to get it whether you like it or not," he whispers. I shake my head no because with him being so close and touching me I can't seem to get the words out. "Oh, I believe you will," he says. He pulls back and nods his head toward the table beside the bed. "Do you see the dagger over there?"

I look at the table and instantly know what kind of dagger that is. It could end a fae's life in a matter of seconds, and if he uses that on Kalen's body he will be gone from me forever. "Yes," I reply.

"If you don't give me your power willingly I will kill him right in front of you while you watch, and then after I kill him, I will take your power by force and enjoy every minute of it." He pauses and runs his hands down my body. "I seem to remember you liking it rough."

The anger inside my body has been building for far too long and I know I can't contain it any longer. I head butt him so hard in the face that he actually stumbles back a few steps. I know I can't escape him, but showing that I am a force on my own is what I want him to realize.

"Yes, I do like it rough, as you can now see," I claim, breathing hard.

He laughs and nods his head in approval. He takes a nearby towel and wipes away the blood. "So what will it be, Meliantha?"

If he takes my magic I know I can heal myself, but he will also be stronger. If I don't give him my power he will kill Kalen, and then all will be lost. I don't trust him to leave Kalen's body and I don't trust he will leave Kalen alive, but what choice do I have? I storm right up to him and his eyes go wide at my advancement. I am not weak or scared, and I am *not* going to let him intimidate me.

"Take it," I demand.

His wolfish smile grows and his body begins to change as a dark cloud settles over him. The talisman I have heard so much about begins to appear around Kalen's neck, starting out hazy and translucent, but then becoming solid. The dark sorcerer takes a deep breath and sighs. He takes the talisman off and begins walking towards me. I stand my ground and I refuse to flinch as he places the talisman around my neck. I can immediately tell that my power is being siphoned from my body by the tiny pin pricks swarming all over my skin, sucking and pulling. I fall to my knees from the agonizing pain and I can sense the darkness coming to claim me. I try keeping the darkness at bay by digging my nails into my palms and concentrating on the pain. I have to stay awake or the sorcerer will get away, or worse, he'll kill Kalen. The weight of the necklace is removed and I can't stop my body from swaying uncontrollably form side to side. My head hits the floor hard and now my vision is nothing but a blurry haze.

A face comes into view above me and I can feel the crushing weight of a body on top of mine making it hard for me to breathe. I can see Kalen's face, but I know it's the dark sorcerer smiling down at me with evil intentions. He takes my bottom lip in between his teeth and he bites down hard while sucking away my blood. I can taste the metallic essence of my blood going down the back of my throat and it makes my stomach roil.

I try to fight, but my body is unresponsive and I can't move. I'm stuck here to endure what he does to my body and all the while I am struggling to fight back. He moans and licks his lips, "You taste so good, Meliantha."

I'm screaming on the inside but nothing escapes my lips. What am I going to do, and how am I going to save Kalen if I can't even move? The dark sorcerer puts his hands underneath my dress and runs them up my legs to my waist while bringing my dress up along the way. I can't let him have me, not again. The darkness is beginning to creep around the edges of my mind, and it's like my soul is leaving my body. He starts to pull my underwear down but then abruptly snaps to attention and lets them go.

"It seems we have company, my dear. I hate we couldn't finish the fun, but if you want your prince alive you have to find me." He bites my ear lobe this time sending a sharp pain down my body. He grinds his body into mine one last time before getting up and walking toward the door.

"May the games begin," he taunts before leaving the room.

I try to keep my eyes from closing, but the darkness is too close. I hear heavy footsteps quickly climbing the stairs and they are making their way to me in the bedroom. I feel warm hands gently pulling my dress back into place, and then being lifted into someone's arms.

"I'm here, Meliantha," a voice whispers in my ear. I recognize the voice as being Finn's, and then Ashur speaks through my mind.

"We're both here, Princess, and we're not going let anything else happen to you."

"Thank you," were the last words I said before my body gave up and took me into the darkness.

Chapter Sixteen

Meliantha

"Wake up, Mel." I bolt awake from the feel of someone shaking me by the shoulders and I gasp for air. The room comes into focus and I am lying on my bed in the cottage. Ashur, Elissa, and Finn are surrounding the bed staring worriedly at me. My body feels fine except for the hollow ache in my heart. I close my eyes to remember how I got here and then in a flash everything comes rushing back. Kalen is gone and the dark sorcerer took his fill of my power. I failed to save Kalen, and now I have to find him. Fear and desperation fuel my every existence and I jump out of bed to gather up my warrior gear. Even though Ashur and Finn are in here, I cease to care as I change out of my dress and into my gear as quickly as possible.

"Maybe you should rest," Elissa advises whole-heartedly. She stands in my way as I reach for my bow. "He's gone Meliantha."

The words sting because I *know* he's gone, I was there, but I'm not going to allow him to be gone from me forever. I take a deep breath and I look at all their faces. I'm determined to find him. Even if I have to search for years, I *will* find him.

"I don't care what any of you say or do, but I *am*

going to find him, and none of you are going to stand in my way. Got it?" They all nod and back away without a word. I don't want to have a confrontation with any of them, so I'm grateful they have decided to keep their mouths shut.

I grab my bow and arrows and my thick, long, wool cloak. It'll keep me warm on my journey, wherever that may be. I pack up some extra clothing and blankets, and I place them in my riding satchel that will hook onto Prince Ashe's saddle. I hastily leave my room to gather food and supplies in the kitchen. I load up as much food as I can into the satchel and I'm satisfied when it's full. This should last me a week, at least.

"I'm coming with you," Ashur says. He's dressed in full warrior gear, weapons and all, and he glares at me like I have no say in the matter.

"You need to stay here with Elissa," I reply, exasperated. We're running out of time and I need to be on my way. I don't know how long I was out, but I know I need to get started on the search.

Elissa walks into the kitchen and shakes her head.

"No, Meliantha. He's going with you." She comes over and wraps me in her arms. "I will be fine here. I'm going to the palace to raise the alarm. Go and find your prince." She gives me a nudge to the door and I eagerly comply. Ashur has his things ready to go so I open the front door and Aki is waiting right there in front of me, poised and ready to go. I'm glad to see him because I know he is a good tracker, and he is our best chance at finding Kalen.

"Come here, Aki." He rubs against my legs and lets out a soft whine. He misses Kalen and I can feel his anguish, but most of all I can feel his determination to get him back. "Thank you," I whisper in his ear.

"Let's go!" I call out to Ashur. I wish Finn would have said goodbye to me, but he disappeared off into his room once I left my bedroom. I don't blame him, but it would have been nice to see him one last time in case I don't come back.

We head to the stables and as soon as I see my horse, Prince Ashe, I run straight toward his stall. He paces excitedly and it lets me know that he's glad to see me. I can tell he's been taken good care of him because he looks well fed and his coat has a bright sheen to it. I open the stall door and he nuzzles me along the way.

"Hey there, boy. We have a long journey ahead of us, and I'm going to need your agility and swiftness to get through it. Can you do that?"

He rears back excitedly and huffs in my face. "I knew you could," I encourage him. I saddle him up while Ashur saddles up his horse. Aki is pacing around the stables and I know he is ready to get moving. So am I.

"I'm ready when you are, Princess," Ashur calls out.

"You hear that, Prince Ashe. Let's go!" I command.

Aki runs ahead of us and we follow closely behind. He knows his alpha's scent well so tracking him should be easy. We head away from the palace and out the Winter gates. Several of the Winter warriors tried to stop us, but we sped past them without a second glance. To where we are going I have no clue. All I know is that I will travel through the Land of the Fae a million times over if that is what it takes to find Kalen. If Elissa hasn't spread the word then I am sure it has now. We ride for several hours without a moments rest until there is no more energy left to be spent. Aki is tired, and I know the horses are as well.

We have reached the Mystical Forest and have decided to set up camp. It's dark out now, but the moonlight shines through the trees giving the forest an ethereal glow. Ashur and I are about to lie down and rest when we hear a rider approaching. Ashur swiftly pulls his sword, and I already have my bow in hand and ready to fire in a matter of seconds.

I recognize the fierce rider coming this way by the long, white-blonde hair billowing out in the wind. It's Finn. What is he doing here? I lower my bow as Finn comes to a stop before me and dismounts from his horse. "I thought you could use more help," he suggests. I could use the help, but I wouldn't feel right asking for his. How can I ask him to help me search for the man I left him for?

"I can't ask you to do that, Finn."

He lets out a sigh and takes my hands in his while looking me in the eyes.

"You didn't have to ask. I'm here because I want you to be happy, and getting your prince back will make you happy. The Land of the Fae depends on you both," he admits.

He is right. The Spring Court can't be formed without Kalen. The Land of the Fae will falter and grow weak if I don't find Kalen and bring him home. I pull Finn to me and he encloses me in his arms. "Thank you, Finn. I don't know what I would do without you," I say genuinely.

He kisses my head and lets me go. No more words were spoken as we set up camp for the night. I lie down on my blanket while Aki snuggles up to my side. We're going to find him, I whisper to the stars above. I hope…

"Princess?"

The sound of a tiny voice in my ear startles me awake and I bolt upright. Dozens of sprites are flying around the camp and the buzzing of their wings sound like a swarm of bees on the verge of attack.

"I'm sorry I startled you," the little sprite apologizes. Ashur and Finn are awake and by the scowls on their faces it would appear they are slightly annoyed by the intrusion.

I smile at the little pink sprite and I beckon her closer while holding out my hand. She settles onto my palm and I bring her up to my eye level.

"It's OK. I just wasn't expecting to have such a grand audience. What's your name?"

Her voice sounds child-like, but if I had a guess, I would say she is older than me by centuries.

"My name is Ansley, and I came to warn you. The forest isn't safe." That caught the attention of my men and they stride over quickly.

"What are you here to warn me about?" I ask.

She looks from me to Ashur and Finn.

"There's evil in the forest. It's parading around wreaking havoc in its wake. It's no place for a princess like you."

Now I have more motivation than anything to find the dark sorcerer. He not only has taken over Kalen, but he's tormenting the lives of innocent fae creatures. "Thank you, Ansley, but that evil is exactly why I'm here. I have to put a stop to it."

Her eyes go wide and she flutters up in the air to come closer. "Please be careful, Princess," she cries. "We are leaving the forest to seek shelter somewhere else. We no longer feel safe here."

The sprites all around me look scared and unsure, so I do the only thing I can think of to do. I motion for the sprites to gather around me so I can address them all.

"Dear friends, I want you all to go to the Summer Court and stay there until I return. I have several sprite friends that will take care of you. Tell them I sent you, and you will be safe."

They all murmur their gratitude and fly away in the direction of the Summer Court.

"You sure do have a way with the fae creatures, don't you Princess?" Ashur grins.

I grin back while loading up my things.

"I do, but I love to help them," I admit.

Aki is huffing and looking off into the forest. I know he is ready so we pick up the pace and pack up our camp. We only rest for a couple of hours, but I feel energized to go on for several days. It's still dark outside, but the horizon toward the Summer Court is slowly turning pink with the approaching sun.

We all three mount our horses and both Ashur and Finn nod their heads showing they are ready. Aki runs ahead and we swiftly follow him into the unknown depths of the Mystical Forest. The forest is huge and I have never ventured off into the heart of it until this day. I have only traveled along the outskirts of it to get to the Fall and Winter Court from my home in the Summer. I have heard of the dangerous fae creatures that live in the forest, and I do fear of what will happen if we encounter them. I sneak a glance at both Ashur and Finn and I know they are thinking the same things as well.

We ride hard throughout the day heading deeper into the Mystical Forest until we come across a small village that looks dark and desolate. It reeks of death. I have never seen this place before, but I can tell this isn't what it is supposed to look like. I can smell the foulness of black magic permeating the air and the taste of it is even worse. The village we are in is a leprechaun village by the symbols engraved on their doors. I was taught all the ancient symbols and these are surely ones of the leprechauns. I have met a couple of them in my lifetime and they are very superstitious creatures; hence, the symbols on their doors that stand for protection and luck.

I dismount my horse and bend down to touch the ground. With my ability for nature, it keeps me in tune to the land, and this area of land is screaming for help. I look around the village and I don't see a soul, but I can sense they are near. They probably ran scared the moment the dark sorcerer's evil took hold. I need to know what happened and I do not want them afraid of me.

I speak loudly, addressing the entire village.

"I am Princess Meliantha of the Summer Court, and I am here to help you! Please don't be afraid and show yourselves to me!"

A few minutes later the leprechauns begin to come forth. One by one they slowly make their way out of their hiding spots. They all wear the traditional red coats and red hats. The mortal realm classifies them by wearing green, but here that isn't so. The women also wear the traditional red, but instead of wearing breeches, they wear long dresses that fall just below their calves, and cinched at the waist with a thick black belt.

They circle around us and with our height we tower over them all. Leprechauns usually only reach about three feet in height and are known to be excellent boot makers. I look down at their faces and they all look angry and scared. "What happened?" I ask the crowd, even though I have a good guess.

A rough, gravelly voice speaks.

"A man of great power swept through here and killed our land. Our once thriving village has now been poisoned with evil."

He comes forward and I can tell he must be an elder by the sheer knowledge showing in his eyes.

"May I ask your name, elder leprechaun?" I ask.

He bows his head and replies warmly, "My name is Griffin, Your Highness, and I'm honored to meet you." I wonder how he knows I am a royal.

I place my hand on his shoulder.

"As am I, Griffin."

He smiles.

"I remember the day you were born. Word traveled fast that there was a purple-eyed fae among the Summer. We knew then that you were destined for great things."

I look around the crowd and they all bow their heads. I look around at the land and it pains my heart to see it like this. I can fix it, but it's going to take a huge amount of power, and I have never healed anything to this extent. As much as I hate to frighten the leprechauns, they have to know who they're dealing with.

I announce sadly, "The evil that has corrupted your land is because of the dark sorcerer." Gasps erupt from the crowd, but I continue, "He has finally returned again and is determined to destroy our lands, and take over the Land of the Fae. I can heal what has been done, but the evil won't permanently be gone. The dark sorcerer is powerful and he'll continue to raid our lands until we defeat him."

"How will we protect ourselves?" Another leprechaun calls out. This time it's an elder female leprechaun that has spoken.

I acknowledge her first and then glance back across the crowd.

"If you fear for your safety, I'll gladly offer the protection of my court." Shouts of appreciation sound off all around us and I take a deep breath before informing them of how dire the situation actually is. "You see, the man who destroyed your home isn't only the dark sorcerer, but Prince Kalen of the Winter Court. The dark sorcerer has taken over the Prince's body and is keeping him hostage. He has done this to keep us from completing our bond. Our bond is supposed to form the Spring Court just like my sister, Queen Calista and King Ryder, had formed the Fall Court. If we don't complete the bond, the Land of the Fae will fall prey to the darkness."

"What can we do to help?" Griffin, the elder leprechaun, asks. They all nod their heads enthusiastically hoping to help, but I honestly don't think there is anything they can do. Their willingness to help warms my heart and I wish to the stars there was a way they could help.

A little leprechaun boy runs forward holding something in his hand. "What about this? Will this help?" he yells.

He puts something in my hand and I instantly recognize it as Kalen's thistle birch cord. My eyes instantly water and I clutch the cord tightly in my hands. These brown leathery cords are made from thistle birch trees found in the Winter Court. They are supposed to provide strength and luck to warriors in battle. All of the Winter warriors wear them, and I know Kalen always wore his.

"Thank you, little one. This will most definitely help me along the way," I answer with a smile. His grin is huge as he saunters off back into the crowd. I take the cord and I secure it around my wrist. This will give me strength and luck in my search for him. I turn my attention back to Griffin.

"Thank you, Griffin, for your help, but…" I hold my arm up where the cord is tied snugly to my wrist, "This right here is all the help I need."

He nods his head and motions to the village.

"How can you fix what the dark sorcerer has done? The land is dead."

I open my mouth to answer, but Ashur silently interrupts, *"Can you really do this, Meliantha?"*

I respond without looking at him. *"I hope so."*

"Don't worry. I'll do all that I can," I reply to the leprechaun.

I look around the crowd at their hopeful faces and I pray that I don't let them down. Ashur and Finn look worried, but I smile to reassure them. I walk away from the crowd to the center of the village. The life and energy of the land is suffocating from the black magic. I can hear their screams as I bend down to touch the ground. It rips at my heart and the tears automatically begin to flow. The pain of the land is my pain, and it's eating away at my soul.

With both hands placed firmly on the ground, I call upon my magic and it instantly begins to surge beneath my skin. The power blasts from my fingers and into the ground. I can see it spreading throughout the land and everything that had turned black from the poisonous touch of the dark sorcerer is now vibrantly green and splayed with flowers. The village bursts with color. The sounds of the leprechaun's cheers bring me joy, and I revel in their happiness.

"Meliantha, that's enough! Stop!"

I can hear the screams from Ashur and Finn, but I am too drawn into my magic to stop. My body is warm and light making me feel as if I'm floating above the ground. Using too much power can make you drunk off of it, but I think I'm way beyond drunk when the pain starts. My muscles begin to ache while the power inside me dissipates. Dizziness overtakes me and my eyes begin to lose focus. I fall over, expecting to hit the ground, but instead I'm scooped into Ashur's arms and cradled against his chest.

"I told you to stop!" he screams inside my head.

I look around the village and a sigh escapes my lips. "It's so beautiful," is all I can say before exhaustion takes over my body.

Chapter Seventeen

ALASDAIR

- Dark sorcerer -

"What the hell are you doing?" Breena screams as the fae surround her to take her away.

"Something I should have done a long time ago," I sneer at her. Her eyes go wide when the realization hits her that I will not save her this time. Her piercing screams echo in the night and fades the farther I walk away. It feels good to be rid of the worthless bitch. She has caused nothing but trouble since the day she opened her legs to me. I have endured too much of her whining and complaining, and no amount of fucking is worth all of that. Now that I have Meliantha's power flowing through my veins it feels like there is nothing I can't do. Thinking of the way Breena's face looked as I left will always stay with me. I laugh thinking about it because now she will spend the rest of her life doing what she does best-screwing everything that walks by her path. I find the outcome fitting.

I deliberately made my way through this part of the Mystical Forest for two reasons: One, to get rid of Breena, and two, to torment Meliantha. Meliantha will soon realize I am leading her around in circles. Destroying the leprechauns land was easy, but now the fun will begin. Once she follows my trail, she will fall prey to the fae that live in these parts. Due to their possessive nature over women, they will not let a prize like her go. They will have a feast with her and Breena because in these parts it's rare for these men to get a hold of a fae woman.

I would love to see how she gets out of this without becoming victim to their power. It's almost impossible. Her companions, no doubt, will have a say about it and will most likely be killed if they interfere. I strongly believe my game will stop here, but I've been surprised before. I plan to make one more visit before I put this game to a close. The most terrifying group of fae creatures will be in this village I plan to go to next. I have several of them in my army and I have seen what they can do. They can be brutal when provoked, and they make the best killers. I would love to have more in my army and I plan to get more of them tonight. These creatures live to kill and if Meliantha makes it past my last stop then there is no way she'll survive where I lead her next.

I have lain low the past five years, but now is the time for me to grow. If Meliantha makes it past this last stop, then she's much stronger and wiser than I anticipated. If it comes to that, I will finish her off myself. I will give her a taste of the prince, and then break her down to nothing when I kill him before her very own eyes.

Chapter Eighteen

Meliantha

"Never again, Meliantha," Ashur chastises me. He climbs up on his horse with a scowl on his face while Finn walks up behind me and lifts me onto Prince Ashe. I don't need the help but he insisted that I take it.

"You had us worried, Mel. You've never done that before and we didn't know what to do to help you. Please don't do it again," Finn begs, looking concerned. I don't want to put them through grief and worry, but I have to do what I can to help. If that means going crazy with my power then so be it.

I feel a little weak, but looking at the village around me I do not regret a single thing I have done. The land is healed and its joy is coursing through my veins bringing me a new surge of hope. I give Finn a reassuring smile, "I'm okay, Finn. It just took a lot out of me, but I'm fine now. Trust me."

Ashur snorts and Finn raises his eyebrows in disbelief. His skeptical glare is penetrating, but then he nods his head and leaves me to mount his own horse. I panicked when I found out I slept for twelve hours and that it was late in the afternoon. My healing dilemma has set me back farther than I wanted. The longer the dark sorcerer has a chance to get away, the longer it'll take to get Kalen back.

My things had already been packed and ready to go for when I woke up and I was amazed to find that the leprechauns had prepared us a grand feast before we left as well. The food was amazing and they also sent us some for the journey ahead.

"Be careful, Princess. We all bid you a safe journey and a fond farewell," Griffin announces.

All the leprechauns in the village have gathered to see our departure. Ashur, Finn, and I were each given a four leaf clover for luck and were told to keep them on us at all times. I entwined mine with Kalen's thistlebirch cord that I have now wrapped around the braid in my hair.

I address the crowd, "Thank you everyone. Remember what I said, if you need protection, I'll gladly offer it to you." I look at them all and say, "Farewell my friends."

They shout their goodbyes and I wave them farewell as Prince Ashe leads me away. Even though I hate the circumstances of my visit, I am glad that I had the opportunity to meet them. Today makes the third day we have been on the hunt for the dark sorcerer. I wish I knew what the courts were doing right now, and if they have sent warriors to find us. I honestly hope they haven't, but I'm sure that with me and the prince missing they will most definitely have a search out for us.

Aki is running with great speed while the rest of us follow closely on his heels. The farther I go in this journey the more my stomach twinges in fear. The first stop with the leprechauns is going to be but a taste of what the dark sorcerer has in store for me. I fear for Kalen's safety and I believe with all my heart that I can save him, but I also fear for my own safety and the safety of my friends.

This twisted game the dark sorcerer has conjured is only going to get tougher. I had thought the dark sorcerer would lead us to the Black Forest, but that doesn't seem to be the case. The path we are taking is moving us away from the Black Forest, and it's looking as if we're headed in circles. I'm determined to remain strong, but leave it to the dark sorcerer to screw around with me any chance he gets.

We're riding hard and swift, and thankfully, Prince Ashe doesn't appear to be tired at all as we make our way through the forest. I worry that I may be pushing him too hard. I know what I'm doing is putting everyone through hell, but they have to understand that I refuse to give up.

"Don't be mad at me, Ashur," I plea silently.

He glances over at me and his expression softens.

"I am not mad at you, just worried. You will kill yourself trying to save everyone and everything, Meliantha. You need to take care of yourself for a change."

He does have a point, but it's in my nature to want to protect the people I care about. It is my duty to protect all fae creatures of the land. If I have the power to help them, then I need to help them.

"I know, Ashur, and I promise to take care of myself. I just want you to understand that I will do anything to save Kalen. I'm sure you would do the same for Elissa if the situation were switched."

He sighs.

"You're right, I would. There is nothing I wouldn't do for her, but I am your Guardian and it is my job to protect you. I am going to repeat what I said earlier...NO

MORE! Do we have an understanding?"

"Yes, Guardian," I reply sullenly.

"Thank you."

I know he worries about me, but I know how to take care of myself. I tell him that constantly, but he never listens to me. Ashur is an amazing guardian and I am honored to have him by my side. Truthfully, I don't know if I can keep my end of the bargain, but at least I didn't make a promise. Promises are sacred and all I agreed to with Ashur was just an understanding. I'm hoping he doesn't pick up on his mistake.

I notice the land beginning to change and I can see an opening where a huge lake lies up ahead. There are several different types of fae creatures that inhabit the waters in the Land of the Fae and most of them are ones to steer clear of. I don't want my warriors to be swept away by sirens or water nymphs.

"Stay away from the water!" I yell.

Ashur and Finn look amused, but I don't think they would have those smiles if they met a watery grave. Aki skirts alongside the water banks and stops when he reaches the bridge. The bridge expands across the water to the land beyond where a dense fog has taken over. The fog makes it to where we can't see the end of the bridge or what might be waiting there when we cross.

"Are you sure you want to cross here, Meliantha? I don't think it's a good idea if we can't see what we are heading into," Ashur points out.

"I agree with him, Mel. I don't like the way it looks around here at all," Finn agrees.

If we don't follow the dark sorcerer, I will lose Kalen forever. I have to go across this bridge. What lies ahead is going to be a challenge, but I am ready for it.

"I have to go," I say to both of them, pleading. "I have no choice."

They both sigh and shake their heads.

"Well, at least let me go first," Ashur snaps. He trots along not waiting for a reply, and I quickly follow him while Finn trails along behind me. The bridge is wide enough for us all to ride side by side, but I know Ashur doesn't want me in front in case there is an attack. We are edging towards the end of the bridge and Aki impulsively jumps through the fog. He starts to growl menacingly and that can only mean one thing…danger lies ahead. I'm not leaving here without him.

I nudge Prince Ashe firmly in the ribs and he bounds past Ashur into the fog ahead. I hear his protests behind me, but that is the least of my worries right now. Once the fog clears I am abruptly aware of why the dark sorcerer led me here; unfortunately, it is not to use my healing abilities. I'm slowly being surrounded by a dozen men and they are closing in fast. Chills spread throughout my body and the realization of why I am here fills me with dread. I can hear Ashur and Finn yelling as they come through the fog behind me.

"Meliantha! Close your eyes!" Ashur demands silently.

Finn's response is just as fast. "What the hell?" he screams. Our situation just became monumentally bad, and I fear that our chances to get out of this one are undeniably slim. What am I going to do? I close my eyes tightly while gripping onto Prince Ashe's reigns with all my strength. Keeping my eyes closed makes me feel vulnerable, but I don't have a choice. If I look at these men in the eyes my life will be forfeit.

"Whatever you do, do not open your eyes. That bastard led you right into the hands of the Tyvar," Ashur says desperately in my mind.

I knew who these men were, but deep down I was hoping it wouldn't be so. My palms begin to sweat and my heart is beating out of my chest. If I don't stop my erratic breathing I am going to pass out on my horse, and passing out around the Tyvar is a very bad idea for a woman. The Tyvar are extremely handsome faerie men and are very enticing to the female eye. They admire the pleasantries of the female body and will lure women away from their homes with their powers of seduction. Their powers are strong and can turn any woman into a sex slave just by a simple glance. Also, the women they take never survive long.

With the Tyvar being only men, the women they have captured are usually passed along endlessly from man to man, wearing them out quickly. Since a lot of fae women aren't around this part of the Mystical Forest, the Tyvar usually find their captives in the mortal realm. But with me being a fae, and being stronger, their nights of pleasure would last a hundred times longer than it would with a mortal. Is this what the dark sorcerer had in mind for me, to be a sex slave for the rest of my life?

My eyes are closed but I hear footsteps coming closer to me. I gasp when I feel large hands encircle my waist and pull me smoothly down from my horse. I'm surprised by his gentle touch, but I did learn that these men take care of their women when they capture them. It still doesn't make me feel any better. The Tyvar's voice sounds smooth and seductive when he murmurs, "Well, well, what do we have here?" I almost opened my eyes to see what he looked like, but then remembered I have to keep them closed. This is going to be harder than I thought.

"There are too many, Meliantha. They have us surrounded. What do you want us to do?" Ashur asks hesitantantly.

"I want you to stay calm, Ashur. I don't want you or Finn hurt, and if you fight..."

I can't finish the thought because the Tyvar who helped me from my horse starts to trail his hand along the side of my face and down my jaw to my neck. I shiver under his touch, but not with pleasure. I think he mistakes it for pleasure because he moves closer. I take a step back, but I am blocked by Prince Ashe, and can move no further. Aki is growling down by my side sounding like he is about to attack, but I hastily send him a mental message to stay calm.

"Get your fucking hands off her, now!" Finn yells.

I hear him pull his sword so I yell, "Finn, stop!" I couldn't bear it if anything happened to him or my guardian. The Tyvar laugh all around us and I can hear them apprehend both Ashur and Finn by the sounds of flesh hitting flesh and their growls of anger.

"Come with me," the Tyvar fae utters. He takes my elbow and pulls me gently along beside him. I know they will not intentionally harm me, but now my fear lies with what will happen to my men.

"Where are we going, Ashur?"

"It looks like we are headed straight for their camp. There are so many of them, Meliantha. If they pull you under their power, there is no way I can save you. I would rather die than see what they do to you."

The sound of his voice in my head breaks my heart and it takes all the strength I have to keep my chin from quivering. I don't want Ashur and Finn to see me turned into a sex slave, but I also don't think the Tyvar will let them go either.

"There has to be a way out of this. Being a sex slave is not my destiny and I refuse to give in to it. I will find a way," I encourage him.

"Well you better find a way fast because we're approaching the center of their camp and there has to be over a hundred Tyvar gathered around."

Damn it! What can I do to get us out of this mess? The Tyvar fae guiding me still has a hold of my elbow, so I decide to ask him.

"Do you mind telling me where you are taking me?"

"I am taking you to our leader, Bayleon," he replies in a low voice.

"Why?" I ask curiously, but I have a feeling my fate has already been decided. I want to know what's going to happen to me because not knowing is going to make everything so much worse.

The Tyvar answers, "Any female we capture gets taken by our leader first and foremost, and then to me next since I am second in command. It is the way of our people."

I try to act calm as the realization of what is about to happen to me sinks in. On the outside I think I am playing it off well, but on the inside I'm screaming. *"ASHUR, they are taking me to their leader to give me to him, as in...give me to him in the sexual sense. Then after that I will be passed to the man holding onto me. I don't know what to do!"*

I'm sure if I could see Ashur right now he would be flinching from my screams in his head. I have to figure something out, NOW. I can hear the murmurs and feel the lust pouring off of the Tyvar as I walk through the crowd. Their desires are thick in the air caressing my skin making me feel exposed and bare.

"You are almost to their leader, Princess."

"No need to worry, my lady. We will take very good care of you," the Tyvar fae says. I swallow hard and I take in a deep, shaky breath. Yeah, I'm sure you will, I think to myself. I know how they plan to take care of me and I beg to differ. I huff in return and he laughs, low and seductively in my ear. "I promise you will enjoy it," he whispers.

I hold my head high and I thrust my chin forward.

"I don't think so," I hiss back. Inside I am terrified of what's going to happen to me and my men, but I refuse to show defeat. We come to a stop and the group grows quiet. I can hear someone approaching and my body instantly goes rigid. I'm frozen in place and my chest tightens so I can't breathe. I know my hands are shaking and the Tyvar holding my arm gently takes my hand and holds it tight. If I knew he wasn't planning on seducing me, I would find the gesture endearing, but all it does is make me more terrified.

An exotic and sensual voice speaks and I notice that his voice sounds exactly like my escort. "I see you brought me a visitor, Bastian. I must say you have done very well, brother. Where may I ask did you find this beautiful she-warrior?"

That explains why they sound alike...they're brothers. "Aye, she is a beautiful fae woman. Her face is by far the most beautiful I have ever seen. I found her after she crossed the bridge into our territory with her two warriors," Bastian replies.

The group of Tyvar hollers out their victory of my capture and hearing it makes me cringe in fear. I don't want to imagine what it would be like to be taken by so many men day and night. Bastian releases my hand and passes me along to the leader, Bayleon. He moves closer and I can feel his breath against my face. If Bastian wasn't behind me I would have moved back. "Open your eyes, my lady," he urges.

"No!" Ashur and Finn both scream simultaneously. I hear a struggle going on behind me and it kills me that I can't help them. I worry for their safety and it sounds like something bad is happening to both of them.

"What's going on, Ashur?" I demand.

"Finn tried to get to you, but they knocked him out cold. He seems to be coming around as we speak. Don't worry about us, Princess. Whatever they threaten you with you better not open your eyes. They never physically force women to open their eyes, but they will threaten you to do it. Stay strong, do you understand?"

"Yes," I reply shakily.

I shake my head at the leader and with a strong voice I say the one word they are not going to want to hear.

"No."

Bayleon releases a sigh and if I could see him I'm sure he would be shaking his head. "I see we are going to have to do this the hard way," he suggests. "If you do not open your eyes I will have one of your men brutally tortured and killed. I can promise you that. I'll even let you pick which one lives if you would like."

I gasp in shock and my knees go weak. I knew they would go to any lengths to get me to open my eyes, but I didn't think they would go to this level. The fae have to keep their promises, and Bayleon promised to kill one of my men if I did not look at him. I have no choice. I have to open my eyes or one of my men will be killed.

Before I have the chance to answer, I hear Ashur's voice in my mind. His desperation makes the tears build up behind my eyes.

"Don't you dare open your eyes, Meliantha. I will gladly offer myself for your safety."

I can't see him, but I shake my head in response.

"He promised to kill one of you, Ashur. I can't lose you or Finn, I just can't."

"Time is wasting, my lady," Bayleon taunts.

I take a deep breath and answer as calm as I can, "I will give you what you want, but in return, all I ask is that you let my friends go. I will give myself to you for their freedom."

Finn must have woken up because his screams pierce the air. "NO, MELIANTHA! I refuse to let you do this!" I clench my teeth hard to keep from crying out as I hear another struggle taking place.

"Very well," Bayleon agrees.

"They will be let free and escorted from our territory. That was a wise choice, my lady. What of your wolf? Do you want him freed as well?"

I can feel Aki rubbing against my legs and I can sense that he wants to stay with me. I don't want him trapped here so I say, "My wolf has a mind of his own so let him come and go as he chooses. He won't be a bother to anyone."

I can hear Ashur and Finn struggling against the Tyvar as their voices drift farther away. I can't believe I will never see them again, and what's worse is that I didn't even get the chance to say goodbye. There is a way I can at least tell one of them.

"Please forgive me, Ashur, but I have to do what I can to keep you both safe."

"Please don't do this, Meliantha?"

I have never told either one of them how I felt because admitting what was in my heart made me feel vulnerable. Being with Kalen and experiencing love again has opened my soul to a whole new world — a world I had once known. If this is my last chance to tell them how I feel, I am going to do it.

"I love you both so much, Ashur. I know I have never told you before, but I do. Please make sure you tell Finn that I love him too, and that I am so sorry. Goodbye, my Guardian."

"No!" was all I heard before I put my shields in place with an unbreakable wall. The absence of my guardian feels like a hole in my chest, but soon I won't even remember him when the Tyvar's power takes hold of my body. The only thing that will be in my mind is lust and sex.

"Let us go to some place more private, my lady," Bayleon suggests. He takes a hold of my right arm while Bastian takes up with my left. I can barely walk for being nervous, but they keep a tight grip on me leading the way. If I knew I could escape without looking at any of them I would be out of here in a second. I gave the Tyvar a quick glance when I crossed over the bridge, but it was only for a few seconds before Ashur yelled at me to close my eyes. I guess that glance wasn't enough to take me under.

I don't know where I'm going but I can tell we have entered inside one of their dwellings. It's a drastic change from the outside. This part of the Mystical Forest is warm and humid, but inside where we are is cool and dry. It feels better in here, but I would rather be out in the blistering heat than in here about to be taken.

My left arm is freed from Bastian's grip and Bayleon gently picks me up and sets me on what I assume is the bed. It's soft and fluffy beneath me, but nothing feels comfortable to me right now. He removes my bow and arrows that I have strapped to my back, and he also takes my armor off one piece at a time. He lightly touches my skin each time he removes an article of my armor, and he also seems to be enjoying taking his time with it. After the tormenting is over I'm left with nothing on but my undergarments. I might as well be naked.

"I've never seen a female warrior, my lady." Bayleon says, sounding fascinated. I would love to show him my warrior skills, but I know I can't fight all the Tyvar and make it out alive. He pushes me back gently to where I am lying on the bed and crawls his way slowly up my body. The realization of how screwed I am finally sinks in and I can feel the panic beginning to rise. Bayleon places both hands against my cheeks and whispers against my lips.

"Open your eyes."

This is it. This will be my final doom. I have failed my people and now the Spring Court will never exist. I wish with all my heart that I could see Kalen one last time. The last tears I will ever shed have left my eyes as I now prepare to open them to my doom. Bayleon comes closer and I know he is about to merge his lips with mine when I slowly open my eyes to meet his. His midnight blue eyes bore into mine, but then they go wide in surprise. This is my end.

Chapter Nineteen

Meliantha

I can feel the power flowing all around me, but then...nothing. His power was trying to take over my body, but something held it back. Why didn't his powers work on me? Bayleon's eyes go wide as he pulls back to gaze at me bewilderingly. He narrows his midnight blue eyes, penetrating mine to the depths of my soul looking for answers.

I peer over at Bastian and he's standing in the corner of the room looking just as confused and transfixed. Bayleon and Bastian look exactly alike, and being that they're brothers, they must be twins. Their looks are all fae, but the Tyvar are more angelic and ethereal looking in appearance than the warriors of the courts. It's deceiving because any woman who gazes upon these men will think they are angels when actually they are the complete opposite. I can see how many women are seduced by their looks alone without their power. Both Bayleon and Bastian have long, silky golden blonde hair that hangs perfectly straight past their shoulders. Their eyes are the most beautiful thing about their faces. They're so big and full of color that you could get lost in the depths of them with one single look. If I wasn't immune to their powers I know I would have already been lost. I don't see where they would need their powers of seduction to seduce women. I'm sure any woman who happens to gaze upon them would be more than happy to come willingly.

"Who are you?" Bayleon asks. "You're not just a she-warrior. What are you doing here, and why have you come?" he asks, astonished.

I don't understand why I can thwart their power, but knowing that I can sends relief and hope surging back into my body. With my newfound strength I am able to finally speak with confidence.

"I'm Meliantha, Princess of the Summer Court. I was led here by someone and that is the reason I'm here. I am trying to save Prince Kalen of the Winter Court."

Bayleon nods his head, "I believe I have met the fae you speak of. His complexion was different like yours, but he also had a female with him."

I snap to attention.

"How long ago was this?" I ask hurriedly.

Bastian saunters over and uses this time to speak.

"He was here early this morning and left just as quickly. He has a strong lead on you if you are trying to track him."

The dark sorcerer is doing everything to delay me from getting to Kalen, like leading me through tasks that he deems unbeatable, and who knows what else. The longer it takes, the more desperate I know I will become. I don't want to make mistakes by being careless. It doesn't feel like this search is ever going to come to an end. Will there always be something that evil bastard throws in my way.

"I'm trying to track him, and my wolf has been helping me follow him. Do either one of you know about the prophecy?" I ask. They both nod their heads so I continue, "The man you saw was the dark sorcerer. He is not of this land and he is not fae. Evil runs through his veins instead of blood and his goal is to take over the Land of the Fae and bring ruin to all that live here."

"Why did he look fae when we saw him?" Bayleon asks.

I take a deep breath to calm my nerves before speaking.

"The dark sorcerer has trapped himself inside Prince Kalen's body, and that is why he looked fae. He's leading me on a wild chase across our realm to torment me. You see, I can't complete my destiny without Prince Kalen."

Both men seem to contemplate everything I have said and then they both look at me with admiration in their eyes. Bastian is the one who comes to the realization first.

"I know how you were able to thwart our powers! You are one of the Four!" he exclaims.

I never thought that being one of the Four would give me special advantages, but I am thankful nonetheless. I nod slowly at them and they both get down on their knees and bow their heads. Maybe I should have said this before and saved all of us the torment, especially with Ashur and Finn. Now they are out there thinking the worst, and doing who knows what to get me back.

"What can we do to help?" Bayleon asks.

"I need you to let me go," I plead whole-heartedly, looking at both of them.

Bayleon gets to his feet and reaches for my hands to pull me up. I didn't realize how tall he was when I had my eyes closed, and now I have to peer up at him. He turns my hands over, palm up, and kisses them both lightly. Please let them understand and let me go, I wish to myself. Bayleon looks me in the eyes, sadness and longing evident in his midnight orbs, and vows.

"I will let you go, but *only* if you do me one favor."

I can see the honesty in his eyes, but favors to the fae can mean anything from something easy to something extremely difficult. I begin to grow weary and a frown takes over my face. "I am not asking for much," he admits, smiling.

I breathe a sigh of relief.

"Then what, may I ask, is your favor?" I ask curiously.

"I have never had the pleasure of a woman who hasn't been enthralled by my power, so all I ask from you is…one kiss."

"One kiss?" I repeat, confused.

He nods his head, "Aye, one kiss. Our mother once told us before she died, that there is no greater joy than the pleasure of true love. She said that we have been cursed with our powers of seduction." He moves closer to me and continues. "By kissing you, it will give me a taste of true love."

I furrow my brows and stare at him. How can he get that from me? I don't love him. I'm about to ask him, but he stops me with his next words. "I know you do not love me, but I will be able to feel the love you share for your prince when I connect with you. It'll be a gift I will cherish for the rest of my existence."

"Is there not a way you can stop using your powers on women and experience love for yourself?"

He shakes his head wearily and looks down at the floor. "Nay, that is why we are cursed."

I am shocked by his admittance, because I never would have thought the Tyvar would consider their powers a curse. I can feel the sadness in his soul, and I wonder if all the Tyvar feel this way or if Bayleon is the only one. I'm sure a lot of them thoroughly enjoy bedding the women until they die, and thankfully, Bayleon isn't one of them. If kissing him is the only way to get out of here, then I'll gladly give it to him. Doing so feels like a betrayal to Kalen, but I think he would prefer I kiss one man instead of bedding a hundred of them. I know I would prefer the kiss. I will do anything to save Kalen, and if it only involves a kiss then so be it.

Bayleon is still looking at the floor, hands in mine, when I squeeze them to get his attention. He hesitates before finally looking up to meet my eyes. "You can have your kiss," I say softly.

His midnight blue eyes glow and a smile takes over his angelic face. He reminds me of Finn with how ethereal he looks. Thinking of Finn spikes my need to get out of here quickly, and to let him and Ashur know that I am safe and well. I don't want them getting killed trying to save me, but when I get out of here I'm going to do what I should have done in the first place. I am going to finish out this journey alone.

Bayleon moves closer and with him being so tall, I angle my chin higher to receive his kiss.

Before touching my lips, he whispers, "I need you to think of your prince and the love you feel for him. Take all of that love and build it up here." He releases my hands and places one of his over my heart. "Are you ready?" he asks.

The love I have for Kalen has never left my heart, but

I do as he says and concentrate on all the love and all the passion I have for the one man I desire most. I let those feelings build until my heart feels like it's going to explode. I close my eyes and nod my head, ready for Bayleon's kiss.

"I'm ready," I confess, shaky and breathless.

He moves closer and takes my face in between his hands. His lips feel warm when they close over mine. I part mine slightly, giving into him fully, and he uses this invitation as time to deepen the kiss. I try to picture Kalen in my head while another man takes claim to my lips. The way Kalen looks when he smiles and the way his eyes smolder when he looks at me are fresh in my mind. My lips move against Bayleon's and I know that if I am to get out of here I have to make this gift memorable. I have to put everything into it, and that means doing the only thing I can think of to do — pretend it is Kalen that I am kissing.

I envision the man before me is the strong and handsome Winter Prince that I have fallen madly in love with. I take us to the place in our vision where everything is colorful and free, the place where we will make our court and begin a new life. I deepen the kiss of my own accord and the man before me moans into my mouth and pulls me in tighter to his body. I wrap my arms around his waist while our tongues intermingle in a sensual embrace. His breathing becomes frantic and so does mine. Things are beginning to get really heated when Bayleon breaks away from the kiss, and I am thrust back into reality. Imagining he was Kalen might not have been the best idea because things were beginning to get carried away really fast.

Bayleon tilts my chin up and presses his forehead

against mine.

"That was the most amazing feeling I have ever felt, Princess. Your love for the prince is powerful," he says, amazed.

I give a small laugh, "Yes it is, and that is why I must go. Am I free to leave?"

He smiles at me warmly and nods, "Aye, you are, and thank you for giving me the taste of true love. I know it must not be easy to give yourself to me when you love another. It warms my soul and has made me see things in a new light. Are you sure you don't want to stay for the night? Your warriors are gone which means you will be travelling alone at night."

Traveling at night is not the safest thing to do, but staying here with an army full of lustful Tyvar definitely isn't. I bow my head in respect, "Thank you, Bayleon, but I really think I should be on my way. I have lost so much time already."

"As you wish, Princess, but I would like to escort you to the edges of our territory to see you off," he advises.

I smile, "I would be honored."

I am given a few moments to gather my things and begin dressing. I find all my armor and I begin placing it on my body. My bow and arrows are on the floor so I pick them up and strap them to my back. I notice the floor is hard packed soil so curiously I look around for the first time. The only light in here comes from the torches that are lit and mounted on the wall. They actually give this room a romantic appeal, and I thank the stars that I will be out of here soon. Bayleon is waiting by the door for me, but before I take another step further I sneak a glance over at Bastian. He looks at me with such longing and sadness.

I never gave thought that he might have the same feelings as Bayleon. Judging by the way he looks I would say he does.

Am I really going to do this again? Here I go with putting another's needs before my own. When everyone finds out what I have done they will never let me live it down. My heart goes out for these men and it makes me sad that they live like this every day not knowing what real love feels like. Bayleon nods his head in understanding before walking out to leave me alone with Bastian.

Bastian is standing there motionless, awkward and confused, and I can't help but feel pity for him. This is the last time I'm going to do this, and I am only doing this now because he was gentle with me earlier. The sincerity in his soul was genuine and easy to see. Bastian's eyes widen at my approach and I waste no time in crushing my lips against his before he has any time to speak. He stands frozen at first, but then returns the kiss with a passion of his own. The love in my body explodes out in waves and I know Bastian can feel it all. He lifts me off the ground and crushes me tight against his body. I don't know how these men survive without love, but it does however give me joy to be able to share this with them. His lips are warm and soft as he embraces my lips with his own.

When the kiss is over Bastian sets me down and I notice a sparkling tear rolling down his cheek. I wipe it away while he smiles warmly at me.

"You didn't have to do that, Princess."

I smile back. "I know, Bastian, but I wanted to."

He leans down and kisses me once more on the lips. "The fact that you wanted to kiss me makes it all the more special. Thank you, Princess Meliantha. I will treasure this moment for all eternity."

"You are most welcome," I reply whole-heartedly.

He walks me out of the dwelling and Bayleon is waiting for us just outside. He smiles at us and takes my arm while Bastian takes the other.

"I'm going to escort you, too," Bastian says with a smirk. I gasp in wonder as I peer around the Tyvar camp. My eyes were closed earlier, so I was unable to take a look at my surroundings. I wouldn't necessarily call it a camp, but more a village of sorts. I curiously look back at the dwelling I just came from and I am amazed by the way it's built. His home looks like it was carved out of a mound of earth. It is set inside a hill and covered with vibrant green colored mosses and grass. I noticed there are no flowers on the vines that cross over and around his dwelling. There also are not any around the territory either. I secretly call upon my magic and I send it to the baron vines that lie across Bayleon's dwelling. Flowers begin to sprout of various colors and I silently laugh as we make our way through the village. Neither Bayleon nor Bastian has looked back so they will definitely have a surprise when they come back here.

We're walking through the camp and all the Tyvar fae immediately stop what they are doing and stare at us in amazement. I look several of them in the eyes and they all freeze in place, wide-eyed and open-mouthed. Both Bayleon and Bastian laugh and it snaps everyone out of their stupor.

"Carry on, everyone!" Bayleon shouts while waving his hands in the air.

Everyone goes back to doing what they were doing until someone catches my attention and I freeze. "What the hell is she doing here?" I exclaim, nodding in the direction of the woman I see hanging all over a Tyvar fae. The woman I speak of happens to be the evil Winter bitch Breena. Why is she here?

They both look in Breena's direction and then down to me with somber expressions. Bayleon is the one who answers, "She was left here by the man you consider to be the dark sorcerer. He said she was a gift, but obviously he used her to get you here."

Well, it worked getting me here, but the dark sorcerer is going to be none too pleased when I catch up to him. When I do find him I will make sure to tell him how much of a spineless bastard he is by having everyone else do his dirty work for him. He hasn't succeeded yet with bringing me down.

I usually love helping people because it makes me happy, but when I look at Breena I have no desire in my soul to help her. She betrayed our people and *she* is the reason Kalen is gone, and for that she can rot in hell.

"Oh, I know he used her to get me here. That's how he works," I express fiercely.

The angry side of me wants to just walk right up to Breena and kill her, but the compassionate side tells me to try and save her. Unfortunately, it is too late to save her. She has already been enthralled by the Tyvar's power of seduction. She deserves this fate though, and deep down I am glad for it. I am actually doing her a favor. Dying by the Tyvar will be way more enjoyable then dying by my hands.

"What would you like us to do with her?" Bayleon asks.

"I don't care what you do with her. If she wasn't here

I was planning on killing her myself. She betrayed our courts and sided with the dark sorcerer. She is of no concern to me anymore," I say with venom.

Bayleon and Bastian nod their heads in understanding and we continue our way down to the fog beyond where Aki and my horse, Prince Ashe, are waiting patiently. Seeing them lifts my spirits and knowing that I will be back on my way to finding Kalen sends the adrenaline spiking through my body.

Aki is wagging his tail excitedly while Prince Ashe is pacing back and forth. I know they must have been worried. They head straight for me and my escorts let me go so I can greet them. Aki reaches me first and I bend down to hug his neck while he licks my face. His excitement makes me laugh so he continues to bombard me.

"Thank you for staying, Aki." He huffs and licks me one more time before moving away so that I can greet Prince Ashe. I rub his muzzle and the sadness he feels dissipates when he senses that I am alright.

"I'm OK, Prince Ashe. Are you ready to go?" I ask urgently.

He bumps me with his muzzle in reply. My saddle is in place along with my satchel. I climb upon his back and look down at both brothers and smile.

"Thank you for letting me go," I say to both of them.

Bastian walks up and places his hand on mine when he speaks. "I hope you have a safe journey and that you find your prince. Farewell, Princess Meliantha." He lets go of my hand and steps back to give Bayleon the chance to say his goodbye.

Bayleon comes forward and takes my hand. He kisses

my hand gently and says, "I wish you a safe journey as well, Princess. When the time comes and you need more warriors, we will be there to fight by your side." His face turns serious with his last words, "I *promise* to always be there if you need me."

I'm astonished by his promise because it puts him in my debt if I need help. Tears sting my eyes and I let them fall.

"I'm going to hold you to that promise, Bayleon," I say while laughing through the tears. I squeeze his hand one last time before letting go. I came in here thinking I was going to be a sex slave, and now I'm leaving and have acquired a powerful ally. I think the tables are starting to turn in this demented game the dark sorcerer has me playing.

The beginnings of night have already begun and it's time for me to be on my way. I wave to both men before Aki heads off in the direction we must go. I look back one more time to see Bayleon and Bastian waving, at least until the fog takes over and they are no longer in sight. It's a strange feeling, but I honestly think I'm going to miss their company.

Chapter Twenty

Meliantha

The direction Aki leads me is the opposite way from the bridge I crossed over to enter the Tyvar territory. It is late in the night and my eyes are feeling heavy from lack of sleep. There will be time to rest when I have Kalen back, so for now, I will push through it as hard as I can. The forest is dark with slivers of moonlight peeking through the trees making it look beautiful, yet ominous somehow. The night has cooled off, but I can still feel the humidity of the forest sticking to my skin. The forest is eerily quiet and the only sounds I hear are the clomping of Prince Ashe's hooves on the ground below. The silence reminds me of how alone I truly am.

I haven't been riding long, but I think I've gone far enough to where I can let Ashur know that I am well. If I spoke to him earlier I'm sure he would have found a way to catch up to me. I hesitate for a few minutes because I know he's going to demand to know where I am at. He won't understand my reasoning for wanting to be alone.

"Ashur?" I call out sheepishly to his mind.

"Meliantha! Thank the stars you are all right. Where are you? Are you OK?" He speaks frantically in my mind. I knew he would be worried and it breaks my heart that he is probably been going crazy for the past few hours not

knowing what was happening to me.

"I'm fine...the Tyvar let me go," I confess.

"WHAT?! What happened? How did you get the Tyvar to let you go?"

"It's a long story and I will tell you later. Where did they take you and Finn?"

"They took us across the bridge and blocked us from coming back across. They did something to the fog to keep us from entering. Tell me where you are and we will come to you."

I knew he would want to come find me, but I can't let him or Finn risk their lives for me anymore. What was the reason for my training if I can't defend myself without a warrior's help? I honestly think I am strong enough to handle this journey on my own.

"Meliantha?"

I take a deep breath before responding.

"I am so sorry, Ashur, but I'm going to find Kalen on my own."

"No, you are not!" he screams in my mind. The blast from his scream actually makes me flinch.

"Yes, I am. I just wanted to let you know I was safe and away from the Tyvar. Go back to the Winter Court and let everyone know what's going on. I will see you soon, my Guardian."

I quickly put my shields up to block him out of my mind. I hate to have to do that to him, but all I wanted was for him to know that I'm well. I honestly hope he does what I say and heads back to the Winter Court. Knowing him and Finn they will keep searching for me until they find me.

As we are riding along, Prince Ashe slows his pace

and his ears perk up in attention. Aki is sniffing around and growling towards the trees off to our left. My adrenaline instantly spikes putting me on full alert. Even with my enhanced vision it's hard to make out every single thing moving around; however, I know my vision is clear when I see several sets of glowing red eyes staring back at me. Sweat forms over my brow and my lungs begin to constrict from being frozen in place. Please don't let these creatures be what I think they are. I know one thing, I'm not going to wait and find out.

"Aki, Prince Ashe, let's go!" I yell. Even though I know both of them are tired, they move swiftly through the forest and away from the danger behind us. We ride hard for a several minutes and I am constantly taking peeks behind me to see if we're being followed. I breathe a sigh of relief when it looks like I'm safe. I make Prince Ashe slow down because his chest is heaving in and out from breathing hard and I don't want him to fall down from exhaustion. Aki looks fatigued as well and I know we have to stop at some point to rest. Redcaps are not the kind of fae I want to cross paths with and that is exactly who I think those red eyes belong to. Stopping for the night is out of the question because getting caught by a Redcap will most surely result in my death. They will feast in my blood just like they do with every other kill. A shiver runs through my body at the thought of what they do. A twig snaps behind me and I instantly freeze in place atop Prince Ashe. They couldn't have caught up to me so quickly could they?

I can't contemplate any further because pain explodes in my head and my vision goes blurry before I even have the chance to turn around. Something hard and heavy hammered me on the head and I can feel the warm, sticky blood pouring down my neck like a faucet. Everything after that moves in slow motion as I am falling to the ground.

I land directly on my side and the brutal force of the fall has knocked the air out of my lungs. I gasp for air trying to get in a breath when I see a pair of blood red eyes glaring and smiling at me with a mouth full of large, razor sharp teeth.

Growling fiercely, Aki is beside me and ready to attack. He leaps at the Redcap giving me enough time to grab my bow and load an arrow. My wolf is thrown into a tree with a loud thud and his growl of pain pierces the night air. His cry tears at my heart and I want to help him, but I know I have to take this Redcap down before he kills us both. The pain in my head is throbbing and my vision is starting to fade. I grab my bow and I unsteadily get to my feet. The Redcap is rapidly advancing, so without any more thought, I let my arrow fly. It snags him right in the heart and he falls to his knees in front of me. Victory is not mine because I fall to my knees as well. The pain in my head is unbearable, my eyes begin to grow heavy, and then…darkness.

The pain in my head has lessened, but I can't move any part of my body. My arms and legs are strapped down and I can't see a thing because of the thick fabric wrapped around my head. It feels like I am strapped to a wooden table of sorts. I jerk my arms and legs against the restraints but they only grow tighter cutting into my skin. My hands and feet begin to go numb making them tingle like pins and needles, and now I can no longer feel them.

I didn't realize how helpless it would make me feel to be strapped down. I can feel the panic begin to rise so I bite my lip to keep from crying out. I killed one of the Redcaps and now they are going to want revenge. I wonder if this is what the dark sorcerer had in mind for my demise. I'm worried about Aki because after he took that brutal hit I don't remember much after that, or even if he's still alive. I hope with all my heart that he is well.

I can't see what kind of room I am in, but from the smell and the moisture in the air I would say I'm in an underground prison. The clanking sound of a door opening gets my attention so I listen carefully to see if I can figure out what's going on. The heavy footsteps on the floor appear to be two men who have entered the room. The footsteps come closer and I instantly freeze in place. I absolutely detest not being able to see anything. If I'm to die I want to see it coming.

They speak in their own native dialect while they check the straps of my restraints. I curse myself silently for not learning their language when I had the chance. I never thought I would come into contact with Redcaps; so therefore, I decided not to learn their language. If I knew it, I would probably know what was about to happen to me. Dread settles in my gut, but after everything I have been through I can't let it be the end now. I have lived through the dark sorcerer taking my power, the Tyvar's power of seduction, and for what…to die by the Redcaps.

If I can make it out of the Tyvar's territory unscathed, then I am sure there is a way to get out of here. Hopefully.

The table I'm on moves and the Redcaps roll me out of the room I am in. It takes a few twists and turns but then they open another door that leads to the outside. I know this because I can see light shining through the blindfold and feel the warm air across my skin. I wish I knew what was going to happen and where they are taking me. As I am being wheeled around several large, rough hands brush across my skin. It took everything I had not to flinch from the feel of their dry, scaly hands running across my skin. I hear their murmurs all around me.

"Where are you taking me?" I finally ask. I don't know if they will understand me, but I try anyway.

"Ah, the lass can speak," a gruffy voice answers. "Twas beginning to think ye were mute."

"I didn't know if you would understand me," I reply honestly.

He huffs, "Aye, lass. My name is Grishom, and I am to take ye to our clan leader, Shamus."

"Why are you taking me to your clan leader?" I ask dismally.

Grishom is quiet for a few seconds and I'm beginning to think he's not going to answer me until I hear his gruff voice in my ear, "Tis time to decide yer fate, little lass."

Decide my fate? What does that mean? I remain quiet the rest of the way until the table I am on is pushed upright to where I'm basically standing against the table. I smell the rank breath of a Redcap before me and the odor of it makes me gag. It felt hot and sticky across my face and if I had food in my stomach it would already be all over him. He laughs and takes his large, talon hands and unties the blindfold from around my head.

I have only heard rumors of the Redcaps only having talons for hands and by the way this one feels up against my head I would say it's true. The Redcap takes away the blindfold and I narrow my eyes against the light of the outdoors. I blink rapidly a few times to get used to the light and when I do, I am horrified at the sight before me.

There are dozens of Redcaps surrounding me and they all look haggard and defeated. Blood is dried in splotches on their faces and their red eyes have taken on a dull sheen. Their skin is dry and cracking leaving sores in its wake, and the smell emanating from them is absolutely revolting. They all look like sturdy old men, but some of them have brighter red caps than the others. I look down at their hands and they are exactly the way I was told they would be, talons and all. Their pikestaffs measure twice as tall as them and they are all wearing heavy armor along with iron-shod boots. Even with all that armor, they were hasty enough to catch me on horseback. No wonder they are great killers, they're swift enough to out run a fae horse.

One of them approaches me and I assume him to be the leader, Shamus. His cap is pulsing and sending rivulets of blood trailing down his face. The metallic scent of his victim's blood is permeating around him and the smell is horrid. It looks disgusting, but I can't seem to tear my eyes away from him. He holds a dagger in his hand and holds it like he is about to strike. My heart rapidly accelerates and I begin to sweat profusely. I can feel it running down my back and dripping down from my forehead, blinding me with its saltiness. I take a deep breath and prepare myself for my fate.

The clan leader points his dagger at me and announces across the crowd, "Blood is to be paid with blood. This young lass has taken a clansman's life, and it must be paid with her own. 'Tis the blood that will save our clan."

Before I can protest, he slices the dagger to the bone across both wrists. I hiss in pain as my blood flows rapidly down into the buckets placed below. I welcome the numbness of my limbs for dulling the pain. I don't know how long it'll take for me to bleed dry. With my healing capabilities, I know I can heal very quickly.

Shamus, the clan leader, separates the Redcaps into two groups and they each take a turn soaking their caps in my blood. Shamus goes first and soaks his cap. Their world seems to be blurring together as I begin to feel light-headed and dizzy from the steady flow of my blood leaving my body into the buckets below. I refuse to die, I scream to myself.

I summon my magic and it swiftly travels to my wrists, healing them quickly. I close my eyes to breathe a sigh of relief at the same time Shamus gasps in surprise. I open my eyes quickly to see him looking at me in amazement. His cap is now a deep crimson shade of red and his eyes are glowing like the flames of a fire. Did my blood replenish him that much? Gasps erupt around the crowd and they stare at their leader, mesmerized.

"Who are you?" he demands. Again, maybe I should have screamed before who I was.

"I'm Princess Meliantha of the Summer Court," I announce looking around the crowd. Murmurs and gasps erupt from all of them and they stare at me wide-eyed.

"Why are ye here, and how can ye blood be so

powerful?" Shamus asks, speaking above the crowd.

"I was in search of the dark sorcerer before I was taken by you." His eyes go wide, along with the rest of the clan. By their angry and weary expressions I would say they've had a recent visit by the dark sorcerer. Again, he has led me into a trap. I look across the crowd and say, "He has taken something of mine and I want it back." I glance at the buckets of my blood on the ground and then back to the Redcaps. "My blood has healing magic, and that's probably why it healed you and made your caps bright."

The Redcaps continue to soak their caps, and one by one their whole appearances change. It's amazing to see how they went from haggard, to rejuvenated, in a matter of seconds. Smiles take over their faces and they look at me in sheer amazement. Grishom takes a step forward and hollers across the crowd, "Tis a gift, it is." He looks at the clan leader, "Ye can't take the lass' life. Tis a healer, she is."

I'm beginning to like Grishom. He has a kindness in his eyes when he looks at me. Relief flows through me as the murmurs across the crowd yell in agreement. Am I going to be set free? Shamus holds his hands up for the crowd to be silent and I shake in anticipation waiting on the verdict. He looks at me and explains, " Tis many of my men betrayed their clan. Tis the evil of the dark sorcerer that has corrupted their souls. He took many and left us here weak." The dark sorcerer must have taken them when he came through here. I know how it feels to be betrayed by those you love.

"Am I free to go?" I ask, hopeful.

Shamus shakes his head and furrows his brows in

concentration. He looks across the crowd and then back to me and says, "Ye still took a life, but if ye offer ye blood once every new moon then ye shall be set free."

Every new moon is once a month and offering them blood one time a month for my freedom is a small price to pay. They must really be in desperate need of saving. Never in history have I heard of a Redcap letting a prisoner go. They're widely known for their murderous ways.

It appears this is going to be my only choice. "I promise to give you blood every new moon in exchange for my freedom," I answer whole-heartedly. Hollers of happiness explode across the crowd while they dance around in glee. It's eerie seeing my blood flowing down their faces as they scream in joy. Grishom begins loosening my restraints and helps me away from the table.

"How will you get my blood every month?" I ask the clan leader.

"I will send one of my men to collect ye blood," he replies happily.

I nod my head and rub my wrists. They still tingle slightly, but the wounds have closed up completely. I haven't seen Aki or Prince Ashe since I have been here and I'm beginning to get worried. I hesitate for a second before mentioning my concern, "Where are my wolf and horse? Are they well?"

"Aye, they are well. They will be brought to ye, along with yer things," Shamus points out.

I take in a deep breath and a smile takes over my face. I am so happy right now I feel like I could cry. I was afraid that Aki would be seriously injured after the hit he took last night. I collapse to my knees and I bow my head to mutter a silent prayer. I hear Aki's whine and I look up to see him racing towards me.

Grishom is headed this way carrying my bow and arrows and leading Prince Ashe by the reigns. I smile at them both and I send my love to them in a silent message. Aki is ready to begin searching again so I hastily strap my bow on and mount Prince Ashe.

"Ye be careful, little lass," Grishom smiles.

"I will," I smile back. He slaps Prince Ashe on the rump and we head off on our way. We come across a creek and it is the perfect place to take a rest and drink some cold, clean water. I pull out some snacks of dried meat and berries and I pass them along to Aki and Prince Ashe. It's hard to find the desire to eat when my stomach is in knots with worry. Our rest is quick, but I have the sinking suspicion that my next task is going to be dealing with the dark sorcerer himself. We are finally fully rested so I climb upon Prince Ashe's back and he continues a steady gallop beside the creek. We follow it for a few miles until Aki starts growling and pacing back and forth. I haven't seen him do this before so I walk over to him to see what's wrong. I can feel the trace of magic as I approach and it gets stronger the closer I get to Aki. I am appalled when I see the shimmery haze up ahead glistening in the sunlight. The dark sorcerer has done the one thing that will put me at a complete disadvantage. Through that doorway he made, it will lead me to the unknown of the mortal realm. If he wants to be a coward that's fine, but I am not and so I go. I take a few deep breaths before squaring my shoulders and stepping through the portal into the strange world beyond.

This game ends now.

Chapter Twenty-One

ALASDAIR
- Dark Sorcerer -
Before the Portal

I waited patiently for morning to come wondering what torture Princess Meliantha was going to have to face. She killed a Redcap last night and was captured by the clan. It appears she was also injured during the fight and has remained unconscious throughout the rest of the night. If caught, the penalty for killing a Redcap would be death. They will most likely bleed her dry and then kill her. Oh, how I would love to see it. The Redcaps are going to revel in her blood, and I know because I have tasted it myself. It's intoxicating.

Once she's out of the way, I plan to deliver the prince's ashes straight to the Winter Court's doorsteps. I laugh thinking about the way their faces will look when I throw the remains of their precious Prince at their feet. I close my eyes to enjoy the silence when I am interrupted by the thundering steps of a Redcap headed this way. The Redcap is one of the creatures that turned traitor to his clan and has graciously pledged his loyalty to me. The others I have sent to the Black Forest to join my army. Their clan is slowly dying and it didn't take much to persuade them to join me. All it took was a promise that I would provide them with kills.

The Redcap approaches swiftly with a scowl on his face. The news must not be what I want to hear.

"What has your clan decided?" I ask darkly.

He growls, "The lass is to be set free, Master."

"Damn It!" I roar loudly.

I know she's powerful, but what is it about the bitch that gets everyone bowing down to her? I pace back and forth contemplating on my next move and cursing myself for my game not having the effect I thought it would have. I open my mind to all the possibilities, and then...a smile crosses my face as a new plan surfaces to the forefront. Oh yeah, I think I will thoroughly enjoy this.

I open my eyes to look at the Redcap.

"It doesn't matter now," I say slyly. "I know just what to do to get the princess falling to her knees before me. I think we can also arrange a little treat for you as well." The Redcap looks at me with an evil grin and rubs his hands together. "Let us be on our way. The princess will be following us soon."

If the Redcaps are letting the princess go, then it will not be long before she gains ground. The Redcap and I come across a creek and we follow along its edges for a couple of miles. "This is where the fun begins," I grin at the Redcap. I place my hands in front of me, palm out, and I call upon the black magic swirling inside my body. I close my eyes to picture the place I want to go. Once I grasp it, I let my magic soar. I can feel the veil between realms slowly thinning while the air in front of me begins to shimmer and thicken.

"The portal is ready to enter," I inform the Redcap.

He enters first and I follow quickly behind. I look around at the place I had chosen to come to. Ah, yes, I say to myself as a smile takes over my face. This is exactly where I want to be. Meliantha will be out of her element here. The ground is frozen beneath my feet and is covered in snow. The air burns my lungs as I take a deep breath in and out. I notice the cabin up ahead and I can see two people moving around inside. I look at the Redcap beside me and his blood red eyes are glowing brightly with the need to kill. The intensity of his desire for blood penetrates the air.

"Take your kills Redcap, but do so outside. I don't want the inside to be contaminated with the stench of mortal blood," I warn.

"Yes, Master," he replies happily.

The Redcap approaches the house quickly and I watch in fascination. Redcaps are brutal with their killings and it is always a joy to watch. He tears open the door and his heavy footsteps can be heard all the way to where I'm standing. Screams erupt from inside and they echo throughout the trees. This is why I love it when mortals live in remote places. There's no one to hear them scream. The Redcap emerges from the cabin with both a male and a female grasped in his hands. He has them by the neck and they are trying with all their strength to get loose.

Mortals may be weak creatures with no magic, but they do know how to fight back. I can hear the sounds of bones crunching and snapping as the Redcap breaks both of their necks. Blood splatters across the snow as he rips both heads from their mortal bodies. He takes his cap and moves it back and forth between both mortals- absorbing the blood from each.

"I want you to dispose of the bodies when you are done, Redcap. I also want you to stand guard outside when you come back," I command.

"Yes, Master," he says with a gleam in his eye. His cap is pulsing with the life force of the mortals he killed and blood is dripping down his face and onto the ground. I nod my head at him, but then something grabs my attention. An idea spurs in my head and I know that what I have found will come to great use. I remove the chains from around the wheels of what the mortals call a 'car' because I will need them for what I have planned. Time is running out so I move hastily to get things prepared.

"Are ye sure 'tis what ye want?" the Redcap asks.

I huff in annoyance.

"Yes, you fool. Now go stand guard and leave me be."

He leaves the bedroom and shuts the door and I can hear his footsteps as he exits the house. The chains I grabbed earlier are now binding me to a chair. They're tight and constricting making it hard to breathe, but I know I won't be in this body for long. Prince Kalen will be the one sitting here tightly bound when I leave his body. Since I'm running out of time I believe it's the perfect moment to have a chat with the prince before the lovely princess shows up. I fade out of his body and the moment I do he gasps for air. He looks around frantic and confused until his eyes settle on mine. I take my true solid form before him and he scowls at me while trying to get free.

"What the fuck have you done?" he yells, struggling against the chains.

I smile wolfishly at him and laugh. "Oh, plenty of things your Highness. I've thoroughly enjoyed watching your princess go through hell to find you. She's quite strong, you know, but now I have to see what she'll truly go through to save you. Although, it's not going to matter because whatever she does I'm still going to kill you."

"Where is she?" Kalen demands.

I'm momentarily distracted when I feel the ground shake from outside. I believe the princess has arrived right on time, and bested my Redcap in the process. I knew he would meet his end once Meliantha showed up.

I shrug my shoulders at Kalen and sigh, "Oh, I would say she should be arriving right about...now."

I hear her light footsteps as she enters and searches the house. I smirk at Kalen and he growls. Fighting his restraints his voice echoes through the house when he yells, "Meliantha, NO! It's a trap! Get out of here, now!"

I laugh at his outburst because all it did was make her get here quicker. She's now in front of the door, but the second before she kicks it open, I disappear into the shadows to wait for the perfect time to appear.

Chapter Twenty-Two

Meliantha

I've enjoyed doing things in the mortal realm, but this surely doesn't qualify as one of those times. I groan as I step through the portal when the icy air blows across my cheeks. Why can't I get away from the cold? Aki follows me through, but Prince Ashe stays behind. Once I step back through the portal he will be right there where I left him. Portals are easy to make because all you do is summon your magic and it can separate the veil between realms. Humans have been known to step through portals so we try to make them in not so populated areas, or at least most of us do. The Tyvar do this frequently in hopes of human women stumbling through. I don't approve of these ways, but there's nothing I can do to stop it.

I look around at my surroundings and once again I'm in a place surrounded by snow. There is, however, a light up ahead that appears to be coming from a cabin. I know the dark sorcerer is doing this to mess with me and to wear me down. Following him to a cabin in the snow is supposed to remind me of Kalen, and it does, but I'm not going to let it distract me.

Aki follows close by me as we approach the cabin. We are a couple hundred yards away when I notice two sets of footprints in the snow. Aki sniffs around and growls low. One of the sets belongs to a Redcap, and the other no doubt belongs to the dark sorcerer in Kalen's body. This Redcap must be one of the ones that turned traitor when the dark sorcerer went through their village.

The closer we get to the cabin I see the Redcap standing guard outside the door. Blood is staining the snow and my heart fills with sadness at the thought of innocent mortals coming to their death by a Redcap. The terror and fear they must have felt had to be phenomenal. I wish I could have been here to help them. I clench my teeth while the anger begins to build inside me. I reach for my bow making sure I am as quiet as can be. The Redcap may a bit farther away than I am used to, but I know in my heart I will not miss. I load the arrow and I take a deep breath. I stretch my bow, pulling against the resistance, and I sight my aim for the Redcap's heart. He's standing perfectly still, eyes trained forward, and not knowing there is danger in his wake. I release the arrow and it flies swift and straight piercing the Redcap right through his armor and into his heart. If I wanted to surprise the sorcerer I think I just messed up. The heavy thump of the Redcap falling dead to the ground shakes the earth below making my appearance known.

Once he turns into ash I peer around cautiously before walking towards the cabin. Aki makes his way beside me when I approach the door, and I see that it has been torn off its hinges and lying on the floor across the room. I take light steps while searching through the house knowing very well that this is going to be a trap. All that matters is that Kalen is here and I have to save him. Aki perks up at the same time I hear Kalen screaming my name.

"Meliantha! NO! It's a trap! Get out of here, now!"

My adrenaline spikes at the sound of Kalen's voice. This is the true Kalen screaming at me. He has to be crazy if he thinks I'm going to leave him here. I hear the dark sorcerer's evil laugh and the anger it spurs inside me fuels my venom. I load my bow with an arrow while following the sound of his evil laugh.

I kick open the door and I'm momentarily shocked at what I see. Kalen is sitting there strapped and chained to a chair, and my heart rate instantly spikes when Kalen's ice blue eyes find mine. The dark sorcerer is nowhere in sight, but I know he is here because I heard his laugh. I lower my bow and I rush over to Kalen.

"Kalen," I whisper as I stare into the depths of his eyes, drinking him all in. These are the eyes of the man I love, and not the evil ones of the dark sorcerer looking back at me.

"You need to get out of here, Meliantha. He's here and he's not going to stop. The cuff is still on my arm which means he can take me over at any time," he pleads.

It feels so good to see him again, but I know I have to hurry. I frantically search his body looking at the chains holding him to the chair. They're bound tight, but I think I've found a way to undo them at the base of the chair. I move to the front of him quickly and I run my hands over his hair and face for my own assurance. I lean down to give him a quick, chaste kiss.

"I'm not leaving here without you. I didn't go through hell just to fail now."

He looks at me concerned and asks, "What happened to you?"

"I'll have to tell you later, but right now I'm going to get these chains off," I answer with haste. His feet are finally free from the chains so I continue to move up his legs, unwinding as I go. The hairs on the back of my neck begin to stand up and the sense of dread settles in the pit of my stomach. I don't think we are alone anymore. I move quicker and now Kalen is free above the waist. Just a few more unwinds and then I will have access to the cuff around his arm to take it off. Only another few seconds and he will be free…

I freeze in place, chain in hand, at the sound of laughter. It's not coming from behind me, but... in front of me. I look up slowly and the dark sorcerer is looking back at me through Kalen's eyes. That evil bastard. I was so close to having Kalen in my arms, and now it's all over.

I grab my bow and jump to my feet. He laughs the whole time as he makes his way out of the rest of the chains. He drops them to the floor and looks at me with a smug smile on his face. I scowl at him and narrow my eyes. He hasn't bested me yet, and I plan on making it known.

"I wouldn't be smiling like that if I were you. If I am not mistaken, I have made it through all your little games unscathed. You haven't won yet, sorcerer," I snap.

"Oh no?" he taunts raising his eyebrows. "I think I have won a lot, Princess. You may have gotten through the Tyvar and the Redcaps, but there is still *one* thing I know will haunt you for the rest of your life." I stiffen because I know exactly what he's going to say. He bites his lip while looking at my body up and down. "That's right Princess. Knowing that I fucked you long and hard all those times will be embedded in your mind every single day." He looks at me with a gleam in his eyes and smirks, "But that isn't the only way I know I've won…"

The sense of danger spikes my adrenaline and I quickly raise my bow when I see him reaching behind his back. "Easy there Princess," he mocks with a devilish grin on his face. He pulls out two black gloves and begins sliding them on his hands. Why is he putting on gloves? My body trembles in fear because I can only think of one reason why he would need gloves being in a fae body.

"You know you're not going to shoot me, Meliantha. If you do you'll kill your one true precious love, but then again, it would save me the trouble of doing it myself. Or better yet, you could always join me. I could stay in the prince's body and it would be like nothing ever happened."

"I would rather rot in hell, and besides, I've seen what you do with your women," I hiss.

He shrugs his shoulders, "Breena deserved it, and I would say she fits in perfectly with the Tyvar. I'll admit that I'm surprised you left her there. With the way you like being a martyr I figured you would do anything you could to save her." I keep my attention focused on him and I still have my bow at the ready. I feel the warnings in my gut screaming at me that something is about to happen.

I shake my head, "I'll do anything to save the people I love. She was going to die anyway either by my hand or someone else's."

He nods his head and narrows his eyes at me. "You're a lot stronger than I thought. I'm going to give you a choice, Princess. Either come with me now and your prince lives, or you can deny me and he dies. Which choice do you want?"

"I told you before. I would rather rot in hell!" I roar with venom in my voice.

"Then I guess you've made your choice," he decides.

The dark sorcerer pulls out the iron dagger from behind his back. With the gloves on Kalen's body they'll be protected from the iron, but if he cuts him with it, it'll spread in his blood and kill him in a matter of minutes. I'm frozen in place as the realization of what's about to happen hits me like a ton of bricks. Deep in my soul I think I've always known he would never leave Kalen's body, but I just wanted to believe that I could save him. The dark sorcerer lifts the dagger high facing it downwards. All he has to do is thrust it down and it will go right into Kalen's heart. I begin to panic and the tears begin to fall as desperation consumes my body. I struggle to breathe as the thought of losing Kalen overtakes my mind. A life without him will be no life at all. I can't lose him now, not when he's right here in front of me. My power is strong, but I don't know if it's strong enough to save him from the iron poisoning if he were to be stabbed.

"Would you like to give Kalen a kiss goodbye?" He asks with a sadistic grin. "I know I would love to taste you again."

Knowing he's been intimate with me disgusts me to the core. The memories will stay with me forever and yes he was right when he said they'll haunt me. I just always thought Kalen would be there to help me through it. I ignore his last question and close my eyes, taking in a deep breath. I have no choice with what I'm about to do because if I don't, Kalen will die. I can't leave him at the mercy of the dark sorcerer anymore. I believe in myself and in my power… I can do this. I *will* save you, Kalen, and this I promise you, I vow to myself wishing with all my heart that he could hear.

I grip my bow tightly and take aim for Kalen's chest. The dark sorcerer looks at me incredulous and laughs. "How does it feel to know you failed, Meliantha? I'm going to enjoy watching you scream when I take your prince away from you."

Even though I'm torn inside, I give him an evil grin and shake my head, "That's where you're wrong. Your game made me stronger instead of breaking me. I didn't fail…you did! I hope you rot in the Black Forest!"

The dark sorcerer's eyes go wide and then everything begins to move in slow motion. He takes the dagger and begins to plunge it down into Kalen's chest, but my swiftness with the bow beats him to it. Before the arrow hits, he looks into my eyes one last time. The roar he lets out is full of venom and malice when he's thrust out of Kalen's body with a vigorous force. The real Kalen screams in pain when he is returned to his body. He looks down at the arrow protruding out of his chest in anguish. I drop my bow and run over to him. I catch him in my arms before he falls to the ground, and I hastily remove the cuff around his arm. I throw it across the room before lying him down gently on the floor. He looks at the arrow and then back up to me with pain in his eyes.

"I'm so sorry, Kalen," I sob, tears streaming down my face. "I'm going to make you better. It was the only way to get him out of your body. He was going to kill you if I didn't do it myself." I pull the arrow out and he screams in pain. My hands are shaking uncontrollably as I place them over his chest. I concentrate with all my heart and soul on healing his wound. My arrows do not contain iron, but they still have the components of mine and Ashur's blood making it a lethal weapon. The warmth of my magic builds inside my body until it is ready to burst forth. It flows from my fingers into Kalen's chest and I can see the light of my magic being absorbed into his body.

He reaches his hand up and places it on my cheek. His voice sounds raspy and weak when he whispers, "Thank you for saving me, Meliantha. Just know that I will always love you." His skin color is turning white and his eyes are beginning to cloud over. No! This can't be happening. I'm sending my power, but it looks like he's getting worse.

"Damn it, Kalen! You stay with me, you understand? I am *not* going to let you die! Stay with me…" I plead, screaming. I close my eyes to concentrate and I use every ounce of energy I have to search into the deepest depths of my magic. My true power is there and I can see it glowing bright and ready for the taking in my mind. I have finally found what I need to save Kalen. I grasp that power with all my heart because all that matters to me is healing Kalen no matter the consequences. He has to live.

I pull the depths of my magic from my body and as I do the strength I once had has diminished to where there is nothing left. I give one final push to send that magic into Kalen's body and when it does, the room explodes with the brightest light I have ever seen. My body is too weak to keep myself upright and I end up falling over beside Kalen. The end is close to coming and there is nothing I can do to stop it. I slowly turn my head to look at Kalen and he is frozen in place with his eyes closed. Tears are pouring down my cheek as I look at the man I tried desperately to save. I'm so sorry, my love. Please forgive me. I swallow hard and it takes all the strength I have left to whisper my final words.

"I love you, Kalen."

I open my eyes slowly to a world of light. The air blowing around me smells fresh and clean and I notice that every single thing here is colored in all shades of white. The ground is white, the trees are white, and even the sky is white. I look down at my body and I myself am in a long, white dress. Am I in the Hereafter? How can I be in the Hereafter if I am alone? There should be other fae here as well, but as I look around there is no one. The landscape before me rolls on for miles and miles in all directions. How did I get here? I close my eyes to concentrate and that is when the memories begin to start flooding back. I fall to the ground in despair when the final memory of my life resurfaces. I remember seeing Kalen pale and motionless on the floor after he said his final words to me. I failed to save him and now he's dead. How could I let this happen? I cry for what feels like an eternity until I hear the sound of the one voice I have been longing to hear.

"Meliantha, please come back to me, my love."

"I'm here, Meliantha. I need you to find your way back."

"Kalen, where are you?" I call out uselessly. I don't know how long I have been here, but every time I hear his voice I yell the exact same question. No matter how loud or how far I search, I never seem to get a response in return. It's as if this is my punishment for not saving him. I still feel hope in my body, and that is what has been getting me through. What I don't know is how I can hear him and not see him? He has to be here somewhere. I shout again, but only louder, "Kalen!"

My voice echoes across the land, but still I am met with only silence. Determination flows through my body giving me a sense of purpose. If I have to spend the rest of my life searching for Kalen I will do it. Wherever this place is, I'm determined to find my way back to him. My heart aches to be with him again to tell him how sorry I'm for not being able to save him. I thought we would be together in the Hereafter, but maybe I am supposed to live out eternity alone since I failed to save him. No, I have to stop thinking like that, I yell at myself. I have to fight the sadness or I'll never find my way. I look around the world where I'm clearly trapped, and I begin a determined pace to the hill of trees beyond. Something about the trees draws me to them so I'll start my search there. I will find you, Kalen.

Chapter Twenty-Three
ALASDAIR
- Dark Sorcerer -
One Week Later

"'Tis there anything else ye want, Master?" the Redcap asks. He's one of the Redcaps that turned on his clan and has now made his home here in the Black Forest. I'm now back here in my dwelling in the Black Forest resting up before the celebrations tonight. I've been here for the past week loading up on power from fae and humans that my army has abducted for me.

"I'm fine for now, but bring me ten more mortals within the hour," I demand.

"Yes, Master." The Redcap bows his head and blood drops down from his cap onto my bedroom floor. A trail of blood follows him as he leaves my room. I love blood, but I don't want it all over my floor, especially mortal blood. The smell of it is pungent and disgusting, and the last thing I want is for it to be on my floor.

"Gothin!" I call out. The troll walks in and bows his head. Out of all the servants I have he is the most loyal. Gothin was cast out of his tribe many years ago and has been a faithful servant to me ever since, even helping me with Calista's capture several years ago.

"What can I do for you, Master?" he asks. He looks around the floor and I think he already knows what I'm going to ask by the expression on his face.

"Will you clean up that shit on the floor," I say as I point to the floor. "The smell of mortal blood reeks of raw waste."

"I'll do it right away, Master." He cleans up the mess and shuts the door on his way out.

When the bitch Meliantha ousted me out of the prince's body it took everything out of me. I didn't know her arrows were laced with hers and her guardian's blood until I felt it pierce through my barriers. The pain was unbearable and it was worse than the pain I felt when Calista stabbed me with her dagger. The longer these women have their power the stronger I think they become. A week has passed and I still feel depleted. Now that the fae know I exist they have been confined to their courts for protection and not venturing out as much; therefore, I have been forced to taking mortal lives instead to sustain me. Their life force is weak, but it gives me power nonetheless.

Also, during this week I've heard no news of what has passed. I sent my dwarf spy out yesterday to find out as much information as he could about what the courts are doing now. He left the dwarf Kingdom and I heard that Durin, the Dwarf leader, has his men out searching for him. He is to be sentenced to death if they ever find him. They eventually figured out he was the messenger that brought Finn's cuff and Meliantha's arrows to the Summer Court that fateful day. If I knew Meliantha's arrows were fortified with blood then I would have confiscated them when I had the chance. I didn't know Durin had made another guardian weapon other than the dagger.

The pain of the arrow in my chest felt like molten lava being sent through my veins. After I was thrust out of the prince's body I was able to stay long enough to see him and Meliantha lying lifeless on the floor before my spirit form was forced back to the Black Forest. My power is the strongest here and I am constantly pulled here when I am weak.

A grand celebration has been planned for this evening in celebration of our victory. The Spring Court will never exist now that Meliantha is dead, and the prophecy will finally tilt in my favor. If the four courts cannot be formed that means my power will supersede all of theirs. I have waited over a hundred years for this victory, and once I get all the power I need from the Four I'll be able to take over the Land of the Fae.

My next step is to plan out how to get the next girl under my grasp. I saw her at the Winter Solstice Ball and her glow was just as bright as Meliantha's. The power has to be taken in a certain order and now that I have Meliantha's power the next girl's power will be ready for the taking. It gets me hard and excited when I think about the things I'm going to make the royals do when I take over. It's time like these that I wish Breena, or hell, even Meliantha was around so I could unleash my dark desires on them. I'm sure I will have no trouble finding another traitorous whore to fulfill my needs. I laugh thinking about it all until a knock at the door interrupts my humor.

"Come in," I answer in annoyance. It would be nice if I could have some peace and quiet for a while without someone bothering me.

Gothin opens the door and ushers in the dwarf spy that I have been waiting anxiously to hear from. I can't stop from smiling because I have been desperately waiting to hear how devastated the courts are over their dead kin.

The dwarf has his head down when he enters and after a few minutes of silence my smile slowly begins to dissipate. The anger begins to build and my patience is running thin. He's scared to tell me something and I must know now.

"Tell me, dwarf. What news do you have from the courts?" I demand in annoyance.

He looks up at me trembling with fear in his eyes. I don't even have to hear it to know what he's going to tell me because…I think I already know.

The game is not over.

Chapter Twenty-Four

Kalen

"Meliantha, please come back to me," I whisper.

A week has gone by and nothing has changed. We're now here in the Summer Court where Meliantha is in a strange slumber that she has yet to awaken from. She lies there motionless and detached while we wait anxiously for her to come back. After she saved me I have been by her side every minute of every day since then. Elvena will be here soon, along with Calista and Ryder, to try and help us get her back. She's going to perform the dreamscape magic so we can enter into Meliantha's mind. Elvena did the same spell years ago to communicate with Calista when she was captured. By doing this we're hoping to communicate with Meliantha and somehow bring her back.

Her hand still feels the same as mine when I pick it gently up from the bed. I hold her hand tight against my cheek so I can breathe in her intoxicating scent of flowers and the pureness of a spring rain. I squeeze my eyes shut to stop the tears that want to fall. Deep in my heart I want to believe I'll get her back. She did everything to save me and now it is my time to do the same for her. Whatever it takes I will do it.

I kiss her tenderly on the hand and I lay it back gently on the bed to rest beside her lifeless body. I run my fingers through her lovely auburn red hair that's fanned out across her golden satin sheets. It shines like the setting of the sun and it feels like silk as it glides across my skin. Her room is beautiful and not what I would have expected. I imagined a room full of purple and flowers, but that's not what it is like in here at all. I guess I overdid it with the purple when I fixed her room at the winter cottage. I laugh at myself thinking just how ridiculous it must have looked to her. I'm sure we will have plenty of laughs about it when I get her back. Oh, how I long to have her back and in my arms. I miss her smile, her temper, and the way she would look at me with such fire and passion from those amazing amethyst eyes.

A knock on the door grabs my attention and I turn to see Ashur entering Meliantha's bedroom. He and Finn had found me just as I was carrying Meliantha through the portal. Apparently, she had chosen to find me on her own after being separated from them. She blocked her mind from Ashur so he couldn't track her, but he tried anyway and that is how he and Finn were able to find us. He told me about the altercation with the Tyvar, but Meliantha never had the chance to explain how she was able to leave. He also told me about venturing through the Redcap camp and hearing about the special blood they had received from a beautiful princess. He and Finn were then able to track her pretty quickly from there and to the portal where they found me carrying her lifeless body in my arms.

We were going to travel back to the Winter Court, but then decided that Meliantha would need the strength of her court to bring her back; therefore, we brought her to her home in the Summer Court. King Oberon and Queen Tatiana were still in the Winter Court at that time so we sent word saying that Meliantha was home, and in dire need of help. They immediately made it back along with the rest of the Summer fae.

Ever since I've been here, the Land of the Fae's calling has been amazingly strong. It's been hard to resist the pull, and I had been secretly hoping it would pull Meliantha out of her slumber. Lost in thought, I forgot Ashur was even in the room until he takes a seat on the other side of Melianatha's bed. He takes her hand in his and caresses it lovingly. If I knew he didn't have feelings for Elissa, I would be furious right now, but I know his bond with Meliantha makes him close to her in ways I wouldn't understand.

Ashur looks at me and shakes his head.

"Why did she have to be so stubborn?" The sadness and guilt he feels can be felt all around him, and honestly, I feel the same way, too. If it wasn't for me, Meliantha wouldn't be lying here in a vegetative state. I know Ashur blames himself for not being there to help, but I don't think there is anything he could have done. Meliantha was determined to save me no matter the consequences, and when she wakes I plan on expressing how idiotic her plan was.

"There's nothing you could have done," I answer him. He shrugs his shoulders with indifference and stares back at Meliantha. I'll never know what it feels like to have a guardian bond, but I can feel how strong it is through Ashur's emotions.

"I know," he sighs. "She was so determined to get you back and I know that if I tried to stop her she would've tried harder to find you. So I did what any man would do that was left in Meliantha's mercy...I let her go. It seems she did fine on her own trying to find you."

I smile, but I know it doesn't reach my eyes. "Yes, she did, and when she wakes up she'll hear an earful about it from me too."

I haven't been able to think straight since this happened to Meliantha. The ache in my chest is unbearable at times and it makes my body feel like it is going to explode if I don't get her back. She needs my help and I feel useless just sitting here waiting.

"When is Elvena supposed to arrive?" I ask impatiently.

"She should be arriving with Calista and Ryder any moment now," he responds sounding hopeful.

Almost time, my love. *I will bring you back*, I think to myself wishing Meliantha could hear me. We sit in silence for about half an hour when the door bursts open and in comes Elvena being quickly followed by Calista, Ryder, and... Finn. Finn blames me for Meliantha being trapped inside her body, and he's made it known on numerous occasions. If I knew Meliantha didn't care for the bastard I would have already killed him. Ashur has had to break us apart many times. I've told Finn on many occasions that I fully blame myself and that I would gladly forfeit my life to save hers if I could. I also made it apparent that he isn't the only one suffering and that he's not the only one that loves her. He's stayed away from me for the remainder of the time I have spent here until now. He scowls at me and I scowl back. I seriously hope he doesn't plan on following Meliantha to the Spring Court when it's formed because I'll surely have something to say about that.

Elvena is the Prophetess and she also happens to be half brownie and half elf. She walks over to us and sits on the bed beside Meliantha. It's been a while since I've seen her, but she's a petite, curly brown haired woman with fierceness in her amber colored eyes. A frown mars her face as she looks intently down at Meliantha. We're all afraid to hear what she has to say about Meliantha's situation.

Elvena is one of the most powerful beings in the world along with the prophetic Four women the dark sorcerer is trying desperately to steal magic from. He's managed to obtain Calista's and Meliantha's power, and now he'll be after the other two. One of those women happens to be my sister, Sorcha, and the other, Ariella.

Closing her eyes, Elvena places her hands on both sides of Meliantha's head. She then begins speaking in the Old Fae language and continues to do so while furrowing her eyebrows. I can't stop from shaking so I stand up and begin pacing alongside the bed. My heart feels like it's in my throat, and I can't seem to breathe as I wait in anticipation. Please don't let there be bad news, I pray. Elvena removes her hands and then slowly slides off the bed. I take in a shaky breath while I wait for her to begin speaking. She looks at us all and lets out a heavy sigh. "She is lost," was her weary reply.

I shake my head in confusion, "I don't understand. What do you mean she's lost?"

She looks at me with sorrowful eyes and explains, "When she tried to heal you she gave you everything in her soul. Her determination to save you was so strong that she wore her body out until there was nothing left." She looks at the floor and then back up to me. Tears are forming in her eyes and her lip begins to tremble. Elvena takes a deep breath before continuing, "She thinks you are dead, Kalen. She never saw you open your eyes so she…she thinks she failed to save you. Her heartbreak and devastation has made her feel lost, and now she's stuck neither here nor there, but in another world all alone. She will wander around endlessly searching for answers until we bring her back."

"How can we bring her back from this? Isn't this a different situation than what Calista's was," Ashur interrupts.

Elvena wipes away her tears and replies, "Yes it is, child, but the same magic I did with Merrick and Ryder when trying to find Calista is still the same. Getting in her head is the easy part, but finding her might be harder than you think. The longer she goes searching for answers, the farther out she will be."

"When can we start?" I ask, impatient to get things moving. I don't want to waste another moment. I look at Elvena and Ashur because other than Elvena she will need both Ashur and me to channel the magic through our bonds with Meliantha.

Ashur nods his head, "I'm ready, Prophetess."

We all three sit on the bed and hold hands. I am not sure what to expect, but Elvena explains, "I'm going to start by speaking some magical words in the Old Fae language, and I need you to focus as hard as you can on the bond you have with Meliantha. You will then begin to feel an extreme amount of pressure building up around your body, and immediately thereafter you will be thrust into her mind. All three of us will be reunited in her mind and in the place she is lost. We will figure out the rest when we get there." Ashur and I look at each other and nod our heads in understanding. "Close your eyes and concentrate," Elvena instructs.

I close my eyes and I envision the bond I have with Meliantha. It isn't complete yet, but I can still feel the closeness I have to her soul. I grasp on to that feeling and I keep it close. I can feel the pressure building around my body and it makes me feel like I am about to explode. I begin to see nothing but a bright white light behind my eyelids, and then...I'm there.

Elvena and Ashur are standing before me and are just as mesmerized as I am of our surroundings. Everything here is white. The grass is soft underneath my feet, but it's white. The trees are white, the flowers are white, and even the sun shining above is giving off a white glow. The only color here is us and the clothes we are wearing. There's no sign of Meliantha and it looks as if this place goes on for miles and miles past the horizon.

"Our best chances are to split up," Elvena says.

"How will we know when someone has found her?" I ask curiously.

Elvena smiles and says, "Whoever finds her and brings her over will automatically send the rest of us over too. That part is easy, child." She turns around slowly and furrows her brows, "So all we need to do now is find her. I don't know how long we have here so we best get to looking."

We each choose a path and begin heading in our own directions. I chose mine because the moment I got here I could feel a pull on my soul demanding me to follow. There are trees up ahead scattered across a hill and they all look like they're covered in snow, but then again everything here looks covered in snow. The trees are still a good distance away, but the magnetic force that's pulling on my soul is getting stronger the closer I get. It couldn't be her, could it?

I pick up the pace and begin running as fast as I can. If I don't find Meliantha in time there's no telling how long she will stay lost before I find her. The trees are so close and I'm now at the base of the hill looking up at them. It's only a matter of seconds before I reach them…one...two...three...I made it.

I crest over the top of the hill, anticipation in each step, and my heart stops the moment I see the most beautiful woman I have ever laid eyes is standing there before me. She's wearing a flowing white dress, but her back is turned to me and she's staring out at the white horizon in the distance.

"Meliantha?" I whisper.

Her back stiffens for a few seconds, but then her shoulders begin to sag. I expected her to turn right around, but she didn't. Why isn't she turning around? "Why aren't you answering me?" I ask, concerned.

"Because you're not really here," she answers. "Every time I hear your voice I always search for you, but you're never here. I've been searching for days to find you, and I'm starting to believe this is my punishment for killing you." My heart aches at the sound of her voice. She is a strong woman, but her voice sounds lost and defeated right now. I can't believe she's been wandering in this world lost and alone, confused, and thinking she didn't save me. Oh, Meliantha.

"My love, you didn't kill me," I reply lovingly. "You

saved me, and I'm alive just as you are. Will you please turn around and look at me, Meliantha. I'm here, and I have come to take you home." I look at her standing there all alone, and it makes me want to hold her and never let go. I'm about to go to her, but I stop when she begins to turn around. She takes a deep breath and turns around slowly. I can see tears streaming down her face when she lifts her head. For the first time ever she actually looks scared, but when she looks at me...everything changes.

She stares at me wide-eyed and makes no move to come closer. My hands begin to tremble and my heart is beating frantically with impatience as I long to touch her. I don't want to rush her, but I have to bring her back before the magic wears out.

"Please, Meliantha. Time will begin to run out if I don't get you out of here," I urge quickly.

Her chest is rising and falling rapidly with her breaths and a huge smile slowly begins to take over her face. Her amethyst eyes bore into mine and I stare lovingly back into hers. "Is it really you," she asks, hopeful.

I smile back at her and nod my head, "Yes, my love, it's me. Now let's go home. Everyone is waiting for you to come back." I hold out my hand for her to take, but instead she shakes her head and laughs. She begins to run towards me, laughing along the way, and so I open my arms wide to receive her. I'm ecstatically counting down the seconds until she'll be in my arms. She slams her body into mine, and covers my lips with hers in a desperate embrace. I kiss her with all the force of my love and she returns the feelings with great fervor.

"I love you," I whisper desperately in her ear.

She laughs and wipes away her tears. "And I love

you," she cries.

I pull her in tighter and she rests her head against my chest. I breathe in the enticing smell of her body and it reminds me of what's to come. She carries the scent of the Spring Court, and I have longed for the day she'll truly be mine. While holding her body close, the world of white slowly begins to fade until I start feeling the pressure of being returned to my body. We are finally going home.

I'm thrust back into my mind quickly and I immediately let go of Elvena and Ashur's hands. They both come awake slowly, but everyone in the room is startled by my movements and stares at me wide-eyed and excited.

"What's happened?" Calista jumps up and shouts.

I rush over to where Meliantha lies on her bed and I lean over her waiting for her to wake. I smile back at Calista, "She's coming back! I found her!" I announce excitedly. Everyone shrieks with joy and surrounds Meliantha with tears streaming down their faces. I, myself can't stop the warm tears from flowing down my cheeks. Meliantha stirs and her eyelids begin to flutter. She opens her eyes slowly and blinks a few times before turning her head to face me. I smile at her and she gives me the most radiant smile back. After years of being apart and being torn away from each other we are finally going to be together.

Our most important journey as one will now begin.

Chapter Twenty-Five

Meliantha

The world of white has faded and in return, my heart and soul has come back together with my body. Seeing Kalen alive was the best feeling I have ever felt in my life. Knowing that I didn't fail feels like a huge boulder has been lifted off my chest. All the sadness and all the despair has melted away as if it never existed. I know my face is radiantly glowing as I smile at the one man I am destined to be with forever.

"You found me," I whispered.

He brings his hand up to cup my cheek and whispers back, "Always, my love."

I tear my eyes away from him to look around the room at everyone celebrating and jumping around in joy. I honestly didn't know if I was going to see them again when I was trapped in the depths of my mind. Calista is hugging Elvena and both of them are laughing and crying. Ashur and Finn have smiles on their faces, but the tension around their eyes lets me know they were worried. Ryder walks over to Kalen and pats him on the back. He nods at me and then takes his place by Calista's side. It feels wonderful to be back in my room, but looking around I realize that this isn't my home anymore.

Elvena comes to the other side of the bed and leans

over to kiss me on the cheek. "Welcome back, child."

I grab her hand to give it a squeeze and then I murmur softly, "Thank you, Elvena. I wouldn't have made it back without your help." She smiles at me once more before taking her leave. I guess this will be the time for everyone to make their rounds. Calista and Ryder both come forward and Calista falls over on the bed and crushes me in a hug.

"I've missed you," she wails. "You were so brave, Mel. All the things you did took great courage, and I will never in my life doubt you." She stays in my arms for a few minutes but then lifts her head to smirk at me. "But I think I can still beat you in a target contest, even though you happen to be a master of the bow," she taunts playfully. Calista has never missed a target and neither have I. I don't think there will ever be a time when we beat each other, but there's no harm in trying.

"I'm ready when you are, sister," I taunt back. We both laugh and she gives me one more hug before whispering in my ear. "I have a surprise for you and Kalen. When you're ready, go to where your heart leads you and there waiting for you is a gift." She gives me a sly smile and winks before letting me go. "Have fun little sister."

I can only imagine what she means about her cryptic message, but I'm beginning to have a few ideas. Once everyone leaves I plan on following my heart and bringing Kalen along with me. We have waited far too long to complete our bond. Finn takes this time to approach, and I can feel Kalen tense beside me. His hand grips mine tighter, but when I look at him questioningly he smiles and loosens his hold.

"They had a few altercations while you were gone, Princess," Ashur informs me telepathically. I quickly look at him and he smiles. *"I kept them in line though."*

"Thank you," I smile back.

Finn sits down on the opposite side of the bed away from Kalen and takes my hand in his. He gives no notice of Kalen when he speaks to me, "Did you mean what you said, Mel… or was it just words?" I know what he's talking about and I know I meant every word. I just hate it took so long to let him know how I felt. I look up at him and smile, "Yes, with all my heart, I meant every word of it, Finn." A tear rolls down his face and he shows no shame with letting it fall. He cups my face in his hands, leans down, and kisses my cheek gently. "Thank you, Meliantha. You will always have a special place in my heart," he whispers in my ear. He pulls back and looks at me once more. "I know I've told you this before, but I'm really going to miss you."

"And I you," I murmur with a smile.

He bows his head to me and quickly leaves my room without looking back. Kalen is silently fuming beside me, but my reassuring gaze seems to calm him down. "I'm assuming with Finn's last statement that he will not be joining us in the Spring Court?"

So that's why he looks so perturbed. I shake my head and laugh, "No, he's not coming to the Spring Court."

"Good, I would hate to have to kill him," he jokes, but with a hint of truth. I'm sure they would fight every day if Finn joined us in the Spring Court. I honestly do believe that in time he will find someone that will love and take care of him.

"He will," Ashur agrees silently.

"I hope it's soon," I reply back.

Ashur takes his place by my side and his face turns from friendly to serious. "Don't you *ever* do what you did ever again?" he scolds. I nod my head in understanding, but it's not enough for him. He opens his soul to show me what I've done to him. The anger and worry he felt comes pouring out of his body and into mine. This is what I put him through and it tears me up inside.

"I'm sorry, Ashur. I was only trying to protect you," I admit desperately.

His face goes soft and he sighs, "I know, but I don't want you to protect me. I'm here to protect you." He closes his eyes and shakes his head. "Women," he grunts.

Speaking of women, my curiosity peaks with the thoughts of Elissa. I wonder what all has transpired since their first kiss. "How are you and Elissa?" I ask curiously.

A huge smile appears on his face and he gladly announces, "She'll be joining me in the Spring Court. We plan to complete the marriage bond soon."

I quickly look over at Kalen and he smiles mischievously at me. The marriage bond. Kalen and I will be bonded tonight, and there's nothing that's going to stop us.

I turn back to Ashur, excited. "I'm so happy for you, Ashur. I've waited so long for you two to be together."

He bows his head and looks from me to Kalen, "I will leave you two to your peace, but soon I want to know everything that happened when we were separated."

I nod my head, "Agreed." Before he leaves, an idea pops in my head so I hastily ask him, but only silently so Kalen won't hear. *"Are my things here from the Winter Court?"*

He replies, "*Yes, they are Princess. Everything has been put away, even your bow and arrows.*"

"*Thank you, my Guardian.*"

He narrows his eyes at me and I give him a huge smile in return. I'm sure he knows what I'm planning, but all he does is shake his head and laughs before leaving my room. "What was that all about?" Kalen asks skeptically.

I look at him and smile, "It's a surprise I can't tell you."

I swing my legs over the bed and I stand up for the first time in who knows how long. I wobble on my feet and Kalen catches me. "Easy there, firecracker, you haven't walked in a week so I'm sure your legs need time to adjust." I was wondering how long I had been gone. I give Kalen's hand a squeeze and then he lets me go so I can walk on my own. My legs tingle a little, but it quickly passes and I am now walking normal. I saunter back to Kalen and I wrap my arms around his neck. I wonder if he's been here with me the whole time.

"What have you done all week while I've been playing sleeping beauty?" I ask.

He laughs at that, but then turns serious as he stares into my eyes. "I stayed here beside you the whole time. I even talked to you hoping you would hear me and come back." I know I heard him when I was lost in my other world, but could it really have been him? His voice kept me going and gave me hope. I honestly believe that if I didn't hear his voice all those times I truly would have lost all hope. I stare up into his watery gaze with one of my own. How could I have ever believed that he would betray me all those years ago? Anyone could have looked into his soul and saw only goodness and love. I was just a fool and couldn't see past the weakness. I whisper, "I think it was actually your voice I heard in my dream world. It's what gave me hope… the hope I needed to continue on. Without it I would've been lost forever."

"But at least I found you. That is all that matters," he claims.

He pulls me closer and then gazes down at my lips. We kissed in the other world, but now that we're here and alone I want to be able to enjoy him. Kalen lifts my chin and caresses my cheek. His soft touch sends chills all over my body and I desperately ache for more. His other hand slides down low on my back and he firmly urges me closer. Anticipating his kiss, I lick my lips as he bends down to press his soft ones over mine. I take his lips greedily with my own and I invite him further in by allowing his tongue to enter deeper. He starts to move over to the bed, and as much as I want to finish our bond I know this isn't the right place. My chest is on fire with the intensity of my passion for him, and even though I yearn for him I pull away from the kiss to cool down the fire.

Kalen groans, "Please don't do this to me, my love. I don't think I can wait much longer."

I lift up to kiss him quickly on the lips. "You won't have to, but you know this isn't the right place for us to finish this."

He nods his head and sighs in understanding, "I know, love. We need to go to *our* home to complete it."

"Yes, we do, but first I need to change," I say, excited.

Kalen never saw me in the purple dress his sister, Sorcha, picked out for me. It was the dress I had worn the night we were to be bonded. I have it hidden under my cloak and out of sight. I couldn't leave without my bow and arrows, but they are however, strapped to my saddle on Prince Ashe instead of on my back.

The journey to our land from the Summer Court was fast and swift with the help of my beautiful horses. I'm amazed at what I see and feel when we reach the border to our land. The sense of belonging warms my heart while the cool spring breeze caresses my skin. I close my eyes to breathe it all in, and then I open them to admire what is there before me. Calista has done a lot more than what I was expecting. My mouth hangs open while I am rendered speechless and unmoving. If I could speak I know I would.

"This is amazing," Kalen exclaims in wonderment.

The stone wall goes on for miles and is covered in flowery vines and mosses. This is the wall that will protect our palace once it's built, and also our court. Calista has been very busy.

The gate is already open waiting on us to enter through. I hop off of Prince Ashe's back and I step over the line of the border, entering through the gate. As soon as I do I gasp in surprise. The magic of the land is strong and it is flowing through my body sending tingles through my veins. I can only imagine what it will feel like when we complete the bond. I look over at Kalen and I know he's feeling the magic too from the wistful expression on his face.

He grabs my hand and I'm amazed when the gates close behind us, protecting us. This place is going to be magnificent when I get done with it. Calista has added flowers here and there, but the surprise she was telling me about lies straight ahead. I look up at Kalen and I find him smirking with a curl to his lip. He laughs and shakes his head. "Calista?" he asks.

I nod my head and smile. Calista has made us a little cottage made purely of vines and flowers. The vines are intricately laced and intertwined to form the walls while millions of flowers are scattered throughout. It's absolutely breathtaking, and I couldn't have asked for a better place to complete the bond.

I can feel the excitement in my blood building and the anticipation rolling off of Kalen. He guides me to the door and gently pushes it open. The cottage is small, but large enough for a bed that Calista has happily put in here. Flower petals of every color imaginable are sprinkled all over the floor and across the bed. I can't help but smile in delight as I enter the cottage. Kalen comes in behind me and closes the flowered door with a gentle nudge.

"What are you smiling about?" Kalen teases. "You're not nervous, are you?"

I narrow my eyes at him and give him a playful scowl. "I've been waiting for this day a long time. I am way past nervous," I laugh. He smiles at me, but then turns that smile to a seductive grin.

"I've been waiting a long time too, Meliantha," he says in a deep, husky tone. He walks over to me and moves my wind tousled hair behind my shoulders. By the lustful look in his eyes I know he's just as ready as I am to get out of these clothes and spend the rest of the evening making love. He unclasps my cloak and removes it slowly, staring into my eyes the whole time.

"You are so beautiful," he whispers. He lets my cloak fall to the floor and steps back to look at my body appreciatively. "You also look amazing in your gown. It's just a shame you won't be in it long."

I smile up at him and bite my lip. "That's not a shame, Kalen. I look forward to having it taken off of me very quickly."

He groans and grabs me by the waist with both hands and pulls me tight against his body. His groin is hard and pulsing against my stomach, and I groan, aching to touch him. I want to see his body on top of mine and looking down at me with those ice blue eyes filled with passion. Just feeling how turned on he is, is making my body weak with a longing desire.

"Well then let's get our bond completed, shall we?" Kalen urges. I don't know how he wants to do this because when Calista and Ryder completed theirs it was during a ceremony. I guess Kalen and I can do this any way we want. He takes my hands and leads me over to the bed. His eyes roam over my body like he can't wait to devour me. He takes in a deep breath and lets it out slowly before speaking, "I want to complete our bond while I make love to you, Meliantha. I want to be connected and bound to you in all ways possible when I seal our eternal fate."

His words make my heart flutter and I couldn't be happier than I am right now to seal the bond with him while making love. To complete the marriage there is a saying in the Old Fae language that must be spoken by both people. These words are not taken lightly because once they are said, they are forever binding.

Kalen is staring at me patiently, waiting on my reply. I bring my hands up to his face and I pull his head down so I can kiss his lips while his arms are wrapped around my waist, holding me tight. "I'm ready when you are, my love," I whisper against his lips.

As soon as I say that his lips crush over mine in a raging display of passion. It's like every emotion, and every desire we have been denied over the years has come rushing to us in a burst of need. His lips are warm against mine while his tongue enters deep, searching to caress my own. My body tingles all over, desperately aching to be touched. He moves back to take his shirt off quickly and throws it on the floor. His muscled body makes mine tighten in all the right places with need, and I long to have his naked body resting firmly on top of mine.

Kalen stares at me with those sensual blue eyes of his while he unlaces the back of my dress, slowly and seductively. He takes his time on the laces, and in the meantime, he's tracing his fingers with feather light touches up and down my bare back. It makes me shiver and the prickling of the chills cascade all over my body. He laughs at my response so I decide to seek a little vengeance of my own.

I lean up quickly to claim his lips and instead of kissing him gently I take his lower lip and I bite down firmly. He moans against my mouth, gripping my waist tightly before continuing on my laces. I love the way it feels to be close to him, and to know that he's mine for the rest of my life. I begin sucking on his bottom lip while I trail my hands down his bare chest to the top of his black leather pants. As I begin to unbutton them his hands start to work faster on my laces. His groin is hard and straining to be let out so I loosen his pants and let them fall to the floor. He is now naked and bared to me.

I release his lips to stare back at him with a fiery expression. I've wanted him so long and now I demand to have him. I take him in my hands and I stroke him gently but firmly. He closes his eyes and sighs as he unlaces the last and final lace while enjoying the tormenting I'm giving him. My dress falls to the floor and I am left with nothing but my lacy underwear.

His hungered gaze looks savagely down my bare body. I let go of his erection to help myself out of the lingerie. I can't wait any longer to have him inside me. Kalen takes me by the waist and moves me over to the bed, guiding me down gently. His skin feels hot and on fire as he settles himself between my legs. He doesn't move, but takes his time to explore my body with his hands. He trails them up and down my heated skin and massages my breasts along the way. His touch makes me tingle in all the right places making me moan in pleasure. The tip of his groin is pressed against my core, but he holds back to tease me for a few minutes more. He gives me a playful smirk and winks, knowing very well that he's tormenting me. I narrow my eyes at him to show my impatience, but I quickly forget when he trails his tongue over the mound of my breast to my tender nipple. He sucks it gently and massages my breast while moving his body back and forth between mine, not entering but teasing.

"I thought we were in a hurry," I urge playfully.

He gazes down at me and smiles before kissing me

tenderly on the lips. "Are you ready now, my love?" he asks.

"Always," I reply softly.

He enters me gently and we both sigh in contentment. He settles his weight above mine when he enters me fully, and I'm filled to the core. I groan in pure bliss as he moves his body in and out of mine in slow delight. I wrap my legs around his waist, holding onto him tightly, and enjoying the feel of him inside me. His long, black hair caresses my face as he kisses my neck and bites gently along the lines of my collarbone before slowly moving down to my breasts. I run my hands down his back and I pull him in tighter against me. My body is on the verge of exploding until Kalen slows his pace and lifts his eyes to stare into mine. As much as I don't want to stop, I know what we have to do now.

Kalen's voice is full of love and devotion when he vows, "You will always and forever be mine, my love. My queen, my lover, and my…wife. *Amin mela lle ilyamemie ar' ten' oio.*" (I will love you always and forever)

Tears begin to burn my eyes as I hear him say the sacred vow. His bond is sealed on his part, so now it's my turn. I take his face into my hands and I stare at him lovingly in the eyes.

"And I will always love you, Kalen. You will forever be my king, my lover, and my...husband. *Amin mela lle ilyamemie ar' ten' oio.*"

He kisses me fiercely as the bond begins to take hold. The magic flowing through our bodies opens my senses and I can suddenly feel the land changing below the ground and spreading throughout our court. It fuels our hunger for each other even more making Kalen move faster in between my legs. Sweat glistens our bodies making us glide together in perfect harmony. His arms hold me tight, and the muscles in them flex and strain as he works hard to hold himself up while moving his hard body ravishingly into mine. We both moan in pleasure until the sensations of orgasm have me arching off the bed. Kalen grips me tighter with a fierce intensity while we're both lost in the sensations of our heightening climaxes.

Sighing in delight, Kalen collapses on top of me, still hard between my legs but satiated. I'm trying to catch my breath and inhaling as much air as I can muster when I happen to notice the changes going on around us. The flowers in the cottage have all doubled in size and their colors have magnified to more vibrant ones. A golden mist swirls about the room and as it comes closer to my body I see that it absorbs into my skin. The magic of the mist is the brightest and purest energy I have ever felt in my life. I can feel the land celebrating its joy of mine and Kalens' union. The land is happy and strong, and it warms my heart to know that I helped save it. Kalen still has his head down and hasn't noticed the amazing display of magic swirling around us.

"Kalen?" I whisper.

"Hmmm," he replies.

"You have to see this," I insist.

He lifts up on his elbows and looks around the cottage. His eyes go wide in amazement and he stares around the room open-mouthed and speechless. The golden mist swirls around his body and he sighs as it absorbs within his body and soul. He smiles down at me, but then gasps when things begin to change. I look down apprehensively until I notice what he's in awe at. I stare in

261

utter astonishment at the changes to my skin. Both of mine and Kalen's skin have taken on a shimmery golden glow. The golden mist not only absorbed into our bodies, but has taken on the shimmery glow on our skin as well. I wonder if all Spring fae will have this happen or if it is just mine and Kalen's body that will go through this change. I guess we will find out soon enough. Calista and Ryder had been blessed with crowns of vines and berries, but this must be the land's way of claiming us as the Spring fae.

A tingling sensation around my wrist draws my attention. I stare in awe as markings begin to appear across the expanse of my left wrist. The word "Taris" is written in the Old Fae language across my wrist meaning "Queen" and is surrounded by tiny flowers and vines that wrap all the way around. The marking is absolutely stunning. I peer up at Kalen and he's just as mesmerized by this turn of events. I search over his body and as soon as I look down at his wrist the markings begin to appear. In the middle of his left wrist the word "Arann" appears in the Old Fae language meaning "King" and is surrounded by the same pattern of flowers and vines as mine. The Land of the Fae has unusual ways of marking its king and queens, but I couldn't have asked for a more glorious declaration.

"How do I look?" he asks, excited. I didn't think he would be so excited to have golden skin and flowers covering his wrist, but he's actually filled with joy at having markings of the Spring Court on his body.

"You look amazing, my love," I reply joyously.

Kalen bends down to kiss me which then begins another round of passionate love making. Every moment we have missed being separated we have now made up for in this one night. Our long night of love making has made us fatigued, but fully and completely satisfied.

Kalen is asleep beside me and as I stare at him I silently thank the heavens and the stars that I was able to save him. He is my love, and the keeper of my heart. The land belongs to us, and we belong to the land. The Spring Court has now been formed and I will take my place as Queen just as Kalen will take his as King. We will make this Court the strongest anyone has ever seen. When the final battle comes...I will be ready.

Epilogue

Meliantha

- Five Months Later -

The Spring Court has flourished and a new life has begun for us all. After the bonding with Kalen we built our palace and have accepted many new fae into our Court. It's been interesting to see how the bodily changes would occur when the various fae would join our court. The skin and temperature changes are what we expected, but something new has developed that I never thought possible. Kalen and I have the flower markings with the shimmery, golden glow, but when our fae swear fealty to our court they are given the same golden sheen to their skin. We didn't know if it would pass to our fae, but miraculously it has. Our people are absolutely beautiful and breathtaking.

Kalen's wolves have joined us here and their pack has blossomed with life. Several new pups have been born and it's been a joy to have them here running around. They have acclimated extremely well to the milder temperatures, and have made their home here amidst the palace walls. Aki has been a loyal protector and still guards me when I venture outside the palace grounds.

I finally told Kalen about the adventures I went through to find him, and he was none too pleased to hear about them. The sprites I sent to the Summer Court have now joined me here in the Spring Court along with my other sprite friends. They tend to all of the Spring's needs and I have never been more grateful.

The flowers grow as far as the eyes can see, making the land shimmer in rainbows of color. I've never felt more at home than I do now amongst the flowers and nature. The leprechauns have joined our court as well and have brought a massive amount of knowledge along with them. They are old and wise and I know their experience and skills will help us grow and flourish.

Bayleon and Bastian of the Tyvar have kept in touch and have sent me several gifts over the past few months which I have absolutely adored. Explaining to Kalen of my time in the Tyvar territory was not a pleasant experience, but I had to tell him the truth of what I did to get out of there. He wasn't happy in the least, but he was thankful I made it out of there in one piece. I also informed him of Breena's fate and that I left her there. He said he understood and that she deserved everything that came her way. I agree, but I think I would have rather killed her myself so I could see her suffer. I don't know what it would have been like to stay trapped with the Tyvar but I sure am glad that I will never find out. Kalen only respects them now because they let me go.

The one thing Kalen has had a severe problem with is my promise to the Redcaps. They have sworn fealty to the Spring Court and I refuse to go back on my promise to them. I will protect my fae to the best of my ability. Shamus, the clan leader of the Redcaps, has kept true to his word by sending a messenger to retrieve their supply of blood from me. Grishom is always the one to come, and

I've grown very fond of him in the process. He says I remind him of the lass he fell in love with centuries ago, and he always makes me laugh every time he says it.

Finn, of course, has stayed in the Summer Court and has now taken over Ashur's place in training the warriors with my brother, Drake. I haven't seen him since that last day in my room when I had awoken from my slumber. I was told just recently that he's very happy and in love with a beautiful Summer fae woman. I wish him all the love and happiness in the world.

My Guardian, Ashur, is happily bonded with Elissa and they live in a nice little house on the palace grounds. It works out great for them because Elissa is usually with me and so is Ashur because of his guardian duties. They are both happy and have just found out they will be expecting their first child in a few months.

So far all is right in the Land of the Fae, or at least until the dark sorcerer strikes again. There are still many things we have yet to learn on how to destroy him. I just hope we figure something out soon before it's too late.

We're lying in the tall grass surrounded by the colorful array of flowers. I'm propped up on my elbows while Kalen is beside me running his hands lovingly down my lightly swollen belly. He has no clue that I hold twins inside my womb. I've decided to keep it a secret, but it never stops him from asking.

Kalen kisses my belly and looks at me pleadingly, "Why won't you tell me, love? I want to know if we have a little Kalen in there or not."

I shake my head and laugh, "I'm not telling you. It's a surprise."

He huffs playfully, and then continues to caress my belly in silence with a huge smile on his face. Actually, we do have a little Kalen in there, but we also have a little Meliantha as well. Elvena checked on me the other day and told me that my twins are a going to be a girl and a boy. I have been floating on a cloud of joy ever since. Elvena was also able to tell me what they would look like. I was shocked when she told me they would be born with amethyst-colored eyes, and that one will be red-headed like me while the other will be dark-headed like Kalen. I will no longer be the only fae with purple eyes, but able to share in this rarity with my children.

A new magic is at work in the Land of the Fae, and I know it'll be strong enough to get us through the dark times ahead.

The End

Acknowledgments

First and foremost, I would like to thank everyone that has supported me and my books. I couldn't have made it without you, and my books wouldn't be where they are today without your support. To my husband, I love you so much and without your help I wouldn't be able to follow my dreams. To my children, I hope that one day you both will follow your dreams just like mommy. To my parents, your enthusiasm and pride for your daughter warms my heart and knowing I bring a smile to your face fills me with great joy. To my nieces, Victoria and Stephanee, thank you for listening to me ramble on and on about my books. I know it drove you crazy. To my lovely friends, I cherish you all and I wouldn't have made it without your guidance. Twink, you are the best.

About the Author

L.P. Dover lives in the beautiful state of North Carolina with her husband and two wonderful daughters. She's an avid reader that loves her collection of books. Writing has always been her passion and she's delighted to share it with the world. L.P. Dover spent several years in college starting out with a major in Psychology and then switching to dental. She worked in the dental field for eight years and then decided to stay home with her two beautiful girls. She spent the beginning of her reading years indulging in suspense thrillers, but now she can't get away from the paranormal/fantasy books. Now that she has started on her passion and began writing, you will not see her go anywhere without a notebook, pen, and her secret energy builder...chocolate.

You can find L.P. Dover at:
Facebook/L.P. Dover
Amazon
Barnes and Noble
Smashwords
Goodreads

Summer of Frost

The Forever Fae Series
Book 3

COMING SUMMER 2013

ALSO CHECK OUT THESE EXTRAORDINARY AUTHORS & BOOKS:

Alivia Anders ~ Illumine

Cambria Hebert ~ Recalled

Angela Orlowski Peart ~ Forged by Greed

Julia Crane ~ Freak of Nature

J. A. Huss ~ Clutch

Cameo Renae ~ Hidden Wings

Alexia Purdy ~ Reign of Blood

Tabatha Vargo ~ On the Plus Side

Tiffany King ~ Meant to Be

Beth Balmanno ~ Set in Stone

Lizzy Ford ~ Dark Summer (Witchling Saga #1)

Ella James ~ Stained

Tara West ~ Visions of the Witch

Heidi McLaughlin ~ Forever Your Girl

Melissa Andrea ~ Flutter

Komal Lewis ~ Falling for Hadie

Melissa Pearl ~ Golden Blood

L.P. Dover ~ Forever Fae

Sarah M. Ross ~ Awaken

Brina Courtney ~ Reveal

DESTINED

By
Jenna Pizzi

Available Now

Chapter 1

Lilly rolled over and looked at her alarm clock, 3:29 a.m.

"Ugh!" she muttered. It's always the same time every time she wakes up. She knew she could forget about going back to sleep. She got out of bed and walked to the kitchen to get herself a drink of water. As she walked through the living room, she could hear her best friend and roommate, Amy, snoring so loudly that she sounded like a buzz saw. *Must be nice to be able to sleep like that*, Lilly thought as she smiled. *One of these days I am going to record her just so she can hear what she sounds like.*

In the kitchen she grabbed a glass from the cabinet then walked to the faucet and filled it. As she held the glass to her lips she happened to glance out the kitchen window. She gasped; there in front of her stood a figure cloaked in darkness, standing only feet from her window, staring at her. Lilly dropped the glass and screamed a blood curdling scream. Amy woke with a start and ran to the kitchen.

"Lilly, what is it? What happened? Are you all right?" She asked with panic in her voice. Lilly didn't want to frighten her friend any more than she already had so she nodded.

"Yeah, I'm so sorry, Amy, I had another nightmare. It's no big deal. I just came out to get something to drink." Amy looked at her suspiciously.

"What aren't you telling me, Lilly?"

Lilly knew she couldn't keep anything from her best friend; they had been through too much together. She leaned against the sink to get her bearings.

"OK, it's just that I could have sworn I spotted someone lurking outside in the courtyard. It's probably nothing. I was most likely still half asleep. I am just so tired."

Amy walked over to her and touched the back of her t-shirt as she said, "Geez, toots, it must have been one hell of a dream. Look at your shirt."

Lilly didn't know what she was talking about, so she grabbed the back of her shirt. It was shredded at the shoulder, as if someone grabbed hold of her and pulled. With a strange feeling of trepidation, Lilly realized that it was the same spot where she had been grabbed in her dream.

"I must have caught it on something; I am not sure what happened."

Amy looked at her suspiciously, but Lilly assured her she was all right. Lilly then quickly cleaned up the broken glass and smiled at her friend.

"I'm all right, really. I'm just gonna go back to bed. Everything will be better in the sunlight."

Lilly had tried to confide in Amy as much as she

possibly could without making it sound like she was completely crazy, but deep down she knew that she couldn't tell her everything, not yet anyway.

Amy was hesitant to leave her friend and return to her room. She had known about Lilly's vivid dreams, or rather nightmares. She'd been there to bear witness to Lilly waking up in a sheer panic only to have no recollection about it. She tried not to make a big deal out of it for fear she would shatter Lilly's psyche. She figured she would wait patiently for Lilly to open up on her own.

The two of them had been best friends since before either of them could even remember. Their parents were friends and therefore introductions were not necessary.

Lilly's parents were killed in a mysteriously set house fire six years earlier, when Lilly was only twelve. She was the sole survivor. They only thing Lilly recalled about that horrid night was that angels saved her by carrying her to safety. Amy's parents were named her legal guardians with the stipulation that when Lilly was old enough she was to be enrolled in the prestigious boarding school Plymouth Academy for the Arts.

Lilly's dreams worsened after the fire. She would often dream about the fire itself. In her dreams, she would see creatures lurking around her house, searching for something, or someone. She could hear them speak in tongues, a language that didn't make any sense to her. In the dreams, she watched her parents as the fire consumed them and their flesh burned. To her it felt as though she were watching through someone else's eyes. She knew it wasn't really her, but in the dreams she became someone else.

The police concluded that the fire was started with an

accelerant, which meant it was set on purpose. They never found the party responsible for igniting it.

Lilly was forced into therapy twice a week following the fire. Dr.Collins, her therapist, believed that he could fix her with Lexapro, an antidepressant for post-traumatic stress disorder. He felt the dreams were her mind's way of releasing the trauma of her parents' deaths and from being the sole survivor of the ordeal.

Lilly never took the pills though; she knew the dreams were more than just dreams. After five years of being in therapy, Lilly continued to see Dr. Collins once a month for follow-up visits. She learned along the way to no longer tell him about her dreams and how they progressed over the years. She didn't want him to treat her as though she was crazy or still traumatized. She knew it was something she'd have to deal with on her own.

Her parents' case grew cold. There were no leads, no connections and no other crimes in the area that fit the circumstances.

Yet she was still forced to go to the appointments once a month. She listened to Dr. Collins drone on and on about how she needed to continue on with her life and not be kept trapped in the past. 'Blah, blah, blah,' was all she heard when she was in his office. Lilly learned it was easier to keep a smile plastered on her face and pretend that everything was nifty until the fifty minute session was up and she'd leave the office feeling no better than when she started.

The dreams weren't always horrible. Sometimes she dreamt of another place and time where she felt and smelled everything going on around her. The scenery always felt so familiar to her. It left her with a hollow ache inside when she woke up, as if she didn't really belong where she was.

Then there was *him*. She didn't know who he was, but she felt as though she'd known him for an eternity. His piercing, sapphire eyes haunted her very soul. Lilly's heart raced every time she peered into them. She found herself lost and longing to be near him. The dreams would suddenly take a turn to darkness and fire. She would hear screaming that would haunt her. Strange symbols would flash before her eyes and she wouldn't understand what they meant. There would always be a whisper in the background, 'Remember, Lilly. Remember who you are.' That's when she would wake, feeling lost and lonely like there was something missing in her life.

§

Amy gave Lilly a hug.

"Try to get some sleep, Lilly, we have a few more days before spring break and trust me when I tell you that you need your beauty sleep." Lilly cracked up laughing at her friend's blatant way of telling her that she looked like hell.

"Thank you, Amy; I can always count on you to tell it like it is."

"That's what I'm here for, sweetie."

Lilly shook her head as she dropped the contents of the dustpan into the trash. She once again looked out the window into the darkness. She no longer saw anyone or anything standing outside. She grabbed the trash bag out of the barrel and tied it up then opened the door leading out into the courtyard and stepped out into the darkness.

She stood there rubbing her hand up and down her arms, hesitating.

Come on Lilly, all you have to do is cross the courtyard and get to the dumpster. You've done this a million times, she tried to reassure herself.

She passed over the place she thought she had seen someone standing, watching her. She slowed her pace as something caught her eye. She bent over and picked up a cigarette butt that was still smoldering. She tossed it and stomped on it. Now she knew she wasn't hallucinating. There had been someone out there. She ran the rest of the way to the dumpster and tossed the bag inside.

A growling sound came from behind her. Slowly she turned and was met by the snarling snout of a wolf. Lilly took a step back and bumped into the dumpster. She stepped on a discarded water bottle and it made a loud sound that only made the wolf growl even louder. She knew the beast was going to attack her, she was trapped. She considered her options. She could run for it, but she knew the wolf could run five times faster than she could. She could scream, but the beast would probably only lunge at her. She slowly looked at the dumpster behind her. *Oh God, I don't even want to think about it*, she thought to herself.

The wolf stepped closer to her. She knew she had to jump into the dumpster. It was her only option. She slowly filled her lungs with the cold March air and before she had a chance to think her way out of it, she jumped and pulled herself into the dumpster. The wolf leapt and nearly caught her foot as she pulled the lid down on top of her. She could hear the beast growling and scratching at the side of her metal prison. Her heart pounded in her chest. She sat waiting, hoping the creature would leave.

Everything fell silent. She could no longer hear the wind outside. Then there was the sound of deep, chilling laughter. The hair on her arms stood on edge, but then the laughter faded and she was left in a dark silence again. She didn't want to move. She wanted to be sure whatever was out there was gone. After what felt like an eternity, she cracked the top of the dumpster open and listened. There was nothing. Whatever had been there was gone. She quickly crawled out and ran back across the courtyard as fast as her legs would take her. She threw open the door, slammed it shut behind her and locked it. She stood with her back to the door, willing her heart to slow down. She closed her eyes and took a deep breath. She didn't know how she would explain what she had just experienced outside. When she felt calmer, she walked to her room and grabbed clean pajamas and hurried to her bathroom. She took a quick, hot shower to wash off the debris from her dumpster dive.

Stepping out of the shower, she grabbed her towel and wrapped it around her. As she wiped the condensation off the mirror, an image appeared on the foggy, cool surface. It was a lightning bolt. Lilly quickly wiped the mirror clean, grabbed her stuff and ran to her room.

She closed her door and sat on the side of her bed. It felt like she was going insane. Everything had been strange for her lately; she had been hearing and seeing things that no one else appeared to hear or see. Her dreams seemed to linger over into her waking hours. Quickly she threw on her clean pajamas and tried to put it all behind her.

Turning on her laptop, she Googled, 'lightning bolt'

to see if she could figure out what the symbol meant. She scrolled through many websites until she came across the exact symbol she'd seen on her mirror.

"Hmm, danger associated with power and energy. Great, what is that supposed to mean, look out for power lines?" She asked aloud.

She switched screens and logged onto Facebook to check for messages since she knew sleep was out of the equation. An instant message popped up on her screen. It was from her boyfriend, Keith. She and Keith had been dating for almost a year. To Lilly it was nothing too serious. Up until she had met Keith, she had no interest in dating anyone. Keith had been persistent until Lilly finally caved in and accepted a date with him. Now, almost a year later, they were joined at the hip and she didn't think she'd ever make it to a class on time if it weren't for Keith. He was on a football scholarship at Plymouth Academy. At 6'3", with his shaggy blond hair and green eyes, he fit the image of the typical Californian surf god. Lilly had to admit he was definitely hot, but she couldn't quite explain it, he just didn't give her butterflies when they were together. There was just something missing that she couldn't put her finger on.

The message read: Can't sleep either, huh?

Lilly stared at her keyboard and began to type. 'Yeah!' She replied. She didn't want to scare him by telling him about seeing someone lurking around outside her dorm. He would be at her door in five minutes, and she didn't want that.

He typed again. 'Well I can come over and keep you company…'

She smiled despite her mood. 'As tempting as that

sounds, I think I am just going to try to force myself to try to go to sleep. Besides, it's after curfew and you'll get in trouble if you get caught,' she typed.

There was a pause before his response. 'Ah shucks! OK! I'll come over in the morning before class and bring caffeine. I love you.'

Lilly stared at the screen for a moment and then signed off without responding. She hated not saying it back to him. She really did care for him and she'd be lost without him always getting her butt in gear every day, but she just couldn't get herself to say those words unless she was absolutely sure she meant it. She turned off the monitor and her bedroom fell into complete darkness, except for the rays of moonbeams shining through her window. She hopped back into bed and watched the moon. She felt strange, almost jittery. She had a feeling of apprehension that couldn't quite be explained. She pulled the duvet cover up over her head and forced herself to fall back to sleep.

§

"Make your choice, Lilly. What will it be?" The voice yelled at her.

Lilly looked around her unfamiliar surroundings. She was in a forest encircled by hooded figures.

"I don't understand. What choice do I have to make?" She asked.

"Will you save humanity, Lilly? Or will you choose love?" A cloaked figure took a step closer. Her heart raced.

"I don't understand. Why must I choose?"

"It is your destiny, Lilly. Choose to save the realms or damn them to eternal darkness for an eternity of pain and suffering."

The cloaked figure pulled someone from the crowd. The person was tied with ropes and bleeding from being bound. The cloaked figure grabbed the man by the back of his hair and forced his face in her view. Lilly gasped, she saw pain in his blue eyes as he pleaded with her to let him die. A hand rested on Lilly's shoulder. She turned to see a handsome soldier standing by her side. His eyes were dark, but warm as she met them.

"You must choose before it is too late, Lilly."

She looked back at the man that was restrained. Her heart ached like nothing she had ever felt before.

The man smiled through his pain and called out to her, "I love you, Lilly. I'll wait forever."

The cloaked figure pulled him back into the crowd and Lilly knew what she had to do. She had to sacrifice her heart.

"I choose life." The world spun around in a mist and everything turned gray.